WILD

WILD
The Ivy Chronicles

SOPHIE JORDAN

WILLIAM MORROW
An Imprint of HarperCollinsPublishers

For my fellow "Mommy" friends:
Jane, Angela, Lindsay, Brenna, Kym, Katherine, Bekah, Amanda,
Jennifer, Lorien, and Josie

HarperCollins books may be purchased for educational, business, or sales promotional use. For information please e-mail the Special Markets Department at SPsales@harpercollins.com.

FIRST EDITION

Designed by Kevin Estrada

Library of Congress Cataloging-in-Publication Data has been applied for.

ISBN 978-0-06-227991-0

14 15 16 17 18   OV/RRD   10 9 8 7 6 5 4 3 2 1

If you are falling, dive . . .

—Joseph Campbell

Chapter 1

"I'M SORRY, GEORGIA, IT'S just, just . . ."

I waited, staring at his handsome face and too white teeth, feeling an overwhelming sense of déjà vu. I chafed my suddenly sweating palms against my jeans and told myself it wasn't possible.

This was how the conversation started when Harris broke up with me months ago. The only difference in this scenario was that this guy wasn't Harris. Not even close. Joshua wasn't my boyfriend. We'd been on four dates. *Four.* So why was he looking at me with that familiar pitying expression? And speaking in that condescending tone? And using *those* words?

This couldn't be happening. Not again.

I shifted on the plush leather seat of his car and played with my pearl necklace, wishing suddenly I was anywhere but here. Since our first date, I'd known there weren't any sparks, but I agreed to a second date and a third because he was the kind of guy I wanted. On paper anyway. A senior at Dartford, he was already accepted into optometry school. He came from a good family. His father was a church deacon. Joshua volunteered at the local food bank. I couldn't have found a better guy. I convinced myself that chemistry wasn't everything. Lasting relationships weren't built on chemistry. Common interests. Like goals. Similar backgrounds. That's what counted.

My phone rang inside my purse. I quickly peeked inside. Mom. I pushed it to silent and returned to the hot awkwardness of the moment. I'd call her back later. After whatever this was wrapped up. I refused to think of it as a breakup. I wasn't invested enough.

I wasn't being dumped again.

Joshua leaned in closer, sliding his arm along the back of my seat. Like he had to get closer to impart whatever he was about to say. A cloud of expensive-smelling cologne engulfed me, stinging my nostrils.

"I'm sorry, Georgia," he uttered, making a *tsk*ing sound with his tongue. "You've got marriage written all over your face."

My cheeks went hot.

He continued, "I'm just not ready for that kind of commitment yet."

I pulled back until the back of my head bumped the cold glass of the passenger window. Suddenly the pasta primavera I'd had for dinner felt like acid in my stomach. I turned my gaze to stare out the windshield at the lawn of dead grass bordering my dorm. The last of the snow had melted a few weeks ago, and the grass hadn't quite recovered yet.

I took a long, pained blink and focused on his face again. "Okay," I began, clearing my throat. "Let's forget the fact that we're not even officially a 'thing,' but . . . are you breaking up with me?"

He nodded sagely. "Yeah. I am."

"Is this because I haven't slept with you?" God knew he'd been trying since the first date. After dinner tonight, he'd invited me back to his apartment. I'd declined. Had he known he was "dumping" me then? If I had slept with him, would he still be "breaking up" with me? *Jerk.*

His face flushed, his tanned skin turning ruddy. "You have a high opinion of yourself."

"No more than you do." I snorted. "I mean, you think I want to marry you after four dates." I shook my head. "Ego, much?"

"Look. You told me yourself that you were with your last boyfriend since high school and you thought you were going to marry the guy." He shook his head and gave me that pitying look again. "I'm not up for being his replacement."

I fumbled for the door handle. "I'm not looking for a replacement."

"You should lighten up, Georgia." He gave my shoulder an obnoxious squeeze. I looked back at him. "C'mon. You're a pretty girl. Stop being so serious and have some fun."

I flung open the door and swung my legs out onto the curb.

He grabbed my wrist, stalling me. "Don't you ever just want to get laid? Try it out with a guy you haven't been with forever?"

Heat swamped my face. Yeah, I'd thought about it. I'd thought about it a lot since Harris dumped me. Especially since both my roommates were having marathon sex with their hot and fabulous boyfriends. Unfortunately Joshua's sloppy kisses and pasty palms hadn't exactly turned me on. I just kept agreeing to go out with him when he asked, telling myself I was being too picky. Too superficial. That sex was overrated. And now I was angry with myself for not trusting my instincts.

Leaning across the console, I toyed with the corner of his crisp collar. His eyes went fuzzy.

"What about it, Georgia?" His voice got all husky. "Want to knock the cobwebs off it?"

Charming.

"Yeah," I breathed against his lips. "I think about sex . . . hot sex . . . a lot. I think about doing it with a guy until my eyes roll back in my head and I forget my name."

He groaned and tried to close the tiny bit of space between our lips, but I pulled back, releasing his collar. "So I better go find that guy, huh?"

Feeling somewhat mollified by the stunned look on his face, I pushed out of the car and slammed the door. Without looking back, I marched up the sidewalk to my dorm and punched in the numbers on the keypad, muttering to myself the entire time, vowing that I was done. Finished. No more dates. No more falling for guys who looked good on paper. They all said the right things at first but after a few dates—*poof.* The prince turned into a frog.

I stopped in front of the elevator and punched the button. I tapped my boot heel impatiently, eager to get in my room and in a pair of comfy yoga pants. I had the place to myself tonight. Both Pepper and Emerson were with their boyfriends and probably would be all weekend. Sadness pinched me at the thought. Then I instantly felt guilty. If two girls ever deserved happiness, they did.

Ironically, a few months ago I was the one with the boy-friend and they were single. I didn't begrudge them their hap-piness, but . . . I was lonely. No Harris. My best friends busy with their own lives. I could only study so much. My grades were better than ever. I'd already finished my Econ project and it wasn't even due until the end of the semester.

As I waited in front of the elevator, the building's outside door beeped open and then clanged shut. Annie strolled in wearing a loose, low-cut blouse and tight cropped pants.

"Hey, G." She stopped beside me, slurping from a ridicu-lously large iced coffee piled high with whipped topping. She eyed me up and down, taking in my outfit. I was dressed to go out in jeans, boots, and a light cashmere sweater. "You already go out?"

"Yeah. I had a date."

"Must not have been a very good date. It's not even nine and you're headed home."

I shrugged. Annie wasn't my favorite person. She hung out with us a little at the beginning of the year. Until we all figured out she was one of those girls who would tell you to wear an unflattering sweater just so she could look better standing next to you.

"It's still early. You should come out with me," she sug-gested. My mind shot back to when Annie abandoned Em at a biker bar. She wasn't the kind of girl to have your back when you went out.

The elevator doors slid open and we stepped inside. "Thanks, but I've got work to do."

"On a Friday? Lame."

"What are you up to?" I went for changing the subject back to Annie—always one of her favorite topics.

"Oh, you know . . . going to a certain club." She lowered her voice to a whisper as she toyed with her straw, even though it was just the two of us in the elevator. "It's going to be funnnn tonight. There are supposed to be some interesting games."

"You mean your kink club?"

"It's not *my* kink club. No one owns it." She rolled her eyes. "It's a place to go if you want to really live and experience whatever you want, whatever you feel like without judgment. A safe place to let go and lose control."

A safe place to lose control? For some reason, an image of my mother frowning and shaking her head rose up in my mind. "There's no such place," I said.

Life was judgment. We lived. We made choices. If we weren't judging ourselves, then others were. That's just the way the world worked. Self-control was everything. It's what kept us civilized.

Annie chuckled. The elevator slid open and we stepped out. "God, you are repressed. You have my number. Text me if you want to join."

I watched her for a moment as she turned and headed down the corridor in the opposite direction from my suite. Somewhere on our floor someone was playing the latest Bruno Mars at full blast.

I entered my room and closed my door. Bruno fell to a low muffle. Emerson's side was a mess, littered with clothes. She might have fallen in love and started taking life a little more seriously now, but her indecision regarding what to wear and her inability to hang clothes back up had not changed.

I flipped on the television and changed clothes, neatly fold-
ing and putting away my sweater and jeans. After tucking my
boots into the corner of the closet, I reached for my phone to
call Mom back. She hated it when I didn't call back on the same
day.

Sitting cross-legged on the bed, I watched a cop chase a
bad guy across the screen as the phone rang in my ear. On the
final ring, Mom picked up. "Georgia, hi!" Her voice was full of
energy. Reminiscent of how she sounded on the intercom all
those mornings in high school.

Attending the school where your mom worked as a principal had been less than fun. Thankfully, she adored Harris—
everyone in my hometown did—or I never would have been
asked out on a date. Not too many guys wanted to date the
principal's kid. Harris had been confident enough to not let it
intimidate him. I'd loved him for that. Of course, his father was
a city councilman then . . . and happened to be the current
mayor now. My mother loved him for those reasons, too.

"How are you? How's school?"

"Good, I'm—"

"Did you change your password? I was trying to get online
and look at your current GPA."

"No, Mom, I haven't."

I might be twenty years old, but my parents were footing
the bill for school and still expected full access to my life—that
included online viewing of my grades at any time during the
semester.

"Hmm. Maybe I hit the caps button. I'll try again later." She
took a breath and slid into the next topic. "Have you thought

more about your summer plans? I've been talking with Greg Berenger, and he can get you on here at the bank. It would be a great way to get your foot in the door for when you graduate."

And there it was. The expectation that I'd come home. Eventually. I'd finish college and start my career back in the bustling metropolis of Muskogee, Alabama.

"Um. I'm not sure yet. Still looking into a few things . . ."

"Georgia Parker Robinson." She must have heard something in my voice because hers just got all principal-mode on me. Not to mention she was whipping out my full name. "This is your future. You need to take this seriously and not wait until the last minute."

"Of course, Mom. I know."

A pause fell. "Is this because of Harris? He won't be here this summer, you know. His mother said he took an internship in Boston."

"You spoke with his mother?" I couldn't help it. My voice escaped in a squeak.

"I saw her at the store. What was I supposed to do? Ignore her?"

"Sorry," I mumbled.

"We both agree that this is just a phase he's going through . . . this other girl is just a fling—"

"Mother! You discussed us . . . *her*?"

Her is a girl I've never even met, but someone Harris started fooling around with a few weeks before he dumped me. It was such a cliché. But then wasn't there truth in clichés? That's why they existed.

"Don't get upset. You and Harris will work this out—"

"I don't want to work it out with him, Mom. He cheated on me. *He* broke up with *me*."

"You're both so young. You don't understand yet. This will only make your relationship stronger down the road."

"Mom, this might be hard to believe, but I don't want to be with Harris anymore."

"Oh, this is so unlike you, Georgia. You're not the type to hang on to pointless anger."

"What do you mean? Why is this so unlike me?" What was I like then? The kind of girl who would let a guy stomp all over her heart and then ask for seconds?

"You've never disappointed me before."

And not marrying Harris would disappoint her? Was that her implication?

She continued, "You always make the right decisions. We raised you to be reliable."

Boring. Harris's word drifted through my mind just then. He'd called me boring when he broke up with me. Oh, there had been other words. Other accusations laid at my feet, but that one stuck in my head the most.

I sighed and rubbed at my suddenly aching forehead, like that accusation was still lodged in there, an annoying pebble I couldn't shake loose. "I'll let you know about the job."

"Please do. The position won't be available forever. Mr. Berenger will hold it as long as he can as a favor to me. I could have expelled his son that time when he stole the test from Mrs. Morris's desk and sold the answers to everyone, remember? I only gave him on-campus suspension."

"Okay, Mom. Tell Dad and Amber hello for me."

"Good night, honey."

" 'Night, Mom."

Ending the call, I fell back on my bed. *Law & Order* was starting over again, the familiar theme music racing over the air.

Restlessness—and a low undercurrent of anger—hummed through me. Mom. Harris. Joshua. Their voices overlapped in my head, making my stomach churn. All three of them thought they knew me so well. *Boring. Reliable. Serious.*

All words to describe me. All words I wanted to fling to the floor and stomp on until they were dust beneath me. Holding up my phone again, I scrolled through names, stopping at one at the very bottom. My thumb hovered over the keypad before reaching a decision and typing.

Me: So what does one wear to a kink club?

Annie: Something you can easily take off . . .

Chapter 2

I HAD A VAGUE recollection of a Tom Cruise and Nicole Kidman movie Mom refused to let me watch but that I watched anyway during a sleepover at Bethany Grayson's house (her mother let her watch anything) called *Eyes Wide Shut*. The movie featured a lavish, hedonistic sex club full of rich, beautiful people dressed in extravagant costumes. Annie's kink club was a far cry from that.

I should have known it after Emerson's one visit. Amid laughter, she had shared her experience . . . which had included a man in an anatomically correct squirrel costume. Chippy was in attendance tonight, too, weaving among the rooms and bumping against females. After stepping off the elevator, I stuck close to Annie, letting her guide me. I drove my own car, the memory of Emerson being abandoned by Annie still fresh in my mind.

Tonight's kink club was being held at a large loft with few rooms. Just a single wide-open space with sparse furniture. Understandably there was little privacy. Not that that stopped people from getting down to business. Several made out. The bedroom consisted of a near-translucent screen that did nothing to shield the orgy happening on the bed.

Couples occupied couches and ottomans. In a corner there was a threesome. They were making out in earnest, but thankfully still in clothes. Their hands were everywhere, diving inside shirts and under dresses. I looked away as I caught sight of panties being slid down one girl's thighs.

"Want a drink?" Annie asked loudly over the pump of music, stopping before a makeshift bar manned by a guy wearing nothing but a speedo, a Captain America mask, and a Superman cape. He was clearly his own brand of superhero. He danced as he shook, stirred, and poured, doing this crazy pelvic-thrust action that drew my eyes and then made me glance away. Repeatedly.

I shook my head. "I'm fine."

Not that I was opposed to drinking. I could have used a cocktail to calm my nerves, but I was a little uncomfortable drinking the purple-colored concoctions Captain No Name was making. He nodded at me with a jerk of his chin and sent me a wink. I smiled back lamely. I wanted a drink to relax me . . . not a roofie.

Annie took a drink from him. Bringing it to her lips, she muttered, "You're a bucket of fun, aren't you?"

"What's over there?" I pointed to where a group congregated on one side of the loft.

"Let's find out." Annie wove through the crowd, smiling and stopping to greet people she knew. At one point, she halted and engaged in a long, sloppy-wet kiss with a guy. Gag. When they came up for air, a long string of spit connected them before breaking.

He turned his attention on me, wiping his mouth with the back of his hand. "Hello, there, I'm Roger."

He extended a hand and I shook it. Smiling, he bent his head, tugging me closer by the hand, clearly intending to kiss me, too.

I flattened a hand to his chest and pushed him away with a tight smile. Yeah, not happening.

Shrugging, he moved on.

Annie laughed. "Uh, you do know you're at a kink club, right?"

I nodded and then shrugged. "Yeah. That doesn't mean I have to be indiscriminating, right? Besides, my tetanus isn't up-to-date."

"You're such a prude." Laughing, she rolled her eyes and led us to the herd of people. Some stood and a few sat huddled cozily together in plump armchairs, cheering and chanting and holding their drinks aloft in salute.

As we approached, I saw that they surrounded a pool table. I stood on my tiptoes and peered between the bodies, catching a glimpse of some movement on top of the pool table. Bodies. There were bodies on top of the pool table. Instantly, I cringed, hoping they didn't tear the felt. Then I cringed again, shaking my head that my first concern was for the pool table.

"Oooh, I gotta see this." Annie squeezed between two bodies. I followed, able to look over her head. I was average height, but in my boots, I was at least six inches taller than her.

My jaw dropped. Two girls were on their backs, shoulders touching, side by side on the pool table. A single guy was poised over them, his knees planted firmly between their thighs. He kissed one of them. Then the other. He took turns, moving back and forth between them. Deep, slow kisses that looked nothing like the kiss I just witnessed between Annie and Roger. He took his time with each girl, taking her face between his hands and holding it in a way that was both tender and firm. Confident and sexy. A man who knew what he was doing.

I couldn't even see his face, but I thought he was hot. A powerful back flexed beneath the fabric of his shirt. His forearms were strong-looking, too. Corded with tendons. Lightly dusted with hair. Something tugged low in my belly in response to him.

Suddenly, someone stood in front of me holding a bucketful of raffle tickets. Annie took one and nudged me to do the same. Without tearing my gaze from the debauched scene, I took a ticket.

The other girl waiting for her turn slid her hand under the guy's black T-shirt and dragged the fabric up so her red fingernails could stroke his bare shoulder. I was right. Holy sexy back. It was broad and muscled. The expanse of smooth, tanned skin made my mouth dry and water alternately. She touched her mouth to his back, her tongue darting out to taste him.

My face flamed and I shifted on my feet self-consciously, horrified that I was getting turned on watching this intimate scene. I was unable to look away. I continued to gawk at the guy. I ignored the girls. I watched him. The way he kissed—like his whole being was focused on the act. The way the bottom of his spine dipped was sexy as hell. His jeans rode low, hugging an ass that looked like it could bounce quarters. Just the sight made my stomach muscles clench and twist. And *that* was a wholly new experience.

A James Taylor song slid on. A hard and fierce beat. His powerful vocals a demanding, urgent wail that added to the tension swirling in the air.

The guy on the pool table lifted up from the lucky recipient of his attentions then. Still on his knees, straddling the one, he twisted around to face the girl who was kissing his back. He took her face in both his hands and that's when I spotted the full, rocking, masculine beauty of his features.

And my world stopped.

I sucked in a breath as recognition sliced through me. It was Logan. Logan Mulvaney. Reece's little brother. Reece, as in Pepper's boyfriend. Logan as in only eighteen and still in high school. About to graduate but still in high school. And here he was. At a kink club.

The fire in my cheeks intensified. This must be what it felt like a split second before spontaneous combustion. Mortification washed over me as I realized I was getting all hot and bothered over a guy I had no business feeling that way about. Off-limits was putting it mildly. It didn't matter that the guy had more experience than I did. He had seen and done more sexually than I probably *ever* would. Rumor was he had already slept his way through the female undergrad population of Dartford and was moving on to grad students now.

I was on the verge of turning and fleeing when his eyes locked on mine.

Hello, awkward.

Now he knew I had seen him. How could I ever act normal when our paths crossed over the course of the next few decades? And yeah, I had no doubt that our paths would cross that long into the future. Pepper and Reece would probably get married and I'd see this guy a couple times a year. First at the requisite wedding events, then the baby baptisms. Birthdays. Holidays. Each time I clapped eyes on him, I would recall this mortifying moment. And I'd know *he* would be recalling it, too. Damn it, where was the rewind button for tonight?

"Ohmigod! It's Logan!" Annie gave a little hop beside me the moment she spotted his face.

Of course, *she* knew who he was. I seemed to recall they had fooled around once. Pepper had mentioned that tidbit. For the first time since knowing this, something ugly spiked inside me. I hated that Annie had gotten to kiss him . . . that they had maybe done more than kiss.

As embarrassing as the whole situation was, I did not spontaneously combust. The earth did not open up to swallow me. Still, I didn't walk away. My feet were rooted to the spot, pinned by Logan's dark blue eyes. With his gaze glued to me, he lowered his head to kiss the girl again. Eyes wide open. Trained on me. He didn't look away from me as he kissed. Not even when the girl on the table brought her hand up and began working him through his jeans. He looked directly at me with a burning-hot stare.

Kissing one girl, his cock being rubbed by another, he stared me down.

I couldn't look away.

"That's hot," Annie breathed near my ear. "He's looking right at you like it's you he's kissing. Or wants to."

I fought to swallow the golf-ball-sized lump in my throat. "No," I choked out, not even certain what I was denying. He *was* looking at me. But he didn't want to kiss me. That would be . . . weird. I was his older brother's friend.

Suddenly someone started shouting: "Ten, nine, eight . . ." The crowd joined in, chanting out the rest of the countdown. "Seven, six, five, four, three, two, one!"

A tall, thin guy wearing a Charlie Brown T-shirt held up his phone as the timer started trilling. "Time's up!"

I exhaled, so relieved to know there was an end to this. That Logan wasn't about to engage in a full-scale threesome in front of this mob. In front of me. Because as much as I disliked the idea, I knew I wouldn't have been able to look away. I would have watched it all.

Which made me wonder who in the hell I even was anymore?

People clapped and hooted as Logan hopped down from the table in one smooth move, landing lightly on his feet. Turning, he assisted the other two girls off the table. One clung to him, clearly eager to continue what they'd started on the table.

"Number 364 . . . 364!"

Logan's gaze found me. Not difficult. I still hadn't moved from where I was rooted.

"All right! Who's got 364? C'mon now!"

"Georgia, did you check your ticket?" Annie grabbed my hand. I'd forgotten about the ticket I'd grabbed from the bucket. I didn't even know what it was for, but I'd hung on to it, clutched it between my fingers as I'd watched Logan's little exhibition. "Ohmigod! That's you!" Annie jerked my hand high into the air. "Right here . . . 364!"

The skinny guy pulled me forward. "Here's 364! Annnnnd."

He made a show of tossing the tickets in the bucket. He selected another ticket and brandished it in the air. "The lucky number is 349! Where is 349?"

Another guy emerged from the crowd. This guy was big. Like lineman big. And tall. My head fell back to assess him. He grinned. "Hey, sweet thing."

Before I could even speak, his hands dropped on my waist and lifted me up on the table. I winced a little as I came down hard. My legs dangled over the side of the table. "Ready for two minutes on the table?"

I opened my mouth, but no words came. For a split second, I tried to convince myself I could do this. Make out with a stranger in front of a group of strangers. I could be that bold. I could let go of my inhibitions for a few minutes and do something just that wild.

He leaned close to whisper in my ear, his fingers tucking the hair back from my face. "You're a pretty piece. If you're shy, we don't have to do this here at all. Would you like to go somewhere else? Take more than two minutes?"

The words finally came. A big fat *no* materialized on my tongue. I opened my mouth to object, but someone else was suddenly speaking.

"Sorry. This one's mine." Logan reached for my arm, fingers closing around my wrist as he guided me down from the table. Relief coursed through me. Until I remembered that I was a big girl who didn't need rescuing.

Lineman scowled at him. I added my own scowl. I wasn't *his* or anyone's.

Lineman stepped between us, blocking me from total

retreat. Logan still held my wrist. "You already had your fun."
He nodded at the pool table. "Now it's my turn."

Logan grinned like he wasn't challenging the thick-necked
guy who probably added steroids to his Chex Mix. "Sorry, man,
but she's not playing the game." Logan clapped a hand on his
muscle-sloped shoulder like they were old friends.

Lineman looked down at Logan's hand on his shoulder and
then back to him. "She took a ticket." He sounded like a petu-
lant child now.

"I—I'm sorry." I finally found my voice. Stammer and all.
"I didn't know what the ticket was for."

Lineman grunted and stepped out of the way. He held up
a finger in my face. "You should always know the rules before
you play."

I nodded, feeling like an idiot. Like a child being scolded
for not following the instructions so clearly written on top of
the paper.

Logan pulled me through the crowd and out into the more
open space of the loft. Only he didn't stop there. He didn't
release me.

His long strides moved swiftly, leading us through the
press of bodies. As if it was his right to touch me. As if his
brother dating my best friend gave him the right to interfere
in my life.

His grip shifted to hold my hand. I tried not to think about
his hand. About how warm and firm and large it felt wrapped
around mine. Harris wasn't big for holding hands, but when
he had it had never felt like this. For a guy, Harris's hands just
weren't that large. Our hands were about the same size.

I shook my head slightly. I had to stop doing that. Stop comparing every guy out there to Harris. It wasn't healthy.

"Where are you taking me?" I demanded.

"Out of here," he said over his shoulder, his voice deep enough that he didn't even have to lift it over the thumping bass for me to hear. I didn't protest. Didn't stop him. Eyes followed us as we moved across the room, and I just wanted to get away from the stares. At least I told myself it was that. I told myself it had nothing to do with the way my hand felt in Logan Mulvaney's. Or that I couldn't get the image of him and the way he had looked at me as he kissed those girls out of my head.

Chapter 3

HIS STRIDES WERE LONG. I took two steps for every one of his, trying to keep up. I spotted the elevator ahead, at the far end of the loft, directly in our path.

A voice called his name. "Logan?"

He stopped, turning partly to face the girl walking toward us. She was dressed all in black. Even her hair was dark as a raven's wing. Dyed, I suspected. The only other color was the slash of cherry-red lips in her pale face. Her blue eyes shifted from Logan to me and then back again. I tried not to shift beneath her intense regard. She was beautiful in a devour-you-alive kind of way.

"It's all right, Rachel," he said. "I'll be right back."

She nodded and turned with a sexy slink of her hips, heading toward the pool table and the crowd still gathered there.

Logan pulled me back toward the elevator. I wanted to ask about her. I didn't think Logan had a girlfriend. After the pool-table scene that seemed evident. Girlfriends, plural, was more his thing. But something had passed between them. Something that wasn't casual. Something proprietary.

He punched a button, calling the elevator, and then looked at me. His mouth lifted in a half smile that was familiar because I saw it almost daily on his brother. It almost put me at ease until I recalled that he wasn't Reece. He wasn't that safe, disarming guy who was head over heels in love with my best friend. This guy was wicked and immoral and trouble with a capital *T*.

He released my hand, waving me inside the elevator. I finally found my voice as he pulled the sliding door shut after us. Leaning against the back wall of the elevator, I swallowed a breath and willed the heat to cool from my face. "Well, wasn't that very caveman of you?"

"Oh, I'm sorry. Did you want to make out with Bubba back there on that pool table in front of all those people?" He jerked a thumb behind him. "'Cause I can let you go back in there if that's what you want. You just looked a little green. I thought you were going to puke."

"I wasn't going to throw up. And you don't need to escort me. Hate to drag you away from the fun you were having, after all. Looks like your girlfriend Rachel might be missing you." Or any number of females inside that loft.

"She's just a friend," he replied casually, thankfully not picking up on my catty tone. But I did. I heard it and I mentally kicked myself for it.

And yet I kept talking . . . still sounding like a judgy little shrew. "Somehow I doubt that you and any girl are just *friends*." I knew his reputation well enough to conclude that. And I'd just seen Logan Mulvaney give the performance of the century on that pool table to back it up.

I crossed my arms as the elevator began its descent.

He crossed his arms over his chest, mimicking my pose. "I've known Rachel since seventh grade."

"Aw. And you hang out at a kink club together now. How sweet for y'all." I opened my mouth to ask if he knew those other girls on the pool table, too, but managed to stop myself.

He smiled, shaking his head. "You're funny, G. Never noticed that about you before."

But he had noticed me. A stupid little thrill coursed through me.

He continued, "I'm guessing Anna brought you."

"You mean Annie?"

He shrugged like it didn't matter that he couldn't get the name right of a girl he had made out with once upon a time.

"I came with Annie but drove my own car."

"Good. You can drive yourself home then. She likes to stay late at these things."

Of course he would know that. Apparently he was a kink club regular.

The elevator settled to a stop and he slid the door open, asking, "What is it with you guys? First, Emerson, and now you're here."

I bristled as I stepped out. "You're one to talk."

"I'll tell you the same thing I told Emerson. This place is over your head. Hopefully, like her, you'll have enough sense to never come back here again."

This annoyed me. Maybe because I always prided myself on being so mature. I reveled when adults would tell my mother how composed and sensible and grown-up I was. It had always been a point of pride—for both Mom and me. But here he was treating me like a kid. And I was older than him!

Over my head.

You have marriage written all over your face.

Boring.

We stepped out onto the empty porch of the building. Empty because why hang out here when there was privacy inside to do all kinds of wild and wicked things? The type of things one did at a kink club. Things I had yet to learn about. Thanks to him.

I chafed my hands up and down my arms.

Everyone thought they knew me so well. Resentment simmered beneath my skin. He didn't know me. Who was he to pass judgment on me?

Maybe I just needed more time to get used to the place. To find the thing that worked for me. Logan ushering me away wasn't going to accomplish that.

"You don't have any say about where I can go." I walked past him and out into the night. It would be too embarrassing to return upstairs now. Not after he dragged me out of there.

"Hey," he called after me. "No need to get all butt-hurt. I'm just trying to help a friend out—"

I stopped and whirled around. "Are we friends, Logan? Pepper and your brother are dating. That's all. There's no other connection between us. I don't know why you feel the need to act all big brother. You're just . . ." I paused, grasping. " . . . a kid."

The minute I said it, I wanted to take it back.

He didn't look like a kid. Or act like one. Especially now.

He repositioned himself, spreading his legs a little wider, bracing his feet on the porch of the building. He didn't look mad or offended. Worse. He looked amused. He actually smiled.

And that grin was devastating. Seriously. No wonder he had such a reputation. Girls must throw themselves at him. His mouth was sexy as hell, too. His lips were well-defined and wide, the bottom fuller than the top. *Oh, the things I bet he could do with those lips. . .*

I blinked at the totally wayward thought.

"You think I'm just a kid, huh?" His deep voice rippled over me like warm wind.

I nodded once.

He stepped down from the porch, coming at me, stalking like some kind of predator. I backed up.

He was just a kid. Just a . . . kid . . .

Aw, hell. My gaze skimmed up and down six feet plus of sexy man. Who was I kidding? He was so totally *not* a kid.

I tried to look down my nose at him the way I had seen my mother do countless times when squaring off with some mouthy delinquent. My sister and I called it her "principal look." If she ever used it on us, we knew we were in trouble. But the effect was lost on him.

Yeah, he stood taller than six feet, but it wasn't that. Logan had an air about him. A confidence rare for anyone, much less an eighteen-year-old guy. He held himself like someone who knew who he was and his place in the world. And that annoyed me. Why was he so damn self-assured?

"How old are you?" he asked, still smiling. A deceptive smile. Cunning almost.

"Twenty. And you're eighteen. Still in high school." I flung that at him almost like an accusation.

"For another couple weeks, yeah." He nodded, absorbing this. "What month is your birthday?"

"November."

"Okaaay," he dragged the word out. "I'll be nineteen in August. My mom held me back . . . didn't want me to be the smallest kid in kindergarten." It was hard to imagine him ever being the smallest kid, comparatively, at any point in his life. "So we're twenty, twenty-one months apart, Georgia." He arched an eyebrow at me, waiting for this to sink in. For me to realize we're actually closer in age than I was willing to admit. That my calling him a kid was just . . . dumb.

I shrugged one shoulder, for some reason unwilling to give him that. "Maybe this place isn't for *you*. Don't you have a curfew or something?"

Pure contrariness had me tossing that out at him. I knew enough about his and Reece's family life to know that he probably never had a curfew. Not since his mom died when he was a kid. His father was disabled and not exactly a check-the-homework-and tuck-'em-into-bed kind of parent.

He laughed deeply then, tossing his head back. It was a deliberate dig, and instead of getting offended, he laughed. It was a hypnotizing sight, the way his throat worked, tendons moving beneath that golden skin. The flash of his straight teeth. My belly dipped and I knew this was why girls my age and older forgot about his age and dropped their panties for him. He oozed sex and confidence. I blinked hard, disgusted with myself.

The sound of his laughter sent goose bumps over my flesh and settled in the pit of my stomach.

He stopped laughing to say, "I've never had a curfew."

Never? I shook my head, telling myself now was not the time to marvel at his lack of supervision. My mom firmly believed no good could come of staying out past midnight. When I went home on break my parents still imposed a curfew on me. As if I wasn't in my second year of college. As if I hadn't been staying out all hours of the night doing all manner of naughty things. Yeah, okay, so I wasn't. But I *could* be.

This reminder of my sheltered existence just made me more determined to live my life on my own terms. To do tonight what I set out to do. To stop living such a boring existence. I was twenty and I'd been living the last four years like a married woman. School. Studying. Sex once a week. *Shit. Liar.* I couldn't even be honest with myself. The last year with Harris we maybe had sex every month.

Standing there looking at this incredibly hot guy who had a hell of a lot more experience than I did *and* was younger only flustered me. I flipped the hair back over my right shoulder, noting that his eyes followed the move, skimming over the long trail of blond hair before moving back to my face. Suddenly, I was glad that I had styled it so carefully for my date and worn it down in soft waves tonight.

"I'll leave. Fine. For tonight." I started to walk past him, but he blocked me.

"Meaning you might come back?"

I edged back from the wall of his chest, careful not to touch him. I think Reece mentioned his brother played sports.

It explained the breadth of his shoulders, which tapered down to a lean waist. The flat stomach. I'd glimpsed Reece without a shirt when he stayed the night with Pepper. It was criminal. Logan was in good shape. My gaze flicked over him. Okay. *Great* shape. He was probably ripped under the black shirt he wore. Just like his brother. Ridiculous six-pack, defined biceps and all. I swallowed against the sudden thickness of my throat. Shoot me. Was I actually drooling over a guy still in high school?

I shrugged. "Maybe."

He rubbed a hand over his scalp, dragging his hand over the close-cropped dark blond hair. "That guy you were talking to? The one you were about to get busy with on the pool table? Georgia," he expelled my name on an exasperated breath.

"You don't have a clue about the things he's into . . . the things he'll do to you."

I shivered a little beneath the weight of his blue eyes. "I can handle myself."

"Does Pepper and Em—"

"Pepper and Emerson aren't my parents," I snapped. "I'm a big girl, thank you very much. I don't need permission to be here."

He looked me up and down, his gaze lingering at my throat. "Sure you do, Pearls. You fit in here about as much as a bull in a china shop."

My hand flew to my necklace. The pearl necklace had been a graduation present. For some insane reason the hot sting of tears pricked the backs of my eyes. *I would not cry. He would not make me cry.*

"I'm tired of people telling me who I am." First Harris. *Always* my mother. I lived halfway across the country and she was still trying to tell me how to live my life. Even Pepper and Em.

And now him. This guy who didn't even know me.

I nodded toward the door. "Maybe I want to hook up with that guy and have him do those things to me. Ever consider that?" I deliberately let it sound like I knew what *those things* were.

"You don't even know what those things are," he retorted, seeing right through me. And how did he do that, anyway? Did I have a sign around my neck that said TOO BORING TO FUCK? Harris's face flashed across my mind. *I need more, Georgia.*

I fumed. I could be more. I was *more*.

"Yes, I do. He told me," I lied. "When he whispered in my ear."

His eyebrow winged. "Really? I heard he likes it when the girl dresses up as a dude and puts on a strap-on. You into that, Pearls? I would have pegged you for the type of girl who's only ever done it missionary-style."

I sucked in a breath. Insulted, yes. Shocked, too. Shocked that he had guessed that about me.

He laughed, nodding. "Yeah. Thought so."

"Asshole," I spit out. Another first. I had never called anyone a bad word before. It wasn't something ladies did.

"Why don't you go home to your safe dorm room and forget about this place?" His look then was part pity and part smirk. I could have handled the smirk. It was the faint pity that got to me. I wasn't pitiable. No way.

How dare he talk to me like *I* was the child? I was an adult. I came out tonight to have a good time. To put an end to my drought and prove to myself that I wasn't boring. I could be spontaneous. I could be unpredictable.

I could be wild.

Before I could stop and think about what I was doing, I stood on my tiptoes, circled his neck with my hands, and pulled his head down to mine.

Chapter 4

THERE WAS THE BAREST minuscule of a second when my mouth touched his that I wondered what the hell I was doing. Then that thought died.

I mean, you don't take a leap off a bridge and then change your mind. It didn't work that way. If I was going to kiss a guy as hot as this, then I was going to give it my all and enjoy the hell out of it.

I still had a hand around the back of his neck and my fingers flexed in his cropped-short hair. My hand slid upward, my fingers enjoying the feeling of hair that was both sharp and soft against my skin.

His lips were softer than I expected. I didn't get an immediate response so I stood on tiptoes and angled my mouth over his.

The idea that I was somehow forcing a kiss on him panicked me. That would be too mortifying. *Please. Please, kiss me back.*

My free hand grabbed a fistful of his shirt and tugged him down, willing him to kiss me. To not let me walk away from this feeling like a complete loser. I pulled back slightly, my lips moving against his. "What's the matter, Logan? Not up for it? I thought you were good at this."

An exhale passed from him into my mouth. *"Brat."*

His mouth opened over mine then. Whether he thought I was a brat or not, my words had done the trick.

He released the kraken. All of the sexual promise Logan Mulvaney radiated spilled into me.

He crouched in one quick motion, wrapping an arm around my waist and lifting me off my feet so that our fused mouths were level.

No me standing on tiptoes or him bending down. He kissed me back. No. More than that. He took over. Kissing me with lips and tongue and faintly scraping teeth.

I released my death grip on his shirt and wrapped an arm around his shoulders, hanging on for dear life.

We were moving. I was faintly conscious of this. I didn't open my eyes to look. I was lost, reveling in his tongue in my mouth, his fingers diving into my hair.

I gave the barest grunt when he backed us against the wall of the building, but that didn't stop the kiss. No. He didn't slow down.

His mouth was hot and aggressive, punishing on my stinging lips. I'd never been kissed so hard. So thoroughly. I felt him everywhere and this was just a kiss. Oh. God. What would the rest of it be like with him? It would wreck me.

"Is this what you wanted?" he growled against my lips.

I mewled against his mouth. He pushed his hips against me and I moaned, shifting slightly so that the juncture of my thighs was lined up more accurately to take the hard thrust of him that made my insides melt to warm pudding.

He increased the pressure of his mouth on mine, his body rocking and grinding into me until I wanted to tear our clothes off and just have at it. It was that or I die from this exquisite torture.

"Talk to me, Pearls," he commanded between kisses. "Let me hear that sweet accent telling me how much you want this."

I kissed him desperately. I was out of breath and drowning and couldn't think to form coherent words. I could only gasp his name as he sucked on my bottom lip. "Logan."

Laughter intruded. I blinked dimly, clearing the haze from my vision and unattaching my face from Logan's. My gaze landed on a couple stumbling up the porch.

"Couldn't even make it into the building before going at it, Mulvaney?" a guy called out amid laughter.

Just like that the spell was broken. I shoved at Logan's chest and stumbled out from between him and the wall, smoothing a hand over my wayward hair.

The couple disappeared inside the building.

"Georgia." Logan stepped toward me, looking a little shell-shocked. But not nearly as much as I was.

My lips had just attacked Reece's little brother. I'd gone beyond wild tonight and descended into things you should never ever do.

"Stop." I held a hand out like a shield.

He stopped, looking from my hand to my face.

"Let's just forget this happened." And never tell a soul.

He looked like he was on the verge of saying something but I never gave him the chance. I did the mature thing.

I ran.

I SLEPT LATE INTO Saturday morning, waking to the stillness of my room. Sunlight poured in through the slats of the blinds, tiny motes dancing on the sunbeams. I lifted my long hair so that it wasn't trapped under me and stared up at the ceiling. Rubbing the sleep from my eyes, I dropped my arms from above my head with a gust of breath.

A door opened and shut somewhere outside my room, echoing down the hallway. A full ten seconds passed before the memory of last night hit.

A sharp inhalation escaped me. My fingers flew to my mouth, tracing lips that still felt swollen. Impossible, of course. You couldn't feel a kiss into the next day.

Except I did.

Logan Mulvaney's mouth had branded mine. I'd been kissed by a total of four guys in my life. I had dated two guys, briefly, before Harris. I couldn't even remember those kisses. I could barely remember their faces. That's how much of an impression they had left. Then there was Joshua. No need to elaborate there. I only remembered him because he was so recent—and slobbery.

I had been with Harris since I was sixteen, and he wasn't much for kissing. Maybe in the beginning there had been some heavy kisses, but once we started having sex, he didn't waste a lot of time on foreplay.

But that kiss . . . Logan . . .

A full-body shudder swept through me. I had felt it down to my toes. Deep in my very bones. It had gone on forever and yet it hadn't been long enough because I still longed for a repeat. I scrubbed both hands over my face as if I could rid myself of these thoughts. Even if I was open to a physical-only relationship with a guy—a fling—I couldn't go there with Reece's little brother. That was wrong on so many levels.

A glance to my left revealed Emerson's bed exactly as it had been the night before. Same clothes strewn about. Clearly she hadn't come home. She'd spent the night with Shaw. Again. A sigh escaped me.

Most nights she spent at Shaw's these days. I tried not to let this bother me. Not only were they a couple, but they were working together now. She had started airbrushing the bikes he built. He'd turned half his work shed into a studio for her so she could even work on her paintings there, too. Still. It didn't stop me from feeling lonely. Shaking my head, I reminded myself that I'd be home in a few weeks. Back in my old hometown. In my old room with my mom and dad and Amber. I wouldn't be lonely then. It would be impossible to feel lonely with my parents breathing down my neck. With my sister barging into my room to invade my closet and wax on and on about her boyfriend, Jeremy, and whether she should follow him to Vanderbilt where he was hoping to get in the year after next. In short: misery.

Pepper and Emerson were staying at Dartford for the summer and I felt a stab of envy. Pepper was taking classes and Emerson was going to work with Shaw and help him get his garage up and running. As little as I saw of them lately, I wish I could stay here, safe from my prying family. I could see my summer in Muskogee unfolding so clearly before me. It would be worse since the breakup with Harris. Mom would want to talk about Harris all the time and what went wrong. Every time I bumped into someone in town, they would ask about him. Groaning, I forced myself from bed. No use dreading it. This was the plan. Even if I wanted to stay here, I couldn't. I'd have to suck it up and put my big girl panties on and start packing to go home soon.

Still groaning, I grabbed a bottle of juice from the small fridge and tore into a breakfast bar. Deciding the endorphins from a run might make me feel better, I changed into my running shorts and top. It was still a little chilly in the mornings, but my muscles soon heated up as I ran across campus to the nearby cross country trail that cut through some wooded acreage.

After my run, I showered and grabbed a quick lunch before settling in to study for my Statistics final. Anything math related wasn't really my thing, but I was a business major so I couldn't escape the requisite courses. I tried to focus on my notes in front of me but the formulas swam and blurred after a while. Sighing, I leaned back in my swivel chair and pressed the heels of my palms to my eyes. For once, studying wasn't working to distract me. When the door to the suite neighboring mine opened and shut and Pepper's and Reece's voices floated through the wall, I was more than ready to take a break.

I knocked once on the partially cracked door, pushing it open as Pepper's chirped, "Come in!"

She bounded over to me and gave me a hug.

Reece waved at me from where he lounged in the bed before tucking his arms behind his head. My chest flipped a little at his resemblance to Logan. After last night, the memory of Logan's face was fresher than ever. They had the same piercing blue eyes. The same square jaw. My gaze drifted to Reece's lips and then jerked away. I would not check out my best friend's boyfriend's lips to see if they resembled his brother's lips. Just. So. Wrong.

"Hey! How's your weekend?" Pepper asked. "Didn't you have a date last night?"

I wrinkled my nose and made a face. "The last."

"Oh, that bad?"

"Just no . . . sparks." I slid a glance to Reece's polite stare. Polite yet intense. Like his brother. These guys didn't just *look* at you. They *looked* at you. Like they were seeing directly into you. Maybe it was embedded in their DNA or something.

"Oh, well. Then better not waste your time there anymore."

I nodded, noticing then that there was a buzzing energy that seemed to cling to Pepper. Like she was a kid who had just been told she was going to Disneyland, but was trying to keep her act together and not totally explode from excitement.

I looked back and forth between her and Reece. An elusive smile clung to his lips. "What's going on?"

She and Reece shared a look before she blurted out with: "I'm moving in with Reece."

I stared for a moment, equal parts happiness and something else filling me. "Wow." I pulled her in for a hug and then moved to hug Reece. "Congratulations. You're moving into the apartment above Mulvaney's?"

"No." She shook her head, her beautiful auburn waves tossing around her shoulders. "Reece offered on a house last week and he got it! It's so cute! It's this little bungalow over on Smithson Avenue. I can't wait to show you." Reece reached for her waist and she moved in closer, sinking down on his lap so easily. So naturally. It had never been that way with Harris and me, I realized. It never felt easy or natural, and a pang struck me in the chest for the four years I'd wasted on something that had been so far from right.

Reece rested a hand on Pepper's jean-clad thigh. It was casual, but there was something possessive in the touch. It hinted at a shared intimacy and that sparked a deep longing awake inside me. I had never known that kind of intimacy. I was no virgin, but some things still felt so foreign to me.

"I can't wait to see it," I said.

"We're moving in next week."

Next week. My stomach dropped. "W-wow. Really?"

A house. That seemed so permanent. So grown-up. I looked between the two of them, marveling that Pepper had this. That she had found the one. Love. I had no doubt, looking at them, that they were the real thing, and I felt a little foolish for thinking that I had had that with Harris. Now I knew. I never had that.

Pepper nodded, her arm draped around him, her fingers idly rubbing his muscled shoulder through his T-shirt. "Yeah." The word slipped past her smiling lips.

"Congratulations," I repeated. "I'm so happy for both of you."

Pepper looked back at me. "I know we planned on living together again next year—"

"Don't worry about that. Emerson and I can put in for a single. Or maybe see if Suzanne wants to join us." Assuming Emerson wasn't moving in with Shaw.

"When are you heading back for the summer?" Pepper asked. "I wish you didn't have to go."

"Yeah. Me, too."

"Then stay."

"My mom would flip. And I don't have a place to stay anyway." Emerson was staying at her dad's condo in Boston. At least that was the cover story. She would be at Shaw's most of the time. Her dad was hardly ever in Boston, so he wouldn't know.

"Oh! I just had an idea." She looked at Reece eagerly. "Georgia could stay in your old apartment above Mulvaney's."

He shrugged and nodded at me. "Sure. It will be vacant. You could stay there a couple months."

"That's really nice of you, but Mom has a job lined up for me back home for the summer."

"If you need a job over the summer, you could work at Mulvaney's," Reece offered. "We have two spots opening up for the summer."

Working at a bar? My mom would have a coronary. "Thanks, but I kind of have to go."

Pepper wrinkled her nose. "To that bank you don't want to work at. You're going to work there?"

Admittedly, Reece's offer was tempting. Staying here over the summer. Having an apartment to myself. Working at

Mulvaney's—having a job where I didn't have to wear a suit and be "on" and impress everyone so they would go back and say great things to my mother about me. It sounded like heaven.

Reece must have seen something in my face. "Think about it, Georgia. Since Pepper and I just bought the new house, the apartment is there if you want it. And with the second Mulvaney's open across town, we're looking for new staff. If you need work, it's there."

I nodded. "Thanks. I'll think about it." And I realized they weren't just words I was uttering to placate him. I really would think about it. Long into the night.

I went for pizza with Reece, Pepper, and Suzanne from down the hall. Emerson and Shaw met up with us, too. Thankfully, I didn't feel like such a third wheel with Suzanne there.

Over slices of Greek and Hawaiian pizza, we all talked about our summer plans. Suzanne was going home part of the summer to house-sit while her parents went on a month-long Mediterranean cruise. I sighed internally. I wish my parents would go on a month-long cruise. Maybe then going home wouldn't feel like such an impending tragedy.

Pepper and Reece talked animatedly about their new place and the newly opened Mulvaney's across town. Okay, Pepper was mostly the animated one. Reece just watched her with a sexy smile on his face.

Aside from the garage Shaw would soon be opening, Emerson and Shaw were excited about a new client who had just commissioned three bikes from them—and Emerson had an offer from a fancy gallery in Boston to feature a collection of her work next month. The happy vibes were almost smothering me.

My phone rang once as Emerson was coaxing me into sharing a slice of tiramisu with her. A glance down confirmed what I already suspected. It was Mom. I let it go to voicemail, determined to enjoy dinner out with my friends.

When I returned to my room later, I played Mom's message. It was a reminder for me to call Mr. Berenger first thing Monday morning.

Sighing, I got ready for bed, telling myself I'd call him Monday afternoon after my morning classes.

Settling into bed, I stared into the dark. Thin orange light bled in through the blinds' slats. I focused on my to-do list for tomorrow and Monday. Study for exams. On Monday I needed to meet with my advisor regarding my course selection for next year. And now I needed to call about the bank job.

Sighing, I rolled onto my side. I needed to get some boxes and start thinking about packing up my stuff, too. Just three more weeks and the semester would be over. There was plenty else to occupy my mind . . . so why did I keep thinking about that kiss? Why did my mind keep going back to Logan? His face was there so clearly. The searing blue eyes. Those lips that were always grinning—except when I was kissing him. And when he was kissing me back.

My hand dragged up my stomach to cup my breast. I was a healthy C cup. There was more than enough for my hand, but I wondered how I would fit in Logan's palm. And that made my breath catch. My fingers brushed my nipple and then squeezed it harder. A small whimper escaped me as my mind played over last night.

I wiggled on the bed, an ache starting between my thighs as I worked my fingers over my breast. My lips tingled, remembering the press of Logan's warm mouth on mine, moving surely . . . his tongue. Wishing it had been more. Wishing I hadn't run away.

Idiot. Wrenching my hand off myself, I rolled over onto my side, punching my pillow with my fist twice, feeling somewhat better and vowing to forget about Logan. He was not the kind of guy I needed to fixate on. I knew the kind of guy that worked best for me . . . If I found him, great. If not, then I was just fine alone. I had a bright future with or without a guy in it.

I drifted off to sleep, feeling angry at myself, which was probably a bad idea. I slept fitfully, weird images plaguing me.

I was drowning in my dream, tangled up in an ocean full of pearls. I kept waving to the lifeguard standing on shore, who was Harris one moment and then Logan in the next. Finally hearing my cries, Logan dove into the pearls and swam out to me, but before he could reach me I went down, choking, lost in a sea of pearls.

MONDAY ROLLED AROUND AND I got so busy that I didn't get around to calling Mr. Berenger. At least that's what I told myself. Tuesday arrived, though, and I still didn't call him.

I couldn't stop thinking about Reece's offer to stay in the apartment above Mulvaney's. It tiptoed around me, gnawing at the edges of my thoughts every day. I turned it around in my head, trying to rationalize how I could make it work, how I could do something like that without my parents totally flipping out on me. Simple. I couldn't.

When Mom called Wednesday night to check on whether

I had called about the bank job, my excuse sounded lame even to my ears.

"Sorry, Mom. My study group ran late. By the time I got out it was past five." I caught a glimpse of myself in the full-length mirror hanging on my door. I was a horrible liar. If Mom could see me, she'd know. My brown eyes had gone really big under my eyebrows and the color faded from my skin—like I was surprised at the words coming out of my mouth.

"This isn't like you, Georgia. I asked you to call him on Monday. I'm starting to wonder if you even want this job."

"I do," I insisted, grimacing a little at my lying reflection. My bothersome eyebrows, several shades darker than my blond hair, lifted high as I made my excuses.

"Well, I certainly hope so. Because your father and I certainly aren't going to let you sit around all summer, hanging out by the pool and getting pedicures. Even Amber has her summer lined up lifeguarding at the neighborhood pool. Responsibility, Georgia. We expect nothing less from you."

When have I ever done anything less than be responsible?

I bit back the caustic reply . . . and others that scalded the back of my throat. I've been the perfect daughter. I've done everything my parents ever told me to do. Everything they expected. In high school, when Mom insisted that I give up the guitar and drop out of choir for the debate team, I did. When they said I should be a business major, I did that, too. When had I ever given her a reason to think I needed a lecture on responsibility?

"I'll call him in the morning," I promised.

"I hope so." She sighed. "Don't disappoint me, Georgia."

Laced beneath the words I hear the words she never says, but are there just the same.

Don't fail me like your father did.

My *real* father. Not the man she married when I was three. No. The father who left me when I was two months old because he couldn't handle the responsibilities of a wife, child, marriage, and job.

My birth father had been a musician. I never met him. He took gigs anywhere he could get them and lived in his van. When I showed an aptitude for music, Mom only allowed me to pursue it until high school. She insisted that with my heavy course load, something had to go and music was it. I knew, though, deep down, that Mom hated that part of me because it reminded her of my father. So I had let that part of myself go, almost ashamed of it, wanting only to please my mother and stepfather.

Don't be him. That's what she was saying. Without saying the words, that's what she *always* managed to say. What I always heard.

And I wouldn't. Long ago, I had vowed to be the opposite of that man. The kind of daughter Mom needed me to be. Someone she could be proud of. Responsible and solid. The kind of girl who went to college and married a lawyer or doctor and took summer internships at a bank.

Harris's voice echoed in my mind right then. *Boring*.

Sounds from the room next door drew my attention and I knocked lightly before entering Pepper's room. She was changing from her work clothes into a pair of frayed denim shorts.

"Hey," she said, snapping up her shorts. "How's it going?"

"Good. Where are you headed?"

"I'm meeting Reece at Mulvaney's. We're going to Logan's game."

Everything inside me tightened at the mention of Logan. "He plays baseball, right?"

"Yeah. It's the playoffs. We missed the last couple games . . . been so busy with opening the new Mulvaney's. I think Reece feels bad he hasn't been there for him lately. He can't miss this one." Her freckled nose wrinkled as though she smelled something foul. "Their father won't be there. I don't think he's left the house in months."

Reece and Logan's father was confined to a wheelchair as a result of a car accident several years ago Not that that was the reason he wouldn't go to his son's game. He was a bitter man who spent most of his time drinking, and wasn't the most supportive or attentive father even before the accident that put him in a wheelchair.

Pepper grabbed her messenger bag and paused on the way to the door. "What do you have going on tonight?"

I shrugged. "Pretty studied out for exams. Guess I'll just start packing up a couple boxes."

"Oh. Want to come?"

Did I want to go to a high school baseball game? Did I want to sit in the stands with a bunch of parents and high school kids and gawk at a teenage boy like some kind of cougar reliving the moment I had kissed him and he had kissed me back?

With another shrug, I nodded once. "Sure."

Chapter 5

THE GAME HAD JUST started when we arrived, and I could tell Reece was anxious to get a seat in the stands. Not an easy feat. It was loud and crowded and we had to climb to almost the very top of the stands and squeeze in between students.

"There he is." Pepper motioned to the field, pointing eagerly and bouncing on the balls of her feet.

I searched, my heart hammering in my chest and then seizing altogether when I spotted him. I didn't know a lot about baseball, but I knew he was the pitcher. Standing on the mound, he stared intently at the player coming up to hit. I'd never seen him wearing a baseball cap before and damn if it wasn't a good look for him.

He rotated a baseball behind his back with the sure movement of his fingers. He held himself still, waiting with seeming idleness, but there was a coiled energy about him that brought to mind the explosiveness of our kiss with a rush of awareness that left me breathless and turned on sitting there on the hard bleacher seat.

I fidgeted, drinking in the sight of him. I'd never seen him so alert, so serious.

Except that moment following your kiss. He'd looked serious then. He'd looked intense, his blue eyes deep and probing and so sexy it hurt.

This Logan was unsmiling as he stood stock-still on the mound, his lean body rigid like a gun cocked and ready to fire.

The batter squared off in front of the base, tapping his bat once and lifting it in readiness, hands flexing as he adjusted his grip.

A hush fell over the crowd as everyone waited, watching. I didn't even breathe. I leaned forward, curling my hands around the edge of the bleacher.

Then Logan let go. His body uncoiled, leg winding up and then back down as he released the ball.

The batter swung, missing.

The crowd surged and cheered, myself included. Then silence fell again. Even from this distance, I could read the batter's scowl. Logan adjusted his cap and rubbed a palm along his snug-fitting pants. I tried not to stare at his butt, but in those pants? Impossible.

I wasn't his only admirer either. As he threw the ball again and the batter missed for a second time, a group of girls a few rows below us screamed his name and followed with several catcalls.

Pepper shook her head with a laugh. "That's our Logan. No heart is safe."

My cheeks heated and my skin hurt. I didn't know why. It's not as though my heart was in danger. Just my lips.

The rest of the game passed with me riveted to wherever

Logan was on the field. Whether he was up to pitch or hitting the ball, my gaze tracked his lithe movements.

At one point, Reece pointed out some scouts sitting in one of the lower rows.

"Are they here for your brother?" I asked.

"Logan already committed to Kellison University."

"That's where he's going in the fall?" Then he would officially be in college. A new college with a new crop of girls for him to divest of panties. He was a jock. They'd treat him like a superstar on campus.

It was a good reminder of just how different we were.

"Yeah." Reece nodded, looking very much like the proud older brother. "We're going to miss him."

"It's not that far," I said. Forty minutes at the most.

"Yeah, but he won't be working at Mulvaney's anymore. He'll be caught up in school. Playing ball." Some of the pride slipped then and Reece looked a little sad that his brother would be moving on.

Pepper sensed this, too. She covered his hand with hers and pressed a kiss to his cheek. "We'll always be family. This is a good thing. He needs to get out from under your dad. And Rachel. Time for him to live a life of his own."

Rachel? I understood the reference to his dad, knowing most of the Mulvaney backstory. Logan often got stuck in the caretaker role for the cantankerous man, driving him places and taking care of the house when he wasn't at school or work. Mr. Mulvaney would finally have to hire someone or accept help from his sister and stop relying on Logan. But Rachel? He had said she was just a friend. Obviously, she was more than that.

"Speak of the devil." Pepper nodded toward the dark-haired girl walking up the stands, searching for a place to sit. She was still dressed in head-to-toe black, her lips that bright coral-red from the other night. She still possessed that hard, almost untouchable beauty.

Students recognized her. They nodded in her direction as she made her way up the steps, her heavy boots clanging over the metal. I couldn't hear their words, but they were followed with laughter and sly glances.

"Rachel!" Reece called, waving her over. Her hard expression gave the faintest crack. She smiled the closest thing to a smile I had seen on her face yet, but that smile slipped when she spotted me. Clearly, she remembered me.

A panicked flurry of butterflies erupted in my belly. Would she mention the kink club? I still hadn't said anything about it to Pepper, and I didn't want it to come out this way.

Reece scooted down, making room for her.

"Hey, Rachel, this is my friend, Georgia," Pepper introduced.

"Hey." She nodded once at me and then looked away to the field as if I was of no interest. I released a breath.

"Hello," I returned. Apparently she wouldn't out me.

Through the rest of the game, I felt Rachel sliding glances my way. I caught her looking several times. It was with great effort that I trained my stare straight ahead. I also made a point not to be overly exuberant in my cheering so she didn't read anything into it. She was probably wondering why I was here. Suddenly I was wondering that, too.

What would Logan think when he saw me? That I was

sniffing around because I liked our kiss? Because I wanted an encore? God. I flushed hot with embarrassment.

The rest of the game passed with Logan's team pulling ahead. They won 7–5, largely due to Logan.

Everyone stood and began filing down the stands. In the crush, a few people slipped between me and Pepper and Reece, putting distance between us.

"What are you doing here?"

I looked sharply to my right. Rachel had hung back and positioned herself beside me as we descended the metal steps.

I shrugged. "Pepper asked me to come."

Her darkly lined eyes stared hard at me. "No."

It was a single word, but it dropped like a stone between us.

I stared at her for a moment, trying to think how to respond. I knew that I didn't want to ask for elaboration. I was afraid what more she might say.

She continued anyway. "You're like all the others, after a taste of him." She looked me up and down before pushing past me, tossing the single word over her shoulder. "Pathetic."

The words gouged me, and I hated it. Hated that I had become this insecure—this vulnerable. My breakup with Harris had stripped me and left me raw and bleeding. I'd been trying to patch myself back up ever since. Trying to figure myself out for the last couple months. There were days when I felt close to luring whoever I was, who I was supposed to be, who I wanted to be, out into the world. And then something like this happened that cut me back down.

Rachel's words felt like a stab into the open wound.

I watched as she moved ahead, weaving her way down to

the bottom of the bleachers and catching up with Reece and Pepper.

I TRAILED AT A sedate pace, determined to keep my distance from them as they approached the dugout. A chain link fence separated the players from the fans, but Reece's deep voice carried as he called for Logan. I knew from Pepper it was important to Reece that Logan knew they came. That Logan knew they loved and supported him.

Logan's head popped up at the sound of his name. His signature grin broke out and he separated himself from his teammates and stepped up to the fence to talk to his brother and Pepper. Rachel soon joined them, too.

Logan pushed back his cap on his head slightly, revealing more of his face. Still so good-looking it made my chest ache a little.

God. This was stupid. Me being here. I couldn't take it back now, but I wasn't going to rush to the fence and be the pathetic thing Rachel just claimed I was.

Logan nodded, smiling almost modestly, and I knew they must be congratulating him, insisting that he won the game. He shook his head and motioned behind him, probably insisting it was a team effort. I could read it in his body language. Logan might be one of the most self-aware guys I'd ever met, but he wasn't full of himself.

He was looking at Pepper, listening to her when suddenly his posture changed. He head shot up, scanning the diminishing crowd, searching.

For me.

I ceased to breathe. Pepper must have mentioned that I'd joined them. Or maybe he just sensed me. I didn't know. I only knew that he was looking for me. I knew it the second before his eyes jerked to a stop on me.

I moved slowly, my steps dragging, unwilling to meet up with them, but knowing I'd have to eventually. I couldn't pass that spot without stopping. The polite thing to do would be to congratulate him, and I was all about politeness. Good manners had been mixed in with my baby cereal.

I'd have to face him and then I would see the same knowledge in his eyes that I had seen in Rachel's. He would think I was pathetic, too. That I came here because I wanted another taste of him. Just like Rachel accused.

Then, miraculously, I was saved. The coach called for all the players.

Logan stared at me one moment longer, his blue eyes unreadable from this distance, before he turned and grabbed his stuff from the dugout alongside the rest of his team. They all trotted toward the locker room.

I stopped alongside Pepper and Reece. Pepper looked at me. "Hey, you just missed Logan. He had to go."

I nodded, fixing my lips into a bland little smile.

Pepper turned to Reece. "Text him and see if he wants to grab dinner—"

"He has plans. Big after-party," Rachel explained, looking at me. Of course, she would be looking at me.

"Oh, sure." Pepper nodded in understanding. "Then it's just us."

We all started down the path that led past the concession stands. The fried goodness of funnel cakes filled the air.

"You stay out of trouble tonight, Rachel," Reece said, sounding so much like a dad that I smiled.

"Always do." With a flutter of her fingers, she headed for the parking lot, her hips doing that sexy slink again. I somehow felt certain she was headed for trouble.

Pepper tugged on Reece's sleeve. "I want a funnel cake."

"I thought we were going to dinner." He pointed toward the concession stand. "And that line is really long."

She played with the hem of his shirt, flashing the world a glimpse of his super-cut abs. "They don't serve funnel cakes at any restaurant I know."

He relented with an exaggerated sigh, pulling her close and tucking her to his side. "This is true." He looked at me. "Georgia? Want one?"

"No, thanks." I inclined my head to the parking lot. "My mom called. I'm gonna call her back. I'll wait by the car."

Of course, I was lying. Needing to use the phone seemed like a good excuse. And I needed an excuse. I didn't want to be stuck standing in line with them in case Logan came back. I couldn't undo coming to this game, but if I could escape without talking to him, I would feel markedly better about the whole thing.

My shoes crunched over the gravel lot as I made my way to Reece's Jeep. I leaned against the door and pulled out my phone and started thumbing through it. I was browsing my sister's Instagram when a pair of baseball cleats stopped directly in my line of vision. I looked up, my gaze skimming Logan's legs before stopping on his face. How did a guy so big move with ninjalike stealth? I hadn't heard his approach, and Amber's latest pictures of gummy bears and her freshly painted toenails wasn't that riveting.

"No funnel cake for you?"

I shoved my phone back into my pocket. "Not in the mood." At least my voice came out normal.

"Were you 'not in the mood' to tell me hello, too?"

Heat crawled over my face. "Hi," I said lamely.

"Why'd you come?" That was direct. Nearly as direct as those piercing blue of his eyes.

I shifted my feet, opting for distraction. "Gr-great game."

"Yeah, thanks." He shrugged one shoulder, brushing it aside as if it were nothing, but his eyes were no less relentless, dismissing my attempt at distraction and demanding an answer.

"Really. It was an important game. Congratulations."

"I know." And yet he didn't seem that eager to discuss it.

"Congratulations. You were—" Incredible. Amazing. Self-possessed and confident. "You won the game. Are you . . . sad a little? It was your last game."

He shook his head once. "There will be other games. In college."

"I heard you're going to Kellison. Congratulations." God. How many times was I going to say that?

A mocking smile played about his lips that made my belly flutter. He probably heard compliments all the time from any one of his countless groupies. I stepped back a pace, bumping into the door of the Jeep, suddenly not wanting to be confused with one of them. I glanced away, worried that he would see something in my face that I didn't want him to see. The thing that Rachel had seen.

I looked across the parking lot, ready for Pepper and Reece to return. I spotted them. They were almost to the front of the concession line now. A woman stood at the counter, five little kids surrounding her as she placed an order. It was going to be a while yet.

I could go stand with them. Then I wouldn't be alone here with Logan.

"Didn't expect to see you here, Georgia. You've never been to a game with Reece and Pepper before."

His voice drew my gaze back to his face. I'd never kissed him before. Never thought about Reece's little brother in the way I did now.

And that made me feel pathetic. Just like Rachel said. Harris called me boring. Rachel called me pathetic. I was two for two when it came to things I didn't want to be.

"Yeah. Well, I didn't have anything going on and Pepper invited me . . ." My voice faded and I felt so lame standing there. Acting like I didn't want to come. That my being here was just a casual thing. After the other night, my being here felt so very obvious and I wanted to punch myself. Hard.

"Hey, Lo!" Another player walked down the row between cars, his bat bag slung over his shoulder. He came over and clapped Logan on the shoulder. "You headed to the after-party?"

The skinny kid looked like a teenager. An honest-to-God high school kid with angry-looking acne and a bobbing Adam's apple. And this was one of Logan's friends? A fellow *peer*? Mortification ripped through me. In that moment, I never felt the gulf between us so keenly. And I felt stupid . . . foolish standing there pretending I was here for any other reason than that our kiss had consumed my thoughts for days.

Logan nodded. "Yeah. See you there."

The boy looked at me curiously, the interest keen in his eyes, before he walked away.

"God," I muttered softly.

Logan must have heard me. His head whipped back around and he stared at me, his eyes alert and sharp like he could read my thoughts.

Thankfully, I spotted Reece and Pepper headed our way. "I gotta go," I said hurriedly, turning to walk around the Jeep, ready to climb in the backseat, not even caring how obvious I was in trying to put distance between us by unnecessarily circling *around* the vehicle.

I felt him move behind me before I felt his hands on my arms. "No, you don't," he growled. "You don't get to run away again."

I squeaked as he hauled me back against his chest. My spine stiffened iron-rod straight against the wall of his broad chest. I felt my eyes go huge in my face. He was touching me. Again. And I was freaking out on the inside. I sucked in a deep breath, determined that my freak-out stayed internal only.

"Let me go. They're coming." My heart hammered violently in my chest and I didn't know if it was because we were about to get busted by my friends or because his body felt so unbelievable against mine. Okay, fine. It was both.

His mouth brushed my ear as he spoke, spiking sensation to every nerve in my body. "Are you embarrassed, Georgia? You don't want them to see me with you? Don't want Pepper and Reece to know about us?"

"There is no 'us.'"

"Oh, but there will be. We both know why you came tonight." His fingers flexed, each digit a burning imprint on my forearms.

"Yeah?" Was that breathy croak my voice? "Why?"

"Because you haven't been able to forget what it felt like to kiss me, and you want to know if the rest of it will be that good, too." He bit down on my earlobe and a whimper escaped my lips. "It will be."

An invisible band squeezed around my chest. I swallowed against my constricting throat. "Arrogant much?"

"It's okay. I haven't been able to forget either. I can still remember the way you taste."

Oh. My. God.

I swallowed a moan and lurched free from him. Swinging around, I faced him and felt my knees go weak at the look in his eyes. Heavy-lidded and deep, his blue eyes looked almost indigo as they stared down at me.

"I know you probably think it'd be some great joke to bang one of your brother's friends, but I'm not going to be another notch on your bedpost . . . some girl you screw once and forget about the next—"

He moved fast then, closing the space that I had established between us. Oh, yeah. He was a jock with ninja-fast reflexes. I needed to remember that.

I gasped as his hand slid around my neck, fingers burying in the hair at the base of my scalp. He lowered his head, dropping his forehead against mine until our breaths clashed and mingled. His fingers pressed and massaged the back of my head, shooting sensation straight to the core of me. Holy hell. Was that some kind of secret pressure point?

His words gusted over my mouth. "You think we'd fuck just once?"

My stomach plummeted at his blunt words.

He took my hand and dragged it between us, pressing my palm to his crotch—against the outline of his cock in his tight baseball pants. It hardened, growing beneath my touch and I felt an answering ache clench between my thighs. *God, it had been so long.*

"This doesn't feel like a joke to me. You don't," he growled in a tight voice. "I want to do things to you . . . things a clean, vanilla girl like you never dreamed of. Things that tool boyfriend of yours never came close to doing to you."

"Ex-boyfriend," I replied automatically.

At my response, Logan pushed my palm harder against him, rubbing the hard ridge of him. A tiny moan escaped me as the ache squeezed between my legs.

He angled his head. "I think you want me to do dirty things to you, Georgia."

My mouth sagged. No one had ever talked to me like that. He shocked every part of me—shocked, horrified . . . and turned me on. I'd never known this with Harris. With any guy. Never wanted sex so badly that I felt like I could weep for the lack of it.

That had to make this just a little bit okay. Right?

I sighed. But not enough to erase the wrong factor. I could not have a fling with Logan Mulvaney.

"No," I said, hating me right then. Hating that even though my lips formed the word *no*, I was thinking *yes* in my head. Yes. YES. "I don't want that."

"Liar," he said mildly.

He brushed a strand of hair back off my shoulder and the simple touch rocked a shiver through me.

I pressed my fingers to his chest and gave him a slight push away. "Don't touch me. In fact, just stay away from me." God. Was that desperate little rasp really my voice?

He stepped back then, the deep blue of his eyes turning chilly. "Fine. Sure. I won't touch you again. It's all on you now."

All on me? What was that supposed to mean? He was leaving it up to me to *ask* him to touch me? No worries there. I never initiate sex. I never had. In fact, the only time I had ever taken charge and initiated anything had been the one time I kissed Logan. And that was never happening again.

That crooked grin appeared on his face again, belying the hard intensity of his eyes. "Any time you want me to make you scream, just let me know, Pearls."

"Oh." It was barely a word. More like a gasp. A sudden image of him and me together, his powerful body driving into mine, branded itself on my mind and my mouth dried. Heat flushed over my body.

"Hey, Logan," Reece called out, suddenly there, almost to the Jeep. I jumped a little. I had actually forgotten they were approaching. It was Logan. He rattled my brain.

With a final wink at me, Logan swung his bat bag around so that it hid the erection pushing against the front of his pants.

I stared after him, feeling rattled and shaken and doing my best to disguise it.

Pepper balanced a sugar-drenched funnel cake in one hand and held on to Reece's hand with the other one. Grin firmly in place, Logan turned to face Reece and Pepper. With no invitation, Logan snatched a chunk of funnel cake from her plate. The latticework of fried bread dangled from his fingers before breaking.

I watched, mesmerized, as he tilted back his head, opened his mouth wide, and dropped the food in. The tendons in his throat, the muscles flexing in his square jaw—all served to make my belly dip.

"Nice," Pepper complained. "That was like half of it."

He picked at another piece and she swatted his hand.

"Great game, Logan." Reece looked at his brother almost earnestly, as if he was trying to convey something . . . be family for him, everything, the parent he so obviously lacked. "Seriously, man. I'm proud of you."

Logan shrugged like it was no big thing. "Will you be at the new Mulvaney's tomorrow?"

"Yeah, I'll be there. You're working afternoon to close at the old location, right? Mike's going to open."

Logan nodded. "Yeah. I gotta go."

Reece moved in for that half-body hug guys did.

"Thanks for coming." Logan's glance skipped to Pepper, clearly including her in the thanks. Me, not so much. I just stood there, feeling as out of place as ever.

Logan's gaze slid to me, warming me all over again. "See you around, Pearls."

Logan walked away then, heading off to his after-party where he would likely use his charm to nail some other girl.

"Pearls?" Pepper inquired next to me around a mouthful of funnel cake.

I lifted one shoulder. "Yeah. It's just a thing . . . he calls me."

"Cute."

I felt Reece's stare on my face, but refused to look, too worried I would see confirmation in his eyes that he knew I was slightly infatuated with his player of a brother.

Climbing inside Reece's Jeep, I wrapped myself in this knowledge that nothing more would happen between Logan and me. First of all, I would have to ask for it and that would be like me asking Mom to share stories about my real father with me. Yeah. Not in this lifetime.

Second, I was leaving soon. When I returned in the fall he would be at Kellison. I would see him less often and not face the temptation of his presence.

I could almost convince myself I was glad about this.

Chapter 6

I KNOCKED ONCE ON my advisor's door before stepping inside. The office smelled like musty books and Taco Bell burritos. A quick glance at the overfull trash bin confirmed that Dr. Chase ate most of his meals there. "You wanted to see me, Dr. Chase?"

He'd written a note on my last paper for me to come see him during his office hours. I'd enjoyed his class this semester. As much as one could enjoy Labor Law and Policy. It just spoke to his teaching ability that he made the course work interesting.

"Yes, have a seat, Georgia."

I still clutched my paper in my hands.

He came around his desk and sank into the chair opposite mine. He tapped at the paper. "This is good work, Georgia."

A flush spread through me. "Thank you."

He crossed his legs, gripping his ankle where it rested on his knee, showing off his plaid socks. "You have a strong control of language. It's a gift. Half the time when I read an undergrad paper, I feel like I'm wading through a jumble of words to get to the point, but you have a better handle of the material than most graduate students."

My chest swelled. I wished my mother were here to hear this.

He continued, "What are you doing this summer?"

"I'm going home."

"And home is . . ."

"Muskogee, Alabama."

"Hmm. Not a bustling metropolis."

"No, sir. I'm looking into an internship at a bank—"

"Filing and making coffee." He shook his head. "It's a waste of your talents. You'll learn nothing. One of the grad students I'd hired to assist me on my research this summer had to back out. I have an opening." His gaze fastened on me, his dark eyes steady through the lenses of his glasses. "It's a rare opportunity, Georgia. The other two students assisting me are grad students and I still need a third—"

"Yes," I blurted. He hadn't even mentioned pay or the research topic, but I didn't care. This sounded a lot better than going home and working at the bank. And the best thing of all? I could stay here. Mom wouldn't love the idea, but she would have to acknowledge it as a great opportunity. It was an academic endeavor that actually paid.

"Excellent. Speak with Doris, the department secretary, and she will gather your information. We'll be in touch regarding our first meeting." Dr. Chase stood.

I rose, too, grabbing the strap of my messenger bag. I shook his hand, maybe a little too vigorously in my eagerness. "Thank you."

He smiled, already looking distracted as he dropped my hand. "See you soon."

As soon as I left his office, I rummaged for my phone and scanned my contacts until I found the person I needed to call. He picked up after the second ring.

"Reece? Hey, it's Georgia. Did you really mean it when you said I could use your old apartment this summer?"

MOM WASN'T THRILLED.

I'd known that she wouldn't be, but she actually required more convincing than I expected.

"Maybe I should call this Dr. Chase," she suggested, "And find out more about the particulars of—"

"Mom, no. What for?" With a deep breath, I softened my voice, "I'm twenty years old and in college. I don't think he's accustomed to getting phone calls from parents. This is legit, I promise. I'll be working with grad students. I'm really lucky to get this chance."

She sighed, and I knew she was relenting.

"I'm sure I can expect a fabulous recommendation from him for future jobs. And this experience will look great on my resume," I added, knowing how Mom thought. "Your friend at the bank will be very impressed."

"Fine."

A huge smile curved my lips and I danced in place.

"What about housing?" she continued. "Do you even have a place—"

"A friend of mine is moving out of his apartment and is letting me stay there over the summer."

"Is it a nice place? In a good part of town?"

"Mom. It's five minutes from campus. It's great." Not a lie. Mulvaney's is right around the corner from campus. I just omitted the part about it being located on top of a bar.

"All right. Georgia. I can see you want this. We were just looking forward to having you home for the summer. We miss you." At that, guilt stabbed at me. My mother, my family . . . they just loved me. Mom especially. She cared about me. I shouldn't resent her for it. My mom wasn't like Pepper's—a drug addict who'd abandoned her only child. Or Emerson's mother who was, depending on the day, either cruel or indifferent to her daughter. My mom cared too much. That was her crime.

"Find out the timeline. Maybe you can schedule a trip home before school starts in the fall."

I nodded, happiness bubbling up inside me. "I will. I'll let you know."

I stayed on the phone for a few more minutes, in such a great mood that I even tolerated her sharing all the latest Harris news with me. Apparently Mom had breakfast with his mother at the club last weekend. I didn't even interrupt when she voiced—again—the inevitability of our getting back together.

Ending the call, I propped my hands on my hips and surveyed my dorm. Suddenly packing wasn't such a dismal prospect.

THE LAST WEEK AND a half of classes flew by. My final paper was turned in. My last exam taken. All my boxes were packed— and not just mine, but my roommates', too. We were all moving out. Moving out and moving on.

I sat on Pepper's bed next to Em, watching as Reece lifted the final box and marched out into the hall with it.

Pepper sank down on the mattress beside us. The mattress was stripped of sheets and made a faint crackling sound with the addition of her weight. The room was completely bare. Naked brick walls stared down at us.

"This is it," Pepper declared with a forced smile.

My eyes ached a little, burning with the threat of tears, as I stared at her. I reached out to caress the loosely braided auburn hair that hung over her shoulder.

"It's not like this is good-bye," Emerson declared after a long moment of silence.

"Yeah, I know. We'll get together every week," I said, my voice a little strangled even to my ears. "We'll always have *Teen Wolf* night."

"That's right," Pepper agreed, pointing at both of us in mock threat. "We watch it together. Reruns, fine, but new episodes are off-limits."

But it won't be the same.

The three of us would never share our lives together in the same way again. Pepper would be living full-time with Reece. Even in the fall when Emerson and I moved back into the dorm together with Suzanne (she had agreed to move in with us), it would never be like before. Em would hardly ever be there. She'd be with Shaw. And it would only be a matter of time before Suzanne had a boyfriend, too.

We were moving on. Growing up. It was right. Good. And I was happy for all of us. *So why did this suck so much?*

Pepper hugged each of us, her arms squeezing tight. "You sure you don't need help moving your stuff to Mulvaney's?"

"No, I got it. Reece already helped me get everything in the car." There was nothing left for me next door. Just an empty room like this one. "I can take it from here. I'll head over this afternoon."

She nodded and we all hugged again like it was the last time we would ever see one another. "At least shoot me a text when you're on your way over and I'll meet you at Mulvaney's to officially introduce you to the staff."

"You don't have to do that. You'll be busy settling into your new—"

"No, I want to. Reece has to go into work later at the new location anyway, so I'm happy to do it."

"Okay," I agreed.

Pepper left then and Em and I turned to face each other. She bumped her knuckles with mine with exaggerated slowness. "So proud of you, friend."

I blinked. "Me? Why?"

"I know your parents were pressuring you to go home for the summer, and I know you didn't want to. Good for you standing up for yourself."

"Working with Dr. Chase is a great opportunity."

She shrugged. "Spin it however you like. You're here and free for the summer." She grinned then. "Now don't get into too much trouble at Mulvaney's." Her pretty grin then turned into a giggle. As if the idea of my getting into trouble was so outrageous she had to laugh.

I laughed as if that was ridiculous. "Oh, you know me. Troublemaker extraordinaire."

I had a flash of myself at the kink club with Annie. I had been on the verge of getting into trouble that night. And that had been the goal. To shake off my self-imposed constraints and not be so boring for once. To be wild. If Em knew that, she might not laugh at the suggestion. She might actually be worried I would do something reckless and get into trouble living above Mulvaney's.

She considered me for a moment, her lovely blue eyes sharp with speculation. "On second thought, a little bit of trouble might be good for you." She held up her thumb and index finger, pinching a small amount of air. "Just a little bit. Nothing to land you in jail or anything."

I seriously laughed at that. I'd never so much as gotten a speeding ticket. "Oh, really? Is jail when you've gone too far then? Is that when things have officially gotten out of hand?"

"Yeah. Jail is a no-no. But you've been the good girl long enough. Maybe you need a wild summer."

It burned on my tongue to tell her about the kink club right then, but I held back. First of all, she didn't approve of Annie, and once I weathered her disapproval for hanging out with the girl who abandoned her at a biker bar, she would demand all the details. Considering most of those details involved Logan Mulvaney and a kiss that left me all hot and bothered, I couldn't bring myself to tell her. The very idea made me wince. "I'll be working . . . doing research, remember?"

"Not every moment of the day. You'll have plenty of time for play."

"I'll be fine," I assured her.

"Who wants to be *fine* all the time?" She snorted, standing and grabbing her bag. "Be crazy. Have a fling. Get that asshat Harris out of your system for good. Nothing like a good romp between the sheets to make you forget the prick and move on. And who knows? Maybe you'll meet the *one*."

I sighed, not quite knowing what to do with this new Emerson. She had turned into the eternal optimist who believed in love and happily ever after.

But some of what she was saying had a kernel of truth. I'd just had a taste of what she was describing with Logan, and Harris's memory was already dimmer. When I did think of Harris these days, it was with more clarity. The relationship hadn't been working for a long time, but habit had kept me chained to him. And the fact that my parents loved the idea of us together.

Could a romp between the sheets with Logan exorcise my ex totally? Tempting. Too bad it couldn't happen. Any other guy, maybe. But not Logan. It would be difficult to have a fling with Reece's younger brother and keep it uncomplicated.

She pressed a quick kiss to my cheek. "You staying here for the summer is going to be good for you."

"Yeah?" I asked as she moved to the door.

"Yeah. Look. You've played the perfect girlfriend, the perfect daughter forever. Maybe you need to spend the summer and just find the perfect you." She smiled at me to soften her words—as though she knew they stung. And they did.

I'd always viewed myself as strong, smart, and independent, but she'd just called me out. I was a fake—not nearly as independent as I had pretended to be. I could think of no reply.

"I'll text you," she said, her smile soft and encouraging.

I nodded, her words tumbling through me with a truth that I didn't want to acknowledge. And yet she'd thrown them out there, forcing me to see them. "Bye."

The door clicked shut after her. Alone in our empty suite, I fell back on the bare mattress and stared at the ceiling, confronting the idea of me being someone else this summer. A girl who didn't have to worry about what her parents thought. A girl without a hovering boyfriend.

I could be anyone I wanted.

Chapter 7

I'D BEEN TO REECE'S apartment above Mulvaney's once before. Pepper had cooked dinner and we'd played cards afterward to the quiet rumble of the bar below us.

The apartment felt like a barren shell compared to that night. They had left the bed, futon, kitchen table, and major appliances. Pepper mentioned they would be buying new stuff for their new place. Even with the basic furniture, all the little flourishes that had made it feel like a home were gone. The photographs and wall art. Reece's bike in the corner. The books crammed into the bookcase. It felt like an echo of what it had been before.

The bar was a low murmur under my feet as I padded barefoot around the space, unpacking and hanging clothes, stopping occasionally to eat some of the fried pickles that the cook had forced on me as I passed through the kitchen to take the stairs up to the apartment. If I wasn't careful, I was going to pack on the pounds living above Mulvaney's kitchen—home of the famous Tijuana Fries, Death Burger, and Fried Pickle Chips with Chipotle Ranch Sauce.

Pepper had made sure I met all the staff earlier when I arrived this afternoon. Those who were on the clock anyway. Mike was the manager. Karla manned the food counter most nights, and the cook, a former cook in the navy, was—unsurprisingly—just Cook.

I'd seen Mike and Karla plenty of times when I hung out at Mulvaney's—mostly back in the days when Pepper was prowling Mulvaney's after first meeting Reece. Since Harris and I broke up, I hadn't been here as often, figuring that any guys I met here wouldn't be the kind I was interested in. Good, studious types that I could bring home to my parents didn't hang out at bars. The next guy I brought home would have to be pretty spectacular, at least in my parents' eyes, to replace Harris. Especially since Mom was still hung up on the idea of Harris and me.

It was after one in the morning when I finally finished arranging the apartment to my liking. I just couldn't sleep until everything was put away and organized. Emerson called me anal. Granted she was a mess and wouldn't know what to do with a hanger, but I had been raised to be tidy and organized. It was simply habit now. My mother was exacting. Clothes had to be color coordinated in the closet. Books in alphabetical order in my bookcase. Disorder and chaos was not tolerated. Again, I think it reminded her too much of my mess of a birth father.

Feeling grimy after putting everything away, I pulled my long hair up into a knot and took a shower, enjoying the fact that this shower was twice as big as the showers in the dorm. I let the warm spray of water beat down on my body and loosen my muscles. Once I was out of the shower, I slipped on panties and a soft tank top.

Still feeling a little restless, I curled up on the futon, pulling my fuzzy throw blanket over me, and watched some television.

After the second rerun of *The Big Bang Theory*, I turned off the TV and tossed out the remaining pickle chips. As I passed the couch, I noticed that I hadn't put away everything. My guitar, still in its case, sat propped between the futon and the side table. I hesitated, staring at it with a funny tightness in my chest.

When I'd pulled it out of my dorm closet, I had almost forgotten its existence. I hadn't left it at home because I was worried Mom would get rid of it. She had tried to cart it off to Goodwill a few times over the years, but I had stood my ground and insisted on keeping it. For some reason, she had always capitulated. Mostly, I think, because she never saw me pull it out and play it anymore. That would have concerned her and forced her hand. So I ignored it for many years. Forgotten like an old pair of shoes.

Sinking on the couch, I pulled it out of the case and brought the comforting weight of it across my lap, my fingers caressing the colorful blue-and-green-patterned strap before moving to the strings. I plucked one. The out-of-tune *twang* filled my ears, and my fingers instinctively went to the knobs, strumming strings and rotating the knobs until the sound was just right.

When I had it perfect, I played a few chords of "Landslide." I smiled, losing myself in that part of me that I had buried for dead long ago. I shouldn't have, but I couldn't stop myself. For a moment, I let myself go. Surrendered to that part of me . . . the part of myself that reminded my mother so much of my father. The part that terrified her.

At the sudden thought of her . . . and him, I slapped a palm over the strings, effectively killing the music my fingers had created so effortlessly from them.

My heart ached, but I forced the guitar from my lap. Forced it from my hands like another moment in my clasp might somehow poison me. I set it down beside the futon, against its case, not even taking the time to put it inside. Later. I would touch it later. Right now I just needed distance.

I turned off all the lights except for the small light above the stove. At the bed, I pulled back the covers. I had one knee on the mattress and was arranging my multitude of pillows to my liking when I heard footsteps, growing in volume.

I froze, eyeing the opening that led to the stairs, wondering who was coming up here this time of night. Surely not Pepper or Reece. The bar had quieted in the last hour and I assumed it was closing up for the night if not already fully closed. The bottom door that led to the stairs had a lock, which I had utilized, but clearly that hadn't stopped this person.

I managed to push up off the bed, but couldn't move otherwise. I stood frozen—prey caught in the crosshairs as Logan ascended the steps to the top floor of the loft.

I recognized him even in the dim light. The long, lean lines of him. The broad shoulders. The weak light limned his hair like sunlight and cast one side of his face in a golden glow. My heart squeezed tightly as I drank up the sight of him, eyes trailing over the square-cut jaw, the shadowed slant of his lips.

I reached for my bedside lamp, fumbling to turn it on.

He beat me to it, flipping the switch on the wall where he stood a split second before I turned on the lamp. Light from both sources flooded the room.

It was inescapable. The blast of light. Him. The full impact of his face. The deeply set eyes with criminally long lashes. The strong angles that my fingers itched to trace. And the dark blue eyes drilling into me.

"Fuuck," he breathed, dragging a hand over his close-cropped hair as his gaze swept over me.

Heat scored my face. I didn't do obscenities all that often. I grew up in a household where the word *crap* got you grounded. With that kind of upbringing, curse words tend to get stuck in your throat. But yeah. *That* word about summed up my feelings on seeing Logan Mulvaney standing in my doorway when I wasn't wearing anything more than panties and a tank.

My chest locked up, not even lifting to draw air as our stares collided.

I unfroze. Straightening, I brought both feet down to the ground gingerly. Like too sudden a movement might break the spell and spur either one of us into movement. And I wasn't certain what that movement would be. Me running from him or to him?

My bare feet flexed on the floorboards as we watched each other like two wary animals. Okay, well maybe I was the only one wary. He just looked . . . surprised but not all that wary. No. He looked like an apex predator ready to pounce.

I shifted my weight and tried not to think about the fact that I was standing there in my boy shorts and a tight tank sans bra. I wore swimsuits that revealed more skin and yet I felt like I was standing before him naked. I never even felt this exposed with Harris. But then I couldn't recall Harris ever looking at me the way Logan was.

His gaze traveled over me. I felt it like a physical caress, roaming my face, my naked shoulders, then down my chest. My breasts grew heavier under his inspection, achy against the cotton of my tank, and my treacherous nipples hardened. I resisted the urge to bow my shoulders and cross my arms over my chest, convinced it would be a sign of weakness. An admission that he affected me.

The deep blue of his eyes darkened. He snapped his gaze to my face. "What are you doing here?" he asked thickly, the tendons of his throat working as he managed to get out the words.

I lifted my chin. "I could ask you the same thing."

"I work here. My brother owns the place." He angled his head, looking at me, waiting for the obvious to sink in.

"Reece said I could stay here over the summer."

Logan sighed and dragged a hand over his face. "Of course."

"He forgot to mention that to you?" I asked, feeling both relieved and a little angry. Relieved because he wasn't stalking me. And angry because he wasn't stalking me.

Great. I've turned into *that* girl. Another Annie who liked the bad boys. The ones wrong in every way.

Logan nodded, resting a shoulder against the wall. "Yeah. He might have left that out. Sometimes I stay the night here when I close up. Since it's so late. I sleep on the futon. Pepper started insisting on it when she and Reece got together."

That was so like Pepper, always looking out for others. I glanced at the clock. Yeah. It was really late for him to be driving home. I know he lived half an hour away.

"Sorry," he muttered, rubbing the back of his neck. He looked tired. "Reece and Pepper moved into the new house . . . I just assumed it was empty up here."

I nodded, my face still burning even though I knew this was a simple misunderstanding. Reece was busy with the move, his relationship with Pepper, running two bars now—and I had sprung it on him that I would accept his offer to move into the loft. No surprise he hadn't mentioned me moving in here to his brother. The fact that Logan and I had kissed, that not a night went by without my touching myself and thinking about him didn't make this awkward. Not at all.

Okay, it was awkward, but it didn't have to be. I could be an adult about this.

He turned to leave, his hand going to the switch to turn the light back off. "Sorry," he repeated.

"Wait."

He stopped and turned.

I swallowed. "It's late. Your brother wouldn't want you driving back this time of night." I sucked in a breath. "And neither do I."

He leaned a shoulder on the wall again, crossing his arms over that broad chest of his. "I'm not angling for an invite to stay the night—"

"I didn't say you were."

He continued to stare, his keen eyes discerning in a way that made me want to fidget.

"Look, you stay on the futon like usual. I trust you."

"You shouldn't," he returned.

I blinked.

"You shouldn't trust me," he repeated, looking me up and down slowly. "I'm not like the guys you're used to."

What guys were those? Harris barely touched me by the end of our relationship. And the last couple of guys I dated pawed at me and slobbered over me and then broke up with me when I didn't jump into bed with them. I didn't want Logan to be like those guys.

My mind made up, I turned and plucked a pillow off the bed. Grabbing my fuzzy blanket from the foot of the bed, I marched to the futon and dropped both items, suddenly annoyed enough not to care that I was in my underwear just a few feet away from him. "There you go."

A corner of his mouth lifted and he shoved off the wall. My heart dropped into my stomach at the sound of his footsteps on the hardwood floor, coming closer.

Suddenly I felt so . . . alone with him. Acutely aware that we were the only two people inside the building.

"You sure about this?" He walked toward me with measured steps and I wasn't so clear what it was he was asking me anymore.

I pointed. "The *couch*," I clarified—maybe just as much for myself as for him. "Yeah, I'm sure you can spend the night there."

"Thanks." He stopped before reaching the couch, looking me up and down again in my scanty attire. The sweep of his gaze caught on my guitar where I'd tucked it between the futon and side table. "This yours?" He sank down on the futon and picked up my guitar, settling it on his lap.

I took a protective step forward, my hand reaching out before I could stop myself. He looked up, lifting his eyebrows, not missing my involuntary move, "I'll be careful," he murmured, a smile playing about his lips. "You play?"

I shrugged uncomfortably. "A little. I used to. N-not really." God. I was babbling.

"No?" He plucked at a few of the strings. "Then why do you have it?"

I lifted the guitar from his hands. "I used to keep it in the back of my closet. Just haven't gotten around to putting it away yet."

"Back of the closet, huh?"

"Yeah." I walked across the loft and opened the tiny closet where the vacuum barely fit and stuck my guitar inside, making sure it was secure before closing the door.

I turned around and gasped, nearly yelping at finding him directly in front of me. He moved like some kind of cheetah. Silent and swift.

His clear blue eyes flicked over my shoulder to the closet. "So you're a 'closet' guitar player?" He grinned. "You know you'll feel better if you just own it and come out to the world."

"Very funny. Do I look like the musician type to you?"

"I don't know." He lifted one broad shoulder in half a shrug. His cotton shirt looked soft and inviting, hugging his chest. There was no mistaking the ridiculousness of the body under that shirt. "What does a musician type look like?"

I had a flash of my father in the one picture I had of him. Aunt Charlene had given it to me. She told me a child should know what her father looked like, and then she told me to never let Mom know I had the photo. I hid the photo in the middle of a book, taking it out often over the years to examine it and search for evidence of me within the features of his face. I would study it for hours. Days of my life were lost to that photo.

The edges were curled with age now, the paper slightly faded. He was wearing an Eagles T-shirt and holding me like

I was something fragile. But there had been something in his velvet brown eyes—eyes so like my own. Tenderness. Love. At least I thought I saw it there. I convinced myself it was there. I was only a few months old, all swaddled up in a blanket. His dark blond hair hung in straight strands to his shoulders. His face was narrow, handsome with taunting eyes. A guitar hung on the back of his chair. Like it had to be close. Like he could never be far from it.

I knocked the image from my head and focused on Logan again, watching me, waiting for my response. "I don't know. Just not me."

I backed away several paces before turning around. Like I was afraid to present him with my back. At my bed, I slid beneath my fresh sheets, my eyes trained on him as he moved back to the couch and began to undress. First his shoes. Then he reached back behind him and grabbed the collar of his shirt with one hand, pulling it over his head in one smooth motion. My mouth dried. Un-flipping-believable.

He was like some guy in one of those calendars my aunt Charlene always hung on the front of her fridge, ignoring Mom's protest that they were vulgar. Maybe I was like my aunt. Minus the five hundred cats. Or maybe that was my future. Eccentric Cat Lady with a calendar full of guys who looked like Logan. God. That was a tragic thought. Especially when I had the reality right here within reach.

Logan was real. Hard and cut. I could probably break my knuckles on his abs. Not that I was going to punch him. I wasn't even going to *touch* him. No, all that beautiful golden skin was off-limits.

Still, my gaze roved over him in appreciation. His stomach was ripped with muscle and a mesmerizing, happy trail led south to the zipper of his jeans. His hands went there, popping open his fly. My pulse jack-knifed against my neck as the teeth of the zipper sang out.

I couldn't look away. I watched, gawking as if he were putting on some sort of show just for me. He shoved the jeans down, revealing a pair of fitted boxer briefs that did very little to hide his package. At least it did very little to hide the shape and size of it. The *growing* shape and size.

Oh, God. He was hard. My gaze flew to his face. He was watching me intently. His mouth curled in that perpetual mocking half-grin, but his blue eyes lacked all mirth. They were smoldering dark and focused on me.

He might be smiling but hard-core sexy-time thoughts were tracking through his head. They had to be.

His deep voice rumbled over the air. "Want me to keep going?"

I licked my lips. "What do you mean?"

"Keep undressing?" His hands moved to the band of his briefs.

"No!" I practically shouted the word, holding out a hand.

He lifted one eyebrow. "You just seemed so interested in the view. Remember . . . all you have to do is say the word, Pearls."

The reminder of what he'd offered me at the baseball park washed over me and my cheeks burned hot. Not that I needed reminding—his words had been taunting me for days—but to know that he hadn't forgotten his offer, that he hadn't been kidding . . .

Any time you want me to make you scream, you just let me know.

Crap. I wanted that. Heat flooded my face and I knew I had to be tomato red. I waved a hand in his general direction. "It's hardly anything I haven't seen before."

The words were all bravado. I'd only ever seen Harris. And that was mostly in the dark. And Harris's body was nothing like his. Harris had been soft. Not overweight . . . there just hadn't been any defined muscle. His flesh always gave way beneath my fingers. Like firmer-than-usual Jell-O.

And there hadn't been . . . *that* between his legs. I could tell, even beneath the fabric of his briefs, that it was different . . . bigger.

Suddenly he was moving, walking toward me.

I shrank into the bed, pulling the covers to my chin, hoping, dreading . . .

My heart pounded so hard I was certain he could hear it in my ears by the time he stopped beside the bed. I hadn't positioned myself in the center of the bed, so he stood just inches from my side and, this close, I could smell him. The faint salt of his skin and a whiff of deodorant. He leaned down over me, his face so close the brilliance of his eyes awed me.

"I can guarantee you haven't seen *me*, Georgia."

His warm voice—those words, the heavy promise implicit in them, made goose bumps pucker across my skin. I gulped. No. I hadn't seen him. Or anything even close to him.

My eyes fixed on his mouth as he inched forward just a fraction closer and extended his arm . . . to turn off the lamp.

The soft *click* filled the air.

The low glow of light from above the stove saved the room

from total blackness, but his features were impossible to make out. There was just the dark outline of him and his voice. That deep, seductive rumble that created friction across my skin.

My fingers clutched the edge of the sheet, my grip bloodless and aching.

"Good night, Georgia."

The words puffed across my lips and then he was gone, moving back to the couch.

Bastard.

He got me worked up and then left me aching. I had no doubt he knew it, too. My only consolation was the sight of his raging hard-on. He was aching, too.

I listened in the near-dark to his movements as he settled down on the futon.

He really wasn't going to make a move on me. I felt my features scowl in the dark, angry at the sharp lance of disappointment shooting through me. I should be feeling relief.

I tossed and turned before settling on my side. Tucking my hand beneath my cheek, I glared into the dark, convinced I would never fall asleep. Closing my eyes, I released a deep breath and focused on forgetting his presence only feet away, convinced that was impossible. No way would I fall asleep with Logan Mulvaney in the same room with me.

When I next opened my eyes, it was morning.

Early-morning sunlight poured into the room. Frowning, I stared at the wide, curtain-free window and the tiny motes of sunlight and dust particles dancing on the air. I searched my mind, trying to remember where I was precisely.

It all returned to me then, hitting me in a rush. I was in

Reece's old apartment. I was spending the summer above Mulvaney's bar.

I held still for a moment, and then remembered all the rest. The most important thing of all—a half-naked Logan Mulvaney was asleep across the room from me.

I sat up with a bolt.

The futon was empty, the throw folded neatly across the back like he had never been here.

I dropped back on the bed, my fingers playing about my lips.

I think you want me to do dirty things to you . . .

Turning my head on the pillow, I glanced at the clock on the bedside table. It was eight A.M. I had to meet Dr. Chase and the other research assistants at eleven. If I got up now, I could manage to fit in a run.

With a groan, I dragged myself out of the bed. A run was just what I needed. Endorphins pumping through my system that made me feel better, stronger. That helped get rid of all residual sexual frustration.

Chapter 8

IT WAS CLEAR FROM the start that I would be the grunt.

After Dr. Chase met with us and outlined our duties for the next couple weeks, we left his office and walked to the library. It didn't take ten minutes for the two grad students to assign me the task of accumulating the necessary statistics for Chase's project on Strategies of Entrepreneurship. A task that amounted to hours on the computer. Snore.

Gillian would write up my findings and actually get the pleasure of interviewing local businesses and conducting phone interviews with entrepreneurs on a national scale. Connor would be combining our data and using it to research social media commercialization tactics.

"So we're all set for now?" Gillain looked first at Connor, then at me, pushing her bright blue glasses up the bridge of her nose.

Connor clapped his hands together. "All set."

I nodded, not really suspecting they were interested in my input. That was the impression I had gotten so far. I was the undergrad here.

"Great." Gillian started gathering her things and stuffing them into her bag. "I'm meeting Caroline for coffee." She looked me squarely in the face as she uttered this. "She's another grad student who applied to work with Dr. Chase this summer. Somehow she didn't get picked." She grinned a small, tight smile then.

My return smile felt brittle.

Looking very satisfied, she rose from her chair and marched away.

"Don't mind her," Connor said as I stared at her retreating back.

I looked at him with a shrug. "At least I know where she stands."

He snorted. "If Caroline had been picked, then she would have been bitchy, too, trying to outdo her. You actually made her day. Right now she gets to go meet with Caroline and act all sympathetic while inside she's just patting herself on the back that she's better than Caroline."

"Wow," I murmured. "It's going to be great working with her this summer."

"Hey." He spread his hands in front of him. "You have me. I'm a nice guy."

I smiled slightly and started packing my things. "Well, I guess I better start on those stats."

He started gathering his things, too, stuffing his laptop into his bag. He fell in beside me as we walked out of the library. "So how did you get this job anyway?"

I slid him a look. He was tall and lanky. His chestnut hair fell low across his forehead, brushing his eyebrows. "What do you mean?"

"Well, you're an undergrad." He tossed his hair back in a move I'd witnessed him do constantly in the last hour. It only ever fell back on his forehead. "Dr. Chase must be pretty impressed with you."

"Dr. Chase liked my final paper—"

"That's it? I mean you didn't hypnotize him?" He waved a hand in a small circle, wiggling his fingers.

"You get you're being insulting, right?" I stopped and looked at him, trying to hide a smile.

"Hey, no offense!"

"I didn't sleep with him if that's what you're angling at. God, what a cliché that would be."

He shuddered. "Oh, I wasn't even going there. He smells like Taco Bell."

"Right?" I laughed as we stepped outside and descended the steps.

"Butttt." He cocked his head in mock contemplation. "You know what they say about clichés."

I stopped at the base of the steps leading up to the library and propped a hand on my hip. "So is this what it's going to be like all summer? You and Gillian looking at me like I'm some sort of incompetent who slept with her professor to get a job? Maybe I should go talk to Dr. Chase?"

"Shit." Connor dragged a hand through his flopping hair, his eyes wide with horror. "I'm kidding. Sorry, I guess I really screwed this up."

I dropped my hand and winked. "I'm just messing with you."

He grabbed his chest. "Damn. You nearly gave me a heart

attack." He released his chest as I laughed and looked me over. "You're all right, Undergrad."

"Thanks."

"Good to know I didn't screw up."

"Screw what up?"

"This. Small talk. Flirtation."

"Is that what you were doing?" I teased. "It was hard to tell."

"Ouch." He chuckled and readjusted his grip on the strap of his backpack. "Yeah. I was trying."

I studied him a moment. He was cute. His face was broad with brackets edging his mouth, like he smiled a whole lot. A good sign.

Sucking in a breath, I decided getting out there again might be a good thing. I couldn't solely fixate on Logan. It wasn't healthy. "You know you could just ask a girl out for coffee. Or a smoothie. I like those."

"Do you want to go get a coffee right now?" His face brightened eagerly as I considered him. It was probably a bad idea. We were working together, but . . .

"Sure," I heard myself saying. We were only working together for the summer, after all, and I needed new friends. A guy like Connor, someone in grad school . . . older, he might just possess the maturity that had been missing in the guys I had been dating recently.

Logan's face flashed across my mind for some reason. I didn't know why. He and I weren't dating. And despite his age, I wouldn't call him immature.

"So how does the Java Hut sound?" Connor asked, tugging

my attention back and motioning in the direction we needed to turn.

"Sure." I smiled. "That sounds great." And I almost meant it.

WHEN LOGAN SHOWED UP on my doorstep again late the next night, it almost felt natural. Well. If not for the crazy way my heart thumped at the sight of him.

His mouth kicked up at the corner. He dragged a hand through his short hair, his eyes tired. "Long night?" I asked.

"Yeah." He blew out a breath and plucked at the ripped sleeve of his shirt. "Only had to break up one fight. It was between a group of girls. I'll take a brawl between guys any day."

I laughed.

"Mind if I crash here tonight again?"

"Sure. It's okay." My voice even passed for normal as I uttered this.

He followed me upstairs and I waved him to the table where I was working.

"You're a night owl," he observed, eyeing my laptop. "Are you studying right now? I can go if I'm bothering—"

"No. Stay." God. Did my voice crack a little just then? I swallowed and tried again, deliberately neglecting to mention that I had stayed up late tonight thinking—fine, *hoping*—he might make another appearance. "I'm not studying for summer school or anything." I sank back down into my chair, tucking a long strand of hair behind my ear self-consciously, and pulling a knee up to my chest. "I'm working for a professor this summer. Doing research for him."

He plopped down at the table across from me. "That's pretty cool."

I nodded, feeling lame and awkward all at once. "Would you like a drink?"

"Sure."

I got up and grabbed him a can of soda from the refrigerator, feeling his eyes on my back.

"So what are you studying? For your degree?" he asked as I returned to my chair. It was a polite question—that thing people asked automatically without really caring, but he stared at me with interest.

"Business."

"And is that what you always wanted to do?"

"Major in business?" I shrugged, thinking about it. Did anyone ever grow up saying they wanted to major in business? It wasn't like your typical fireman-ballerina-astronaut dream. "I guess." It had seemed like a sensible plan. The only thing I had ever really had a passion for was music, and if I had pursued that it would have been a knife in my mother's back. "It just seemed like a smart choice. My parents liked the idea."

He studied me carefully. "Your parents' approval is that important to you?" It was more of a statement than a question.

"Yeah. Sure. You don't think it should matter?" And then I felt like an ass. His mother was dead. His father didn't give a damn about him. Parental approval wasn't high on his list of priorities.

He looked away, staring across the room at nothing in particular. "I guess if I had the kind of upbringing you did, good parents, picket fence, and all that stuff, it would matter to me, too . . ." A decided *but* hung on the air.

I nudged him. "And?"

He lifted his gaze back to mine. "There comes a time when you've got to do what's right for you . . . what makes you happy." His gaze held mine, the blue of his eyes so direct that it cut through everything. I realized then that Logan would always follow his own path. Even if he had grown up with that picket fence, he was that kind of person. Confident and self-assured enough to do what he wanted to do and not give in to the expectations of others.

"What about you? What do you want to major in? Or do you only live and breathe baseball?"

He looked back at me, studying me over the laptop, and shook his head. "I do love the game. Don't get me wrong. There's a rhythm in it. A peace that comes over me when I'm standing on the mound." He took a long sip from his drink. I watched his throat work, mesmerized. "It doesn't matter if the ballpark is full of screaming fans or smack-talkers shouting at me from every direction. It's like I'm on a boat drifting at sea, totally calm, the world fading around me. Nothing hurried. Just the sound of my breath, the pulse of my heart, the ball in my hand. Have you ever felt like that?"

I took a breath, realizing I'd been in some kind of trance, my memory searching for a moment like that. His description had triggered that need in me. I'd never met a guy who talked like him. With mere words he fired a need in me to know that kind of peace.

"Yeah," I admitted slowly. "I have." When I held my guitar, I felt that way. Or rather, I had.

When it became clear I wasn't going to elaborate, he continued, "If I'm lucky enough to make it to the majors, then great. But I have other interests, too . . . other things that bring that same feeling."

And this struck me as wholly unfair. My fingers tightened around the curve of my knee. I looked away for a moment and bit the inside of my cheek, disturbed by this. Nothing inspired me the way he described except for something I couldn't do, and he had *multiple* things that spoke to him?

"I'm actually interested in teaching."

My attention snapped back to him. "As in becoming a teacher?"

He nodded. "Yeah."

"Like being a coach?"

He sent me a look that said *I'm not just a dumb jock, you know.* "No. English."

"English?"

"What are you? A parrot? Yeah, English. Literature." He made a flapping motion with his hands. "I'm into those things that open and have pages in the middle."

I laughed awkwardly. "No, I didn't know that about you. I didn't know that you—"

"Read? Yes, I can read words and everything."

I wadded up a napkin and tossed it at him.

He chuckled and caught it. "I actually read a lot. And write."

I stared at him, not knowing what to do with this sudden new insight to him. He was a jock who . . . *wrote*? But, of course, it was believable. The way he used words. He didn't just talk. He painted a picture with language.

He rubbed a hand up and down the back of his scalp and blew out a breath. "I've never told anyone that before."

"Not even Rachel?" I blurted before I could help myself. Clearly they were close. How could she not know that he liked to write?

He shook his head, his eyebrows drawing tightly over his deep-set eyes. Like even he was confused that he had confessed this to me. "No. Actually I haven't. When we talk it's usually about . . . her . . ." He frowned like maybe this had just occurred to him.

I wet my lips. A fluttery feeling danced inside my too-tight chest as I stared at him. Maybe she thought she knew everything there was to know about him. Every moment I spent with him, I discovered another layer. I doubt there would ever be a time when this guy didn't fascinate me. "I want to hear about your writing. What is it that you write?

"Fiction. Stories," he provided.

"I'd like to read them . . . if you'd let me."

He looked at me for a long moment and then smiled almost self-consciously. I blinked. Impossible. This guy never looked uncertain. "I've never let anyone read them before."

"What?" I toyed with the tip of a pen. "You scared?"

He looked only halfway joking as he replied, "Yes."

I grinned, continuing to play with the pen, rolling it between my fingers. His gaze followed the movement, making my skin pull tighter. "I'll be gentle with you," I teased. "Promise."

He laughed, but his eyes deepened to that dark sea blue I was becoming familiar with. It was that blue that made me feel all funny inside. Like I was dipping down on a roller coaster. His gaze dropped to my mouth. The sexual tension was thick. Choking me. God. He was close. Just a small stretch of table between us. This proximity was killing me. My lungs hurt too much to even draw a full breath.

I rose suddenly, picking up our empty soda cans. "Yeah. You should email me something. Or bring it with you on your next shift." *Or on our next sleepover.*

"Maybe I will."

I glanced back at his face and grinned, shaking my head as I rinsed out the cans for the recycle bin. "No, you won't."

He shrugged. "We'll see."

"Fine. I won't push."

"Hey, I'll make a deal with you. When you play your guitar for me, I'll let you read one of my stories."

My smile slipped and a nervous prickle swept over me. "Oh."

"Yeah. Oh," he echoed, nodding, his expression so knowing and smug that I had to say back to him:

"Maybe I'll do that then." A bluff, and from the glint in his eyes he knew it.

"Great. I'm working on a story right now about this girl that wakes up from a coma to find the world gone. Friends. Family. It's like they disappeared. Or never even existed." His fingers made a poofing gesture. I leaned forward, riveted by the idea of a girl waking to find her world gone. "There's only one other survivor . . . this guy. But she won't accept that everything has changed . . . that they only have each other in this new life."

I leaned back against the sink, staring at him, hypnotized by his deep voice. "She's probably scared," I heard myself saying, sucked into the world of his story.

He angled his head. "Oh, she's terrified," he agreed.

I narrowed my gaze at him sitting so calmly at the table. Why was he looking at me so pointedly? Was he saying *I* was that girl in his story? I bristled, not liking the implication that I was terrified. Or of the analogy of me as a recently comatose girl.

"Sounds interesting. How does it end?"

"I haven't gotten that far yet."

My fingers tapped agitatedly against the edge of the counter. "Hmm. You'll have to let me know."

"I'll do that."

I glanced at the clock above the microwave. "It's late." I walked across the loft and plucked the throw and pillow off my bed.

"You sure you don't mind me staying here again?" He moved to the futon.

I shook my head, smiling tightly. "It's like having a roommate again." *God.* Had I just compared him to one of my former *female* roommates?

As his hand reached behind his neck and grabbed the back of his shirt, pulling it over his head in one move, I swallowed a squeak and hurried from the kitchen to my bed. Yeah. There was no mistaking him for Em or Pepper.

Pulling back the covers on my bed, I couldn't stop my gaze from straying to him again as he slid his jeans down his narrow hips, leaving him in snug boxer briefs, his male glory on display. He was a feast for the eyes. My hand dove for my lamp, twisting the knob and plunging us into darkness. I exhaled in relief. Out of sight if not out of mind.

"Good night, Georgia."

His deep voice was a feather-stroke to my skin in the dark. I hugged a pillow close to my chest, squeezing hard, welcoming numbness into my fingers. "Good night, Logan."

Chapter 9

IT WAS A LITTLE after midnight a few nights later when a knock came from downstairs. I was still up, sitting on the futon watching *Love Actually*. It was one of my favorite movies. Whenever it was on, I always stopped channel surfing and settled in to watch it for the umpteenth time.

I had started to nod off earlier, but something stopped me from getting up and going to bed. Okay, I knew what that something was. Logan was working tonight. I'd checked the shift schedule pinned to the wall downstairs and knew. He hadn't worked lately, explaining the sudden end to his late-night visits. I missed our sleepovers and had been a wreck with nervous energy all day, wondering if he would put in an appearance. Okay . . . *hoping*. No sense lying to myself.

Hopping to my feet, I brushed my hands over my shorts and tank top like I was freeing them from wrinkles. The real clue that I was open to the possibility of seeing Logan again was the fact that I still had on a bra.

Inhaling a shuddery breath, I hurried down the steps.

"Who is it?" I called.

"Uh, this is the guitar police checking to see if you're hiding any guitars in your closet."

Rolling my eyes, I opened the door. "Funny."

Logan stood there in his customary Mulvaney's T-shirt and jeans with his customary grin. My chest squeezed and my skin pulled tighter. Every time I saw him it was like getting reacquainted with his hotness all over again. The memory and the reality of him never quite caught up.

"Hi," he greeted, his deep voice sending a wake of goose bumps over my skin. "Would it make you totally uncomfortable if I crashed here again tonight?"

Yes. "No."

Turning, I led him upstairs, acutely conscious of him behind me. I could feel his stare on my butt and thighs.

I motioned to the futon. "I was just watching a movie, but I can turn—"

"No. I'll watch it with you."

I made a face. "You sure? It's a chick flick."

He shrugged and dropped down on the futon, stretching his long legs out and looking relaxed and at home as he draped an arm along the back of the couch. "My best friend is a girl, remember?"

"Yeah." Rachel. I sank down beside him. "How'd that happen anyway? You don't seem to be the type . . ." My words faded, revealing too much. That I thought about him. That I thought I knew what type of guy he was.

He looked at me for a long moment before answering. "When her brother died, her parents kind of forgot they were a family. Their marriage fell apart. They ignored her for the

most part. I understood that. My mom was dead. My dad . . ."
His voice faded. "I think you know about my old man from
Reece." I nodded. He didn't need to elaborate. "We understand
each other. I try to look out for her. The kink club . . . that's
been her thing."

I snorted.

His lips twisted. "I'm not denying I haven't had my fun
moments there, but lately . . . Well, I can't convince her not to
go anymore."

"She's seems like a girl who knows what she wants."

"No. She doesn't, but she's stubborn. So. There it is. " He
stared at the TV, watching Hugh Grant dance across the room
like it was the most interesting thing in the world. "I can't let
her go there without me."

I stared at him for a long moment, the reality of him sinking in.

Logan Mulvaney was a decent guy. I mean, sure, he got his
rocks off while he was there. I saw that for myself, but he didn't
need to go to a kink club to get laid. I went to his baseball
game. I saw the girls there. The guy was like a rock star with
groupies everywhere. He went to the kink club to keep an eye
on Rachel.

I sucked in a breath, a little rattled from this revelation. It
was hard enough to resist him when he was just a hot guy, but
now he's hot and decent.

"What are you going to do about next year?" I asked. "Are
y'all going to the same college?"

He shook his head with a faintly sad smile. "I guess I have
to let baby bird fly the nest and hope for the best."

I propped my elbow on the back of the futon and studied him. I felt my forehead knit, wondering if he would really be capable of doing that . . . of letting go and not trying to save his friend. "Who knew?"

"What?"

A slow smile lifted my lips. "That you made such a good mother bird."

"Don't look at me like that."

"Like how?"

"Your chocolate eyes all big. Like I'm some good, wholesome guy. I'm not. There are things about me . . ." His voice trailed off. He was no longer smiling. "I'm just not."

I wanted to ask, to press, but I couldn't bring myself to demand more information on the not-good-wholesome guy he was. We stared at each other for a long moment until the tension grew too thick and I looked back at the TV. I still felt his stare on my face, but pretended to be lost in the movie.

Eventually, he started watching it, too. Asking questions. We slid to the center of the futon, our shoulders touching as I caught him up on the various plot lines running through the movie.

"So they don't even speak the same language at all?" he asked, pointing to the couple on the screen. "That's just wacked."

I shook my head. "No, that's the beautiful thing about it. They fall in love anyway. They're in sync without even knowing what the other one is saying."

I glanced from the TV and back at him as I was explaining, freezing when I caught the curious way he was looking at me. "You're a romantic."

My cheeks flushed at the almost tender way he looked at me.

I shrugged. "Me and every other girl."

He shook his head. "No. You'd be surprised how many girls don't care about romance. Or love." And then I remembered this was a guy who spent a lot of time at a kink club. I remembered his baseball game, too. The girls shrieking his name like he was some kind of teen heartthrob. Did they see him at all? Or just some hot jock with all the college scouts after him? A piece of meat they wanted to taste. Yeah, maybe Logan didn't have a lot of experience with girls who believed in love and romance.

I turned back to the movie, uncomfortable with these thoughts and realizing I hadn't been that different from those girls in the beginning either. I hadn't seen beyond his good looks and reputation. "You want a drink? Snack?"

"I could eat."

I went in the kitchen and popped some popcorn. Tucking a couple cans of soda under my arm, I returned with a big bowl.

We sat back on the couch and continued to watch the movie, munching on popcorn and chatting, covering a wide range of subjects. From why husbands always cheat with the secretary to why girls loved guys with British accents.

"It doesn't matter," I insisted.

"Oh. Come on. You can't tell me that if I opened my mouth and started talking like Prince Harry girls wouldn't drop—"

"You're not a proper test case. Girls drop their panties *now* when you open your mouth," I accused.

"Not every girl," he shot back, lifting his eyebrows meaningfully at me.

"Oh!" I blew out an outraged breath and tossed a handful of popcorn in his face.

Chuckling, he grabbed a handful and hurled the stuff back at me. Buttery popcorn pelted me and my laugh twisted into a loud, indelicate pig snort.

At the sound, I clapped and hand over my mouth and nose.

"Oh, that's nice." He threw back his head, the tendons in his throat working as a deep belly laugh rumbled up from him.

I plucked a piece from my hair and flicked it at him.

His hand shot out and walked along my ribs. "C'mon. Do you always snort when you laugh. Let's hear that again."

I looked down at his hand and back at his face, arching an eyebrow. "Sorry. I'm not ticklish."

"What?" He looked at me like I was crazy. "Everyone is ticklish."

"Nope. Not me. I'm an anomaly. It's a freak genetic trait. My mother isn't ticklish either."

"I bet you are," he insisted, looking knowing and smug. And sexy as hell.

I shrugged and shook my head. "Nope."

His eyes narrowed on me. "Well, let's see then."

I held out my arms, inviting him to tickle me again. "Go ahead. I won't laugh."

He stroked his chin, considering me for a moment like he was trying to decide his strategy.

"Come on," I taunted.

"What do I get if I make you laugh?"

"You can sleep in the bed." His eyes darkened and a flock

of butterflies took off in my belly. I quickly added, "I'll sleep on the couch."

"Well, that would be kind of dick of me."

"Chicken."

"Ohh." He shook his head. "It's on. Prepare to laugh."

His fingers started at my ribs again and then drifted under my arms. Nothing. Well, nothing except that flock of butterflies in my belly got so seriously out of hand that I suddenly thought I might puke.

His wide eyes fixed on me with awe. "You're not human."

A burst of laughter escaped me and I held up a finger. "That didn't count."

He moved his head side to side as if deciding. "Debatable, but okay." His fingers hovered clawlike over me.

I clenched my teeth, waiting for his touch again.

"I've got a new tactic." He gripped the hem of my shirt and tugged it up.

I squeaked and grabbed his hand, stopping him.

"C'mon. Don't be a prude. I can't really tickle you properly through your shirt. That's an unfair advantage for you."

"You sure you're not trying to get me naked?"

It was his turn to look offended. "I don't resort to manipulation to get girls naked."

Sighing, I released my death grip on his hand. "Fine. It still won't work though. You'll see."

He pushed my shirt up, stopping just below my bra. He stared at my bare stomach for a moment, holding one finger aloft.

"Go on," I said tightly.

He flicked me an annoyed glance. "Patience. I'm trying a different approach."

That finger landed in the center of my stomach, feather soft. He dragged the blunt-nailed tip down, then up and around. His other fingers joined in. So slow and barely there that a chill ran down my spine. My breathing grew harsh, a hoarse rasp, and I squeezed my thighs together against a familiar ache. This was so not a good idea.

He looked up at me from hooded eyes, braced over me like some sort of hungry beast. At least that's how I felt. Like someone about to be devoured.

"Nothing?"

I shook my head, afraid to speak.

He clucked his tongue. "That's too bad. I guess I lose."

A ragged breath shuddered past my lips. My right hand dug into the side of the futon like I was hanging on for dear life. Only he didn't move away. No. His fingers continued to work a lazy pattern over my quivering skin.

I looked from his face to his hand, strong and tan, so much darker against the peaches hue of my skin.

He traced a fingertip over my belly, his expression intent and serious. Like he was doing important work.

I wasn't even close to giggling. That was the furthest possibility. Moaning would be more probable. Begging him to keep touching? Check. Pleading with him to move his hand lower? Double check.

He bent his head and fixed his gaze on the flesh above my navel, moving his finger in a deliberate, precise manner.

My stomach muscles contracted and quivered. "What are you doing?" I whispered.

"Writing my name."

And then I felt the letters there. His name written on my skin. *L-O-G-A-N.* As though he'd just marked me. Branded me for life. Yeah. Fitting, I supposed. That's how I felt right now.

Poised above me, he relaxed his hand, lowering it to my stomach, splaying each finger wide against me. He lifted his gaze to my face, his stare deep and penetrating, the pupils hardly discernible against the dark blue of his eyes.

A muscle feathered in his cheek and I realized he was holding himself in check. Restraining himself above me. One word. One move and we would pick up right where we left off outside the kink club. He'd told me it was on me. All I had to do was say the word if I wanted this to happen between us. I just needed to open my mouth . . .

"I have to get up early," I blurted.

He hesitated and then removed his hand. Settling back on the futon, he was relaxed and at ease again. "Then we better go to bed."

"Yeah." I grabbed the bowl of popcorn and swept into the kitchen with it. When I turned he had stripped off his shirt, treating me to the familiar, mouth-watering sight of his chest again.

I hurried past the futon and into the bathroom. Staring at my reflection, I brushed out my hair until it crackled and shone. My brown eyes looked both tired and exhilarated beneath my dark brows. This was the third night in one week that I had stayed up so late. My eyes looked bloodshot. And yet there was a flush to my skin and I was breathing hard.

"Get a grip," I whispered to myself. Shaking my head, I made quick work of brushing my teeth. Taking a final look at myself in the mirror, I stepped out into the dark apartment.

"Need me to turn on the light?" Logan asked, his disembodied voice drifting from the futon.

"I can get to the bed." I made my way without mishap to the bed.

Once under the covers, I curled onto my side and strained my ears for the sound of Logan stirring on the futon.

Clearing my throat, I called out. "Good night, Logan."

"Good night, Pearls."

My chest squeezed at the nickname. For some reason it didn't annoy me at all. Not tonight. It felt more like an endearment. I brought my knees to my chest, curling into a tight ball and biting down hard on the fleshy pad of my thumb, fighting the urge to invite Logan into bed with me.

It was going to be a long night.

By some miracle, my exhaustion won out and I fell asleep, waking again to an empty apartment.

I sat up in the bed, blinking my eyes in the morning light and staring at the futon, seeing Logan there as he was last night, desperately trying to tickle me, tracing his name on me like some painter immortalizing his name forever on a piece of art.

My hand drifted to my stomach, convinced I still felt his name there.

Chapter 10

MAY SLIPPED INTO JUNE and summer arrived.

Logan didn't ask to crash at the apartment anymore, and I tried not to wonder why. According to the shift schedule, he was still working. He just wasn't knocking on my door at the end of the night. Maybe it got too weird that night he wrote his name on my skin. Despite the chemistry between us, I wasn't going to sleep with him. Maybe he decided he already had one female friend and didn't need another one. I did force him to watch a chick flick and then sleep on a bumpy futon. Whatever the case, the days passed without any more encounters and I told myself it was for the best.

With the advent of summer, I didn't need a jacket in the evenings anymore. Not that I was out too much at night. The mornings were still chilly though when I stepped outside Mulvaney's into the smoky blue predawn for my morning runs. But by the time I finished my newly amended route that cut through a nearby park rather than campus, I was sweating and the crisp air felt good on my skin.

I developed a new summer routine. After my runs, I showered and headed to campus. I worked in the library through the afternoon. Usually by myself. I hadn't seen Gillian since our first meeting. Sometimes Connor would join me, although he wasn't tasked with compiling statistics. I didn't mind his company. Working on research was a solitary task, and his presence kept me from getting lonely. There were several more coffee dates at the Java Hut, and I guess they were dates because he always paid.

I was usually home before dark. Lame existence, I knew. What twenty-year-old was in bed by ten? That was probably why I agreed when Connor asked me to dinner and a movie. To save me from total, utter lameness.

It was nice. Nice to be out with someone with similar interests. Even if all we ever talked about was Dr. Chase's research project and mutual classes we'd both taken and his grad program and what I might do after graduation. So very adult. So very boring. Nothing like Logan, who said outrageous things that made my face burn fire. But who needed that?

I knew going out with Connor on a Friday night was a risk. I had timed most of my comings and goings around when Logan was working so we didn't have to run into each other. The shift schedule was conveniently posted on a wall in the kitchen, and after I agreed to the date I had checked and seen that Logan was working that night. It had taken sheer willpower not to reschedule with Connor. I refused to be that big of a coward. So what if I saw him again? He wouldn't try anything. He'd made that much clear. Not unless I expressly invited him, and that so wasn't going to happen.

Mulvaney's parking lot was packed. I knew it would be on

a Friday night. As Connor pulled up to the curb and peered through the window at the rowdy line snaking out the back door, he looked concerned. "Want me to walk you in?"

"No, it's fine. I can squeeze through."

"You sure? I don't mind."

"I'm fine. Once I'm inside it's a short walk to the kitchen and no one can go in there except staff. The door to my loft is in the back of the kitchen." At his still dubious expression, I added, "It's safe. Promise."

His gaze flickered to mine, the brown eyes softening. "I had a really good time, Georgia."

"Me, too." I nodded, hating this part. The awkward good-night. Would he kiss me? Did I want him to? He must have read something in my demeanor because he settled back in his seat without making the dreaded move. "I'll text you."

"Sounds good. Thanks for tonight."

When I opened the car door, all the sounds that had been muffled were suddenly amplified. It was like diving into a pool of voices and activity as I pushed through the back line.

"Hey!" one girl exclaimed. "No cuts. We're waiting."

I ignored her and kept moving until I spotted the familiar face of Chris, one of the bouncers checking IDs at the door.

He waved me through, snapping at people to get out of my way and let me pass.

"Thanks," I said loudly over the din. He nodded and flashed me a smile.

I continued ahead, trying to hurry toward the kitchen, but there were a lot of people crowded around the counter, ready to place their orders, and they were very protective of their space, glaring at me like I was trying to cut ahead of them in line.

I felt out of place in my maxi dress. It was sleeveless, held up only by tiny halter straps that wrapped around my neck.

Good for a date, but not exactly what one wore to a bar, and I felt that keenly in the lingering looks I was getting.

"Excuse me," I said to a trio of guys who blocked my path to the hatch door in the counter that I needed to reach. They all wore baseball caps and their faces were flushed from beer and heat.

They stopped talking and looked down at me.

"I'm trying to get through," I explained, pointing beyond them as though that would help make them understand.

The taller guy in the group pointed to his chest. "Through us?"

I nodded. "Yes. Excuse me," I said again.

"What will you give me?"

I blinked.

He pushed back his cap, revealing sweaty dark hair at the crown of his head. "Yeah. You gotta pay a toll."

I laughed nervously.

I was about to start my third year of college. I'd been to plenty of bars. Been hit on by drunk guys. However, I was usually in the company of Emerson or Pepper or Suzanne. And usually it was Emerson's mouth that did the talking—telling guys like this off.

"Come on, guys," I coaxed. "I'm not cutting in line. I just need to get to the kitchen."

He looked at his buddies and cocked his head as if considering my request. "Maybe just a kiss?"

His friends laughed.

Anger flashed through me. Who was he to make demands of me? I get that some other girl with a few beers in her might not have minded the attention. She would probably be happy to play his game, but I wasn't one of them.

He leaned down until our faces were on level. "Come on. Give me some sugar."

I clenched my jaw, tempted to take a swing at that face with those puckering fish lips. My fingers curled into a fist, ready to take a swing at his ruddy, perspiring features. "Get out of my way."

Then suddenly he was out of my face. Logan was there, stepping around me. He shoved Fish Lips hard against the shoulder and knocked him off balance. The guy staggered. Clearly the alcohol didn't help his equilibrium.

Regaining his footing, he came back at Logan with a double-handed shove.

Logan stood his ground, hardly budging from the force. He stared Fish Lips down, indifferent to the two guys on either side of him who suddenly looked ready for a fight. I licked my lips and glanced around to see if help was coming from any of the other bouncers. Three to one weren't the best odds.

And then Fish Lips's gaze flicked to the Mulvaney's logo on Logan's shirt, clearly recognizing him as staff. Some of the tension ebbed from him as he demanded, "What the fuck, man?"

Some of the fight went out of his buddies, too. They no longer looked ready to jump Logan.

Fish Lips went into instant restrained-pissed-guy mode, puffing out his chest and practically standing on his tiptoes to match Logan's six-feet-plus frame. "What's your problem?"

Logan jerked his thumb in the direction of the back door. "You can take your boys and go for the night."

"You're kicking us out, man?"

"Harassing girls is something we frown on, *man*."

Fish Lips looked ready to argue, his hands flexing open and shut at his sides.

One of Fish Lips's friends clapped him on the back. "Let's get out of here."

"Come back in here and harass any girl again and you'll be blacklisted from Mulvaney's," Logan added.

Fish Lips snarled as he started walking away with his boys, his body twisting beneath their hands. "Like I'd ever step foot in this shit hole again."

I turned an uncertain gaze on Logan.

He was staring at me unwaveringly. That stare alone made me feel like I needed to apologize. For what, I didn't know. I hadn't done anything wrong.

I moistened my lips. "You didn't need to do that."

Both his eyebrows winged. "Oh, no?"

I shook my head and then yelped as he grabbed my hand. "What are you doing?" I demanded over the buzz of voices as he pulled me through bodies.

"Escorting you to your room." He flipped up the counter, and instantly we were free of the hot press of humanity. It was like suddenly breaking through the water and taking your first deep breath of air.

"That's not necessary," I said as we walked past Karla working the counter and back into the kitchen. Cook didn't even look up from where he was shaking salt over fries. "I can make it on my own now," I said, digging my key out.

Logan ignored me, plucking my key from my hand and unlocking the door to the loft. Still holding on to my hand, he pulled me up the stairs after him, his feet heavy thuds on the wooden steps. "You really think it's a good idea to live above this bar, Pearls?"

I bristled at his use of that nickname. "It's just for the summer."

"What? Mommy and Daddy won't spring for a pimp apartment. You gotta stay here?"

I bit back a "no." He didn't need to know the particulars of my life—that my parents only paid my way as long as I did exactly as they instructed.

"I'm home now." My sandals hit the steps hard in my mounting anger. "You can go. I don't want to keep you from your job."

"Saving damsels from drunks is part of the job requirement."

We reached the top floor and I tugged my hand free of the warm clasp of his fingers. "Yeah?" I tossed my handbag on the futon and turned to face him.

"Yeah," he tossed back. "I'm pretty sure it's even more important to my brother when the damsel happens to be a good friend of his."

I narrowed my eyes on him. "Did Reece tell you to look after me?"

He snorted and crossed his arms over his chest, advancing on me. Those well-carved lips curved as he spoke. "That goes without saying."

"Oh." I inched back, stopping when the back of my knees hit the edge of the futon. "You think he would approve, then, of you hitting on me?"

Chuckling, he stopped directly in front of me, leaving only a thin line of space between us. "I don't answer to my brother. I've been my own man for a long time."

I had a flash of memory then. Pepper telling me that Reece was only eight when their mother died. Logan would have been just three then. And their father was a mean drunk. Cruel and bitter even before the accident that put him in a wheelchair. Yes. By all accounts, Logan had been his own man for a long time. He had missed his childhood entirely.

The breadth of his chest was so close, vibrating with an energy and vitality that made something inside me quiver . . . stretch soundlessly toward him in response. But it was an invisible thing, buried deep inside me. I refused to let it loose.

I made no move. No sound. The clean, musky scent that I was coming to learn as belonging to him enveloped me, filling my nostrils.

He lifted a hand, dragging his thumb down my cheek. His fingers trailed down my throat, stopping just above my neckline and picking up a lock of hair, rubbing the long strand between his fingers. "I don't check with my brother for approval when I decide that I want a girl."

I swallowed. He wanted me. I knew that, I guess. Even if he had stopped spending the night on my futon. But still . . . hearing him say it like that. While he was looking at me like he wanted to devour me. Like I was the one thing on this earth that he needed.

He continued, "This is between us, Georgia. It's no one else's business." His fingers tightened around my hair, wrapping it around his fist and forcing me closer until our bodies were flush.

Us. It was tempting to believe there was an us. That there could be.

"There is no us," I whispered, my lips brushing his jawline as I spoke. Deliberately. Because I had to. Because I couldn't stop myself.

"Because you won't let it happen," he countered, his fist tightening in my hair, tugging my head back to look him in the eyes.

Was that why he'd been staying away? Because he was mad at me for not putting out? I shook my head and then froze as he bowed his head, burying his face in my neck, nuzzling my skin and turning slightly so that his mouth grazed my ear. "Let it happen, Georgia."

He bit down on my earlobe and pleasure spiked through me strong enough that my knees almost buckled. I grabbed his shoulders, holding on to him. He released my earlobe and breathed into the whorls of my ear, his voice coming out hoarse. "Do you know how you look in this dress? How badly I want to pull it up around your thighs."

I exhaled a ragged breath and shivered, shaking my head no.

His mouth skated down my throat, lips skimming over the straps. "I want to tear these tiny little strings, rip them off with my teeth . . ."

God. I'd never had anyone *breathe* words that hot into my ear before. I didn't think I even remembered conversation happening when Harris and I fooled around, but Logan talked. Something told me he would talk all throughout it. Sexy, dirty words. And I had to be honest with myself—I liked that. I wanted that.

He gave my hair a slight tug, pulling my head back even

farther and arching my throat. "Then I'd do other things to you. With my mouth. My tongue. My teeth. I'd taste all of you, every inch of your sweet peach skin . . ."

A thrill shot through me. I felt his words as effectively as a skilled touch.

With one hand still fisted in my hair, holding me hostage, his other hand was free to roam, free to toy with one of the straps that he had threatened to tear. "Were you on a date, Georgia? Is that why you put on your pretty dress? Did you let him kiss you? Touch you?"

I made a strained, incoherent sound and shook my head.

"No?" he asked idly, giving my head another tug. "He didn't kiss you?"

"N-no."

"Good. Because that wouldn't be very fair to the bastard, would it? Kissing him when it's me you want."

I sputtered, then laughed hoarsely, fighting to hold his brilliant blue gaze and not look away. "God. You're arrogant."

"Honest. There's a difference. If you were honest, you would just say it. Admit you want me to fuck you."

I blinked, startled, both turned on and horrified at his blunt speech. He just called it what it was. What it would be if the two of us were to come together.

He laughed roughly and released me then, stepping back. "But you're too scared to let that happen, aren't you? To be honest with yourself. With me."

This is the part where I could have admitted that I wanted him. That I was honest with myself. I *knew* I wanted him. I just wasn't going to let myself have him.

Flings with eighteen-year-old guys weren't responsible. And yet I held silent. Admitting I wanted him was giving him power over me, and when it came to him I already felt too weak.

His chest fell and lifted slightly and I realized he was turned on, too. My gaze dropped and I noticed the raging hard-on pressed against the front of his jeans.

I yanked my gaze back up, cheeks burning.

"Logan." I hardly recognized my own voice. It sounded so small and tremulous. Not the mature twenty-year-old I was going for. "This is out of hand. You need to leave me alone." *Please*. I didn't say it, but the word hung there because I was afraid I couldn't resist him much longer. If he continued to come around me. Touching me. Talking to me the way he did. I was lost.

He stared at me for a long moment, those vivid blue eyes examining me in a way that made me feel somehow lacking. Then he nodded once, his jaw tense, mouth set grimly. "I'm gone."

I watched, battling feelings of disappointment and helplessness as he turned his back and left me alone in the loft.

I stood there for a long moment, shaking.

And still wanting him.

Chapter 11

I'D GIVEN UP EXPECTING Logan to knock on my door. Each night I would listen as Mulvaney's quieted under my feet, closing for the night. I'd gotten in the habit of keeping late hours. Unfortunately that meant instead of sleeping, I got hungry in the middle of the night. I often found myself raiding my kitchen. Tonight was no exception. I had even made plans for the perfect late-night snack. Pretzel bread was my weakness. I'd picked up some from a bakery a few blocks from campus. I'd already bought turkey and Swiss cheese earlier in the week. Ducking to peer inside the refrigerator, I realized that I was still missing a key ingredient.

Committed to the idea of a turkey and Swiss sandwich on pretzel bread, I slipped on my flip-flops and headed downstairs. I turned on the kitchen light. The bar was silent. Cook was gone, so I was free to invade his kitchen.

I quickly located the brown mustard in the large standing refrigerator. Feeling slightly guilty over raiding Cook's supplies, I smoothed the mustard on the bread with smooth strokes. I'd have to be sure to buy him an extra jar tomorrow to relieve my conscience. I slapped the bread together and hurriedly put the brown mustard back into the fridge. I started to turn for the stairs when voices drifted into the kitchen. Angry voices.

"Get your mitts off me before I lay you the fuck out, you hear me! You're not so tough I can't do it either!"

Still clutching the sandwich in my hand, I moved through the kitchen, peering over the counter with eyes that felt wide in my face.

A burly man sat at one of the tables that faced the counter, gesturing wildly and taking swipes at Logan. He jabbed a finger toward the ceiling. "Last time I checked that's still my name up on the bar and if I want another drink, then get me another drink, damn it!"

I winced. His father. Of course. I could see the resemblance in his ruddy and slightly swollen features, all a testament to years of drink and hard living.

He'd been handsome once upon a time. Like Reece and Logan. The same blue eyes. I could see that even across the distance. His hair was longish and looked like it needed a good shampoo. In fact, all of him looked in need of a shower. His arms were tatted and muscular and I had no doubt that back in the day he had broken up his fair share of barroom fights under this very roof.

"Dad, it's late. The bar's closed. It's time to go home." Logan sounded tired. Older than his years. I'd never been so glad in that moment to know that he was getting out from under his father. This was no kind of life, caring for a parent who did nothing but heap abuse upon your head. At least my mother was the passive-aggressive sort. She never yelled or cursed at me.

He plunked his beer bottle down on the table. "Listen, you little bastard, you might clean up my piss, but that doesn't make you my keeper, now get me another beer. I'll be done with this one soon."

Logan didn't even flinch, which told me he was accustomed to such verbal abuse. "Actually you and Mom were married, so I'm not a bastard."

"Such a smartass." Mr. Mulvaney picked his beer back up and took a swig. "You think you're a big man because you can throw a fucking ball—"

"That's enough. I'm taking you home." Logan grabbed the beer bottle and wrested it from his father's thick fist, but Mr. Mulvaney snatched it back and sent it crashing across the room. It smashed into the base of the counter I stood behind and shattered into a thousand pieces.

I jerked at the unchecked violence, a shiver running through me. Suddenly my stomach felt queasy. I doubted I could go back upstairs and eat my sandwich now.

Logan tracked the destruction, his eyes lighting on me at the end of the trail. The moment stretched as we stared, the knowledge passing between us that I had witnessed the ugliness he lived with day to day. I saw. I knew what he lived with . . . what made him who he was. Someone accustomed to taking care of people who didn't appreciate the effort, who still continued down their paths of self-destruction.

My pulse strummed against my throat as we considered each other in silence. For a split second some unknown emotion passed over his face. Shame? Regret? Then a shutter fell over his eyes and nothing. It was gone. His face was impassive as he unfolded himself from where he was bent over the table his father occupied.

Mr. Mulvaney looked out at me with bleary eyes. "Who the hell are you?"

I fired to action, not entirely realizing what I was doing until I was halfway across the bar. "Hello, Mr. Mulvaney. Care for a sandwich?"

He eyed the sandwich dubiously before looking back at me. "Who are you?"

"Georgia," I replied, deliberately choosing not to elaborate. I wasn't sure how he would feel about me living above the bar he felt so proprietary over even though Reece had taken it over.

"I made it with this really delicious pretzel bread. Made fresh this morning. It's unbelievable."

Mr. Mulvaney's gaze dropped to the sandwich I held wrapped in a paper towel in my hand. If there was one thing I knew about a hard night of drinking, it was that the munchies were never far behind. I glanced down at it and added, "Turkey and Swiss cheese, too."

He held out his hand. "Give it here."

I handed it to him and he started eating, assessing me as he chewed. He swallowed. "It's good." He shot a glare to his son. "Would taste a hell of a lot better with a cold drink. This beer is getting warm. Make yourself useful."

Logan snorted and looked from me to his father and back again. "Too bad we're closed and no longer serving."

Mr. Mulvaney waved at me as he tore into the sandwich again with gusto. "She one of your girlfriends?"

I shook my head even as Logan lifted his gaze to me. I didn't miss the use of the plural. Even his father knew he was a player.

His father snorted. "Oh. It's like that then. Complicated. I had a complicated relationship once. I married her and that only made things even more complicated." He laughed roughly.

He took another bite out of his sandwich and then set it down on his lap, presumably keeping it. He lowered his hands to the sides of his wheelchair and rolled out from behind the table. "Thanks for the sandwich."

"Sure." I gave him a small wave good night, watching as he descended down the ramp. Turning, I found Logan staring at me with an odd expression on his face. "Yeah. Thanks."

I shrugged, feeling uncomfortable. "It was nothing." And it really was nothing. I didn't do anything special. I gave his father a sandwich. Big deal. He could have thrown the food at me and just as easily kept yelling at Logan. He could have yelled at me, too.

"No, my old man . . . he's difficult."

I resisted pointing out that that might be an understatement. My mother was difficult. His father was abusive. And that angered me, tightened my chest with all kinds of impotent rage for the little boy he had been, living under the same roof with that man.

He motioned to the back door and then tucked both hands into his front pockets. He rocked on his heels for a moment. "I gotta take him home." He looked down at the mess and sighed. "I'll come in early and take care of this. Watch your step so that you don't cut yourself."

"I will."

He looked at the back exit again, clearly reluctant to go. He probably just hated leaving the mess. I'm sure it had nothing to do with me. "A buddy of his dropped him off. He can't drive himself . . ." His voice faded.

I nodded. "Of course. I understand. You gotta go."

He lingered, still looking like he wanted to stay. If not for his dad, would he ask to stay the night? I had given up expecting to see him at my door. Especially since we had those ugly words the other night. He'd called me scared in the most scathing way, but right now he looked like he wanted to crawl all over me. Every part of me tingled under his regard, tiny pinpricks of sensation racing along my skin like lit gunpowder.

I tried to cling to my outrage, but after seeing how his father treated him, I just wanted to hold him . . . bring him into my body until the only thing either one of us felt was the gratifying rush of release.

Even as tension-riddled as those nights had been with him asleep across the room, I missed it. I missed our conversations. The laughter. His scent. The physical ache of his nearness. I missed hearing him adjust his weight on the futon. The too-fresh memory of his body stripped down to his boxer briefs as he readied himself for bed made me all kinds of hot and bothered. I shifted on my feet, squeezing my thighs close together.

"Thanks again . . ." He looked like he wanted to say more, but then he pressed his lips flat and left it at that. Big hands still buried in his pockets, he turned and headed down the ramp out the back door, his tread thudding over the barroom floor. I watched him go, listening as he locked up.

I turned my attention back to the mess. Beer had settled into the wood, marking it a darker brown. It wasn't the first beer ever spilled on the floor. Still, I hated to leave it overnight.

I headed back into the kitchen for the mop and bucket. One less burden for Logan to bear—and I refused to let myself consider too closely why that mattered so much to me.

I WAS UP EARLY the following morning. I had agreed to meet Connor at the Java Hut at eight A.M. before heading over to the library. I was busy stuffing a protein bar in my bag and not really looking where I was going as I passed through the kitchen. Staff didn't usually arrive until nine A.M., so when a voice rumbled across the air I yelped and jumped back a step.

"You cleaned up?" Logan stood near the counter leading out into the bar, looking slowly from me to the bare wood floor where shards of glass sat late last night.

My hand clutched my chest. "You gave me a heart attack."

He pointed to the floor. "You cleaned up the broken bottle."

"Yeah, well, I didn't want to leave it overnight." I adjusted the strap of my messenger bag on my shoulder and shifted on my Chucks.

"You didn't have to do that."

"You had your hands full last night." His jaw tensed, and I got the sense he didn't like the indirect reminder of his father.

Most nights it seemed like he had his hands full. Between work, baseball, school, his father. My gaze skimmed him. At least he looked rested. That, unaccountably, made me feel better. My chest loosened with relief for him and then tightened back up again as I studied him. He looked good—better than good—in fresh jeans and a graphic T-shirt. I inhaled and caught a faint whiff of shampoo and his deodorant.

"Well, thanks. You didn't have to do that. It was nice of you."

"Least I could do. Your brother is letting me stay here rent-free."

"Your best friend is his girlfriend. I think that kind of makes you family in Reece's book, and if you haven't noticed, family gets to stay the night in the loft." His mouth kicked up at one corner, and I resisted reminding him that he wasn't spending the night in the apartment anymore.

"I'm not true family," I mumbled. "Picking up is the least I can do."

"Why can't you just admit you're a nice person, Georgia? The kind of person who distracts a mean drunk with sandwiches and cleans up broken beer bottles."

I flushed at the compliment and started to move around him. "You don't know me—"

"You don't think I see you?" His gaze cut into me. Emotion cracked through his voice that sounded suspiciously like anger. "I see you. I see you now like I saw you then. Months ago. When you were still with that asshole, I knew what kind of girl you were."

I froze, those words sinking in. Heat crawled up my neck like swarming bees.

I gaped at him, unable to look away.

I had wondered if he'd noticed me all those times we were within each other's radius. We spoke little, but of course I had noticed *him*. Just like every other red-blooded female with a pulse. I felt his energy like electricity on the air. Apparently he had noticed *me*.

I was almost afraid to know . . . to ask what he saw in me all those months ago when I was still with Harris. I had been a shadow of myself then, around Harris, swallowed up like a sparrow in a storm.

"I saw you." He nodded. "At first I thought you were some princess, indifferent to the fact that your boyfriend was a dick."

I flinched, not liking this description of myself. "I don't know what you're talking about."

"Reece's birthday dinner. We went to Gino's, remember? We all sat at a big table. It was really crowded that night and they were understaffed. The waiter was stressed, trying his best to get orders out. Harris treated him like some fucking peon." He shook his head, his lip curling. "The way he talked down to him . . . you were uncomfortable. I could see it in your face, the way you would touch his arm trying to calm him down."

I inhaled as he painted this image, filling in my memory with strokes of color. I remembered that night as one of several uncomfortable instances when Harris's superior attitude boiled over onto some unfortunate soul. I knew Logan had been there, but I didn't remember him even talking to me then, much less watching me. But then I'd been preoccupied. Harris had been in a mood. He wasn't especially a fan of my friends, and the waiter suffered for that. It embarrassed me now that I could be with anyone like that.

Logan continued, "When we got up to leave he didn't tip him. Remember? You questioned him and he said he didn't tip for shitty service. Right there in front everyone. No regrets for stiffing the waiter."

I nodded, a lump forming in my throat. God. Harris really

was an entitled ass. I inhaled. "You must have thought I was pathetic . . . dating a guy like him."

"Maybe for a minute there I did, but then you said you had to go back to the restroom. I had to go, too. I was a few feet behind you and I saw you"—his voice dipped to a quiet murmur—"I saw you go back and dig in your purse and drop that money on the table."

I remembered that. I'd been relieved I had cash on me. "So you saw that. So what?"

"I'm sure you've heard that saying. 'Character is what you do when no one's looking.' Well, I was looking, Georgia. And I've been looking ever since. The same girl who wouldn't let Harris stiff that waiter is the same girl who cleaned up this mess last night. You did it for me." His gaze locked on me then with an intensity that made my chest swell. "Because you like me."

A thousand butterflies took flight in my stomach at the way he looked at me. I felt like a deer caught in headlights. Denial was impossible. I didn't have it in me to lie. "I have to meet someone," I said hurriedly, suddenly overwhelmed at the idea that I'd been on his radar all this time. Even before I kissed him outside the kink club.

"Sure. Don't want to be late." He stepped aside and waved me through the kitchen.

My fingers nervously flexed on the strap of my messenger bag. Something had changed. He wasn't the same. There was a new resolve in his eyes, a firmness to his voice that made me uneasy.

Suddenly his previous promise to leave me alone didn't feel

like such a promise anymore. At least not one I believed. No. As I walked past the counter toward the exit, I felt his stare on my back and didn't feel safe with the assurance that it was "all on me." For some reason, I felt certain that Logan was done waiting for me to make the first move.

Chapter 12

THE FOLLOWING WEEK WE had an honest-to-God heat wave. Girls who stayed on campus through the summer could be found spread out on towels in the quad in tiny shorts and tank tops. Some wore bikinis. And where girls in bikinis were, guys could be found hovering close by.

Walking past the quad on the way home from the library, I thought about Emerson and how she would have been one of those girls last summer, happy to flaunt her body in a bikini and flirt with hovering guys. Now she was busy with her new life—Shaw and their bikes and her art.

I hadn't seen her since the night I moved out, so I was eager for Pepper's birthday party tonight. It was at the new house. Just a small group. Mostly couples, so I had asked Connor to go with me. I didn't know if we would ever be anything more than friends—okay, so I knew we would never be more than friends—but he was a good guy and seemed excited to go.

Of course, Reece went all out and splurged on Pepper. He catered the party, so the delicious aroma of char-grilled meat greeted us when we stepped inside the house. Pepper let us in, hugging me and whispering in my ear. "He's cute."

I smiled in acknowledgment and accepted the margarita placed in my hand.

"For you," Emerson said, then turned to meet Connor. She didn't treat him to the same bubbly welcome that Pepper had, and instead regarded him with the icy reserve of an overprotective father—but then that was Em. Trust wasn't given but earned.

We soon split off into boy-girl groups, Connor joined the guys and Emerson, Pepper, Suzanne, and I stood in a tight circle.

"You always go for the uptight ones," Emerson accused around the salted rim of her margarita glass.

"He's cute," Suzanne offered. "And looks nice."

Nice: aka, boring. "He's *not* uptight," I insisted, knowing this much was true at least. He was not like Harris.

Em lifted a dark, finely arched eyebrow. "He's a grad student. In the Business School."

"Stop it. You're being judgmental," I snapped.

"Be nice, Em," Pepper chided. "She brought a date to my birthday. She must like him."

I smiled and hoped it didn't look like the wince it was. I didn't like him *that* much. To be fair, when he'd tried to kiss me yesterday at the Java Hut, I dodged his lips. Not a good sign. Deep down, I knew the reason I brought him with me tonight. He was meant to be a buffer. If Logan showed, which was very likely, then I would have a date to keep him at bay. Not that I expected Logan to misbehave. This was Pepper's party . . . at his brother's house. It would be fine.

Especially after the other night. I'd seen him twice from a distance: Once inside the bar as I was heading to my room. And another time as I was in the parking lot getting into my car and he was heading across the parking lot to start his shift. I felt his gaze even though I pretended to be looking somewhere else beyond him each time. Yeah, I knew he had seen me. He'd made no attempt to speak to me. Not even a wave. I had effectively killed things between us—just as I'd intended. And if I felt a tiny bit like crap over that realization, I'd get over it. It wasn't the first disappointment of my life. It wouldn't be the last. Mom had taught me that lesson well. Life was full of disappointment.

My real father had been one of her biggest disappointments. The few times she spoke candidly with me on the subject of him, she had been clear. He was the greatest mistake of her life. She regretted it. Him. *Me.* She didn't say it but what else was I to interpret? Some mistakes were like that. Colossal and irreversible. Logan Mulvaney would not be that mistake for me.

There was the right path and the wrong path, and if I ever had any doubt which was which, I need only ask my mother. She always had an opinion, and I knew she would want me to avoid guys like Logan Mulvaney.

I think you want me to say dirty things to you.

I cringed. Some guys were impossible to forget though.

"Georgia knows I'm just messing with her," Em said, snagging my attention back to the here and now. "If she really likes this guy, then I'm going to love him. You know that, right, Georgia?"

I nodded reflexively and then froze as the front door opened and Logan stepped inside. A thousand prickles rushed over my skin. He wasn't alone either. Rachel was with him. I was never so relieved in my life than at that moment. I had a date. He had Rachel with him. I took a big gulp of my margarita.

Pepper clapped her hands and made it across the room to hug him. Even as tall as Pepper was, Logan easily folded her in his arms. Pepper hugged Rachel, too—an embrace the girl accepted awkwardly. His gaze did a quick sweep of the room before landing on me.

We stared at each other across the living room. The moment struck me as so strange. This guy had been in my sphere for a long time, but I'd only thought of him as Reece's impossibly beautiful, shallow kid brother. Never considered him beyond that. Never thought of him as more. Never been tempted.

And now, in this room, he was the center of my universe. Everything in me prickled with awareness of him.

A hand brushed the small of my back and I sucked in a sharp breath. Connor stood beside me. "You okay? Can I make you a plate of food?"

"Not yet." I shook my head and took another sip of the margarita Emerson had placed in my hand. "Thank you."

Connor looked longingly at the spread of food across the room.

"Go ahead," I encouraged. "Make yourself a plate."

"If you don't mind—"

"No, go. Shaw is already eating."

"Okay." He dropped his hand from the small of my back

and headed for the table of food. When I looked back across the room to where Logan had stood moments ago, he was gone. I scanned the room, skipping over the dozen or so people mingling. Some standing, some sitting. He was gone. But then so was Pepper and Rachel. She must be giving them the tour of the house.

"Not hungry?" Emerson asked.

I shook my head.

"Well, that guacamole is calling my name. I'll be back."

I stood there by myself for a moment. An old Johnny Cash song played low on the air. Connor's gaze met mine as he listened to something Shaw was saying. He sent me a nod and angled his body as though he was on the verge of breaking away to join me. Like a good date should do. Only I realized I didn't want to get trapped in small talk with him just yet.

Before he could reach me, I moved out of the living room and stepped into the hall that led to the guest bathroom. It was past the study with the French doors and guest room. I heard footsteps behind me and hurried, half-afraid it was Connor following to check up on me. Fortunately, the bathroom was unoccupied. I slipped inside, but didn't have a chance to shut the door all the way behind me.

It swung inward, and Logan slid inside before I fully realized what was happening. He locked the door behind him and leaned against it, crossing his arms over his chest. He loomed there, staring at me almost expectantly.

"What are you doing?" I demanded. "You can't be in here with me!"

"What are you doing with that tool?"

"I beg your pardon?"

"You heard me, Pearls. Did you bring him to make me jealous?"

I laughed, but the sound rang brittle, so I cut it short and just stared at him in my best imitation of my mother's cool, principal glare.

"Hardly." Studying his face, I could see that he was serious. For once that mocking humor was nowhere in evidence. "There is no reason for you to be jealous. We're not a thing."

He said nothing, just stared at me with those bitter-hard eyes. The blue was like some kind of frozen marble.

"Not a thing," he echoed, his lips unsmiling. He usually always smiled. Even on those rare occasions when he was serious, he had that derisive smile on his lips. But not tonight. Not now.

Suddenly the bathroom felt claustrophobic. "Look. We don't really know each other. And you agreed to back off—"

"Maybe I changed my mind."

That made me take a step back. I laughed nervously. "Don't be ridiculous. I have a date out there. You have . . . Rachel." So they were just friends, but she had come here with him. "Nothing is happening here." I motioned between us. "Nothing is going to happen here. You need to step away from the door."

"Don't pretend like there isn't something here. Like we haven't been dancing around it for weeks now, Georgia." He jabbed a finger toward me, coming off the door, advancing. "You started this."

I backed up, swallowing, miserable. Yeah. That night at the kink club. That kiss. And then I showed up at his baseball game like some kind of groupie.

I sucked in a deep breath. "I admit we have chemistry, but that's not anything either one of us can't find with someone else. Someone more appropriate."

He tossed his head back and let loose a harsh laugh. "You gotta be fucking kidding me."

I blinked, itchy heat flooding my face like swarming ants. I didn't like being laughed at. Not like that.

He lowered his gaze back to me. "You're fooling yourself if you think chemistry is an automatic thing you can find with anyone . . . It's not something you can find with that asshat out there." He looked me up and down. "I doubt you had it with your last boyfriend either. You always looked too bored when you were with him."

I looked too bored? That was an interesting description considering Harris dumped me because he claimed I was boring.

"You have chemistry with me," he added, "because we'd be good together."

The air fairly crackled around us, jammed full of his provocative words.

I shook my head, marveling, "Where do you get off being so arrogant? How do you know I don't feel it with Connor out there—"

"Because you're in here having this conversation with me. You haven't walked away."

Damn. Good point. I hadn't even tried to leave the bathroom.

"I didn't want to cause a scene."

"I'm not stopping you from leaving." He waved a hand past himself.

"You want to see me walk away?" Bravado rang out in my voice and my chin went up a notch. "Watch. I know it might be a new experience for you . . . girls giving you their backs but here goes."

I strode right past him, dodging around him, my wedge heels biting hard into the floor.

I felt as much as heard him come after me. The rush of movement sparked the air all around us like electricity, and my heart actually hurt for a second in my chest, squeezing so tightly with awareness, anxiety, and I don't know . . . something else.

When he grabbed me and whirled me around, I started to tell him just what I thought about his inability to keep his hands to himself, but I didn't get very far before he released my shoulder and grabbed my face. Words died in a sputtering choke as I stared into those dark blue eyes inches from mine, his big hands holding my face.

"You're right."

"About what?" I said distractedly, focusing way too much on that mouth of his with the deep indentation right there in the center of his top lip. God. I had tasted that mouth. I ached to do it again, only this time I wanted to run my tongue over the indentation. I didn't do that last time. I wanted to lick and savor and nibble at it. Need for him strangled me and I knotted my hands at my sides.

"I'm not used to girls turning their backs on me." He studied me in the hazy orange glow of the bathroom's light.

"B-but you said I'd have to ask for this . . . for *it* from you. You said you wouldn't touch me," I reminded him, needing him to keep that promise now more than ever.

"Sometimes plans change. They have to . . ."

He brought his mouth close, his nose the barest brush on my cheek, our lips not touching, but I felt the puff of his breath as he spoke. "Do you know what you do to me, Georgia?"

"I have a d-date," I sputtered.

Something dark glinted in his eyes, and I was struck with the knowledge that I was way out of my depth with this guy. He knew more. Had seen more. *Done* more.

"Wrong answer," he growled.

"What do you want from me?" I bit out, frustration bubbling up inside me. I gazed at him helplessly, shaking my head.

"You haven't figured that out yet?" He stared at me, his eyes sliding from my eyes to my mouth, down my body and then up again. Alarm bells went off in my head.

His hand circled my neck. "Fuck," he growled. "Then I haven't been clear enough." His mouth slammed over mine.

Chapter 13

HE CLAIMED MY MOUTH in a bruising, teeth-clanging kiss. I tasted lime and salt, and I felt like I was drowning in the sea. My hands flew to his shoulders for balance, then in desperation, I was clinging to him when I should have been pushing him away. He knew this though and wanted to prove a point evidently.

He pulled back slightly, his mouth a hairbreadth from my own. I inched forward, chasing that mouth, but he kept himself just out of reach, pulling his head back, making me come after him, tormenting me, forcing me to take what I wanted. Dimly I realized this, but I didn't care. Not anymore. I was past caring. I only needed.

With a frustrated moan, I grabbed his face in both hands and held him still for me. It was a giddy, headlong dive into sensation. I kissed him. I took. I claimed. Like before. He had sparked a fire inside me and those flames were burning hot now. I did what I wanted.

I sucked on his top lip, my tongue finding that dent at the center . . . tasting it, loving it, savoring it with my lips, tongue, and teeth.

My hands drifted down from his face, fingers curling into his shirt, bunching the fabric in tight fists as I rubbed my tongue against his. He made a growling sound and backed me up until we collided into the door with a thud, rattling the hinges and knob.

I should have cared at the sound, at the noise we were making—anyone passing could hear and wonder. But I didn't. I didn't care. I only felt.

The naughtiness and savagery of it thrilled me. I was making out in a bathroom in a house full of people with a guy who wasn't even my date.

I was wild and free and totally reckless.

His fingers curled around my wrists and lifted them off his shoulders. In one fast move, he pinned my hands against the door on either side of my head.

A small gasp escaped me. He lifted his head to look at me, his eyes so smoldering I felt their burn, their power as effective as his hard body trapping me against the door.

I tried to tug my hands down so that I could touch him again, but he held them fast. He shook his head once at me, sending a clear message. I wasn't to move my hands. I was under his control.

My feminine hackles bristled at this show of dominance, but another part of me stirred, responding to his command over my body.

He kissed me again then. His hands slid down my arms. When I started to lower my arms, he snatched my hands back and held them to the door. "Keep them there."

I obeyed, butterflies erupting in my belly.

Suddenly it dawned on me. This was him. The not-good, not-wholesome guy he had mentioned on the futon in my apartment. It was his hands pinning me hard to the door. I was staring at *him*, my eyes wide open and absorbing every inch of him as his lips ravaged mine.

The pressure of his mouth increased. His lips grew more demanding, his tongue a deeper tangle with mine as his bigger body pushed even closer against me.

I felt his cock through our clothes, the hardness grinding into my stomach and everything in me liquefied.

His hands resumed their slow descent and this time I didn't move mine. I kept them against the wall, a true feat as his passed down my rib cage and then came around to claim my breasts.

I cried out, the sound swallowed up in his mouth as his hands molded to my breasts through the thin fabric of my dress. His fingers unerringly found my nipples through the fabric, pinching and rolling. Bolts of pleasure-pain lanced through me.

His hands moved with purpose. Sure, swift, and just a little rough. I never knew it could be like this—I never knew I wanted it to be.

He bent slightly, his erection grinding right where I most needed him. I moaned again into his mouth.

A heaviness pooled in my muscles and my arms began to weaken and shake, slipping from where I held them against the wall.

As if he sensed their movement, his hands slammed mine back into place against the wall, his voice a hard rasp against my mouth. "Leave. Them. There."

"Oh."

It was the only sound, the only word I could make. My panties were wet. I would have been embarrassed if I wasn't so turned on. I moaned into his mouth, clinging to his top lip, then his bottom, then warring my tongue with his again.

His hands left my breasts and slid down, bunching my hem in his hands and dragging my dress up around my hips. His lips moved against mine as he spoke. "I have wanted to do this ever since you first kissed me."

Before I could fully understand what *this* referred to, he slid his big body down mine and hooked one of my thighs over his shoulder. He traced a finger against the crotch of my panties. Heat scorched my cheeks because I knew he knew how much I wanted him now. As if he didn't have a clue before.

He made a groaning sound and looked up at me, his eyes heavy-lidded and full with the promise of delicious things to come. "You're so hot, baby." He pulled my panties aside so that I was exposed to the air, his gaze. It was shocking, and the most exposed I'd ever felt, but I was so aroused I couldn't move. Couldn't try to cover myself from his eyes. His touch.

Still watching me, he rubbed a single finger over me, gliding it against my moisture until he found that spot. The spot that Harris never seemed to know even existed. Logan found it instantly and pressed down, rolling it slowly. Eyes fastened on my face, he bent his head and placed his mouth there until all I could see was his dark blond head. All I could feel was his lips and tongue, sucking and pulling on my clit, drawing it deep between his teeth. My head dropped back on the door and a shudder built, working its way up my body from where his mouth devoured me.

I brought a hand down, helpless, unable to stop my fingers from lacing through his hair.

I turned my head sideways and caught sight of us in the mirror. Me with my leg thrown over his shoulder and his head buried between my thighs, my fingers speared through his hair. It was the hottest thing I'd ever seen. My eyes looked fogged over . . . like they belonged to someone else entirely.

His mouth eased its pressure on me and I almost wept. So close. I was so close. My grip tightened on his hair as his tongue lightly played on my clit, the teasing strokes tormenting me.

I whimpered his name and he paused to look up at me.

His eyes went dark at whatever he saw in my face. "What do you want, Pearls? Do you want me to lick you harder?"

I nodded.

He ducked back down and drew me into his mouth with a deep, savoring pull. Still, it wasn't enough and he knew it. My hips lifted in an effort to give him more of me, but he just lifted his gaze back to mine. "You want my mouth to fuck you?"

Oh. My. God.

My chest squeezed tight and I remembered his promise to say dirty things to me. He'd meant it.

I nodded.

"Let me hear you say it then, Pearls. Say: Fuck me with your mouth."

I gulped. Oh. God.

His hand tightened where he held my thigh, each of his fingers an individual brand.

I moistened my lips and God help me if his blue eyes didn't follow my tongue and darken even more. I swallowed against the tightness in my throat. "Fuck me with your mouth."

My voice didn't even sound like it belonged to me. It

sounded tinny and faraway. Like I was some other girl pinned against a door with a hot guy between her thighs. And I was. This was not Georgia Robinson from Muskogee, Alabama. I wasn't the lauded Principal Robinson's daughter.

His mouth was on me again, and I bit my lip to stop from crying out. My head dropped back, rattling the door as my orgasm welled up inside me.

He knew exactly what to do. His lips and tongue flayed me until short gasps burst from my lips. I arched my spine off the door, my fingers splaying wide in his hair. The coil twisted and tightened as he worked me over.

A knock thumped on the door behind me. "Georgia, you in there?"

I slapped a hand over my mouth at the sound of Emerson's voice, but Logan didn't stop. If anything, his attentions grew more persistent, frantic, and hungry. He eased a finger inside me as his mouth lapped and sucked at me.

I shattered inside, shudders working up through me as Emerson knocked again, vibrating the wood behind me.

"Georgie?

"Be out in a second," I croaked as Logan stood with a satisfied gleam in his eyes, letting my dress flutter back down over my thighs.

My chest heaved. I couldn't meet his eyes. His fingers grasped my chin and forced me to look at him. "You go out first. I'll follow later."

I nodded jerkily and turned around, slipping out the door, my legs shaky as a leaf in the wind, but at least I was escaping his too-knowing stare.

Only that brought me face-to-face with Emerson.

"You okay?" Her keen gaze traveled over me.

I nodded, blocking the door. "Yes, fine, thanks."

"You've been gone awhile." She smiled ruefully. "Not hiding from your date, are you?"

I had forgotten about Connor. "Something like that."

"I knew you weren't into him."

I shrugged. "He's nice . . . and we've been spending a lot of time together this summer." I wasn't even sure what I was saying. My body was still reeling from the aftereffects of my first orgasm. There'd been close calls before. I had even thought it had maybe happened a time or two, but now I knew. It had never happened before. Even after years of having sex with Harris, I had never had an orgasm

Until tonight.

Em's voice recaptured my attention. "Don't fall into another boring as hell relationship, Georgia. Please?"

My cheeks stung thinking of what I had just done with Logan—what I had just let happen to me. It was a far cry from boring.

I nodded. Maybe too vigorously. Stepping forward, I grasped Emerson's arm. "Don't worry about me. I won't be diving back into another relationship, boring or otherwise," I assured her, eager to lead her away from the bathroom. "C'mon. I'm hungry."

She resisted, pulling back on her arm. She jerked a thumb behind her. "I need to use the bathroom."

The bottom of my stomach fell out. "Uh . . ." My gaze flipped from her to the door and back again. "Nah, come on and get a margarita with me."

"Well, wait a second and I'll join you." Her hand moved for the doorknob and I gave her a hard pull, desperation making me less than subtle at this point.

She angled her head and gave me a funny look. "Georgia, what—"

The door opened then and Logan stepped out, his face expressionless. There was no smile. Nothing in his eyes that revealed what had just happened. He looked normal and casual and not like he was stepping out from a bathroom where he had rocked my world.

"What. The. Hell."

My gaze swung to Emerson. She was staring daggers at Logan and looking at me like she didn't know me at all.

"Don't tell anyone." The words tumbled from my mouth. "Don't tell Pepper."

Pepper would tell Reece. I didn't expect her to keep secrets from him. And Reece could *not* know. This was of vital importance. The only person I could want to *not* know more was my own mother.

I could well imagine Reece ripping into Logan under the assumption that his younger brother had somehow taken advantage of me. I didn't want that. He might have followed me into the bathroom and started this tonight, but I had wanted this. Since that first kiss, we had been heading toward this.

Emerson looked uncertainly between us. "It's no one's business what you do . . ." She stepped forward and jabbed Logan in the chest. "But just so you know. You fuck her over and you can kiss your balls good-bye."

Logan nodded, looking unfazed at the threat. "Understood."

"Emerson," I croaked, heat flooding my face.

She nodded as though satisfied, her features relaxed into a less severe expression. She stepped close to say into my ear. "Jesus. And here I was worried you were sliding into a pit of perpetual dullness. Just be careful."

That said, she slipped inside the bathroom.

I breathed easier. She hadn't said the words, but I knew she wouldn't tell anyone.

Facing Logan again, I was startled to find his expression no longer casual. He looked pissed. "Don't worry. I won't tell anyone either. No one needs to know that you're fucking around with Reece's little brother. It will be our dirty little secret."

I shook my head. "Logan—"

"Go back to your date, Georgia."

My *date*. The reminder hit me with a pang. I had forgotten about him again.

"Logan," I repeated, reaching for his arm, but he pulled it away.

"I primed you. Maybe he can finish you off tonight. Just don't expect him to fuck you like I would."

I flinched and without thinking my hand lashed out, slapping him soundly across the cheek.

His face gave the barest turn from the force before righting to look me over, his deep blue eyes drilling me. "Nice, Pearls." He fingered his cheek. "Didn't know you had it in you."

I stared, horrified. *I don't. I don't have it in me*, I wanted to say.

And yet it was a hard thing to argue when I had just in fact slapped him.

I had never struck another person. As in ever. Not even Amber when she overfed my hamster and killed it. It was just another first, courtesy of Logan Mulvaney. What would be next if I continued to do whatever it was I was doing with him?

A heavy pause full of wild emotions I couldn't even name pulsed like a heartbeat between us. Crazy as it sounded, I still wanted him. More than ever. I wanted him to grab me and pin me to the wall again. God, I was messed up. He'd insulted me. I'd slapped him. These were not normal things two people who liked each other did. And then I understood. Liking had nothing to do with it. This was wanting. Desire. Lust.

He turned away then, his big body striding down the hall, his steps thudding over the wood flooring.

"Great," I muttered, standing there for a moment, wishing I could call him back and erase that last couple minutes. Wishing I could explain the real reason I didn't want Reece to know. That I was only looking out for Logan. Well, partly. True, I wanted to spare him an ass-ripping by Reece. Partly. But there was a part of me that was embarrassed, too. I could pretend and lie to him but not myself.

After a few more moments, I headed down the hall, not wanting to face Emerson again when she emerged from the bathroom. She probably hadn't heard the slap or she would have flung that door open and followed up with a slap of her own. I eased back into the crowd halfheartedly, searching for my date. At least pretending to. Really, my gaze sought Logan, skipping over faces. I didn't see him anywhere—or Rachel for that matter. Had they left?

I located Connor sitting on a barstool, talking to one of

Pepper's coworkers from the daycare where she worked part-time. He smiled brightly when I arrived at his side, and I felt yet another pang of guilt.

I wished I hadn't brought him. It felt so wrong. Especially now. I had just made out with Logan in the bathroom while Connor sat out here eating fajitas and queso, oblivious to the fact of what I was doing . . . and that we had no future. At least romantically. We were colleagues. Plain and simple. I needed to set the record straight with him tonight.

I fixed a plate and picked at my food, feeling Emerson's stare on me from where she stood with Shaw. My appetite had fled, but I attempted to put on a good show. I joined in the toasts celebrating Pepper and Reece's new house. No one (except for Emerson) seemed aware that I was quieter than normal.

When Pepper came to stand beside me, I casually managed to mention Logan. I couldn't help it. Standing there, parts of me still throbbing and tingling from the things he did to my body, I couldn't hold it in.

"Reece's brother leave?"

"Yeah, he and Rachel had another thing to go to."

"What's the story with Rachel?" I was fishing. I had Logan's explanation of their relationship but I wanted another version.

"She's his best friend. Ever since they were kids. Her brother died when she was twelve. They just gravitated toward each other after that. I think Logan got what she was going through and she attached herself to him like coral on rock. Honestly, I'm surprised he's leaving her behind for college."

"She's attending school locally?"

"If at all. Her parents don't care what she does with her life."

"Then I'm glad she has Logan."

Pepper looked at me and I realized that must have sounded more invested than just someone making casual inquiries.

"Their friendship has been a good thing for the most part, it served them both . . . Reece hasn't always been there for Logan. First he went away to school, and then took over the bar. And God knows their father hasn't been an ideal parent. Reece regrets that. He feels like he failed Logan . . . left him to raise himself. But it's time for Logan to stop saving everyone else. His dad. Rachel. He needs to follow his own path." She sighed then.

I didn't miss how she said their friendship was good for *the most part*. "Why do I feel like there's a *but* in there somewhere?"

She winced and gave a quick nod. "Rachel is a bit of a wild child. Boys, booze. When they were fourteen, Logan found her after she swallowed a bunch of pills. He called an ambulance and then made her puke, trying to get her to empty her stomach." Pepper shook her head with a shudder. "No one should have to do that. Can you imagine being fourteen and walking in on that? Her parents weren't around as usual. Logan showed up because she had missed school. Thank God for her he did."

I released a shaky breath, imagining a young Logan bent over Rachel, shaking her to life, making her puke. It was just another picture at odds with the Logan I thought I knew. I spread them all out in front of me like snapshots—jock, teacher, writer. Hero.

"Hey." Pepper nudged me. "Don't share that with anyone, okay? Not that you would, but Reece told me that and I doubt Logan wants people knowing that about Rachel." She released a small puff of laughter. "He works so hard putting up a front that everything's great."

I nodded. "Of course." I knew something about putting up fronts. I wasn't going to advertise that I knew Rachel had tried to kill herself. The girl might not like me, but I wouldn't do that.

Pepper gulped her glass. "Okay. I didn't mean to turn into Debbie Downer with all this heavy talk. This is supposed to be a happy night."

I forced a grin and tried to shake thoughts of Logan. Yeah, he intrigued me, but I'm pretty sure that his encouraging me to bang Connor, followed with my slapping him in the face, destroyed whatever it was we had going.

I reached for a second margarita, deciding that a good buzz was in definite order.

Chapter 14

CONNOR ESCORTED ME TO the door of my loft. It was still early. A little after ten. The bar was packed. I waved at Cook as we passed through the kitchen. He jerked his chin once in greeting while treating Connor to an appraising glance.

"Care for some fried pickles?" I offered, motioning to the kitchen.

"Thanks. I'm full. But that's pretty cool—having a short order cook within shouting range."

"Yes and no. My arteries may not thank me after this summer."

I invited him up after unlocking the door, deciding this might be a good time to clear the air and establish that we were just going to be friends. Once we cleared the top, the opportunity came sooner than I expected though when he tried to kiss me.

I pressed a hand to the flat of his chest, noticing how much softer it felt compared to Logan's. And not nearly so broad. "Connor, I can't . . ."

He sighed and shook his head. "Friend zone, huh? Not the first time it's happened."

I winced. "I enjoy hanging out with you . . . and working together."

Nodding, he held up a hand. "I get it. Don't worry. I'm not going to turn into a bastard when we work together. You're still a hell of a lot better than Gillian."

I snorted. "Not much of a compliment, but I'll take it. We can still hang out, right? We can be friends. Our relationship doesn't have to be strictly work." I'd enjoyed being around him so far this summer. It was nice to have someone to catch a movie or bite to eat with. Pepper and Emerson were busy with their relationships and work.

"Sure." He flashed me a smile that didn't look too pained. "Like I'm going to say no to hanging out with a cute girl. Besides, you can always change your mind. Especially once you realize how much I enjoy to shop."

I wasn't going to change my mind, but I just laughed lightly and smiled at him. It was kinder than digging the blade in deeper and insisting that I wouldn't change my mind.

"And I couldn't help noticing your friend Suzanne," he added. "She's cute . . . and single, I gathered?"

I patted his shoulder. "I'll let you know about that." I wasn't about to toss Suzanne at him until I asked her if she was even interested.

I walked Connor back down and said good night. Closing the door after him, I locked it and sighed, falling back against the flat expanse. For several long moments, I just stared unseeingly ahead. Then with another sigh, I shoved off the door and ascended the steps. Once in the loft, I kicked off one heeled wedge and then another.

A knock on the door below had me turning around. Walking back down stairs, I opened the door, expecting to find Connor there. Maybe he had changed his mind about those pickle chips.

Instead Logan stood there, one hand resting on the edge of the doorjamb, his blue eyes dark and avid in a way that made my chest squeeze to the point of pain.

I stepped back up on the stairs like his presence was too much, his nearness a flame, burning hot and bright. He lowered that arm and I couldn't help noticing the way the sleeve bunched, hugging the nicely muscled bicep.

He stepped up on the top step and shut the door after him. It felt like the stairwell was closing in on us. Our proximity was too much. Turning, I hurried up into the loft.

Maybe I shouldn't have. Naturally, he followed me. But my brain only half functioned around him. My body did all the thinking, reacting on its own. My skin tightened, every nerve ending tingling and prickling in a way that made me want to puke or dance for joy. It was pretty much the same sensation.

"You invited him up here." The words fell on the air like an accusation, but there was a tightness to his jaw that told me he hated even uttering the words . . . like it pained him to get them past his lips.

"You told me to fuck him." For once the profanity slid easily off my tongue. It's what he had said to me and I wasn't even going to try to paraphrase. He hadn't cared. I blinked suddenly burning eyes. Treacherously burning eyes. After kissing me and . . . and all the rest, he hadn't cared what I did with another guy. It shouldn't have stung. He wasn't my boyfriend. But it had stung. It still did.

"Did you?"

I opened my mouth and then shut it with a snap. I didn't owe him an explanation.

He shook his head, his eyes never leaving my face. He started to move again, stalking me. I backed up into the kitchen area, deliberating avoiding the bed and futon. He followed.

"I hate that you might have been with him. That I taunted you into it. I want him to eat my fist if he even touched you, but it won't change anything between us either." His chest lifted on a breath. "I want you, Georgia."

I sucked in a ragged breath. I'd backed up into the kitchen area. The table bumped the backs of my thighs.

"I-I wasn't with him." I didn't have to tell him this, but the starkness of his gaze, the bluntness of his words compelled the words from me.

His features eased with relief. His eyes roamed my face and his voice came out hoarsely. "Tell me to leave."

I blinked, confused and bewildered at the request. He stepped forward another pace until we were chest to chest.

My senses reeled, overwhelmed at his closeness, the push of his chest against my breasts, the breadth of him surrounding me.

"Tell me to leave," he repeated, his hands reaching for the hem of my dress. His gaze held mine for a fraction of a second, but I couldn't find my voice.

In one swift move, he pulled my dress over my head, leaving me pressed between him and the table in nothing but black panties and bra.

The only sound was the distant hum of the bar below us and the rasp of our breath.

"Tell me to leave," he repeated, his voice harder, his eyes like flint.

When I didn't say anything, his mouth covered mine and he simultaneously lifted me up on the table. He broke away for a split second to pull his shirt off, not giving me nearly enough time to appreciate that sight, and then his mouth came back down on mine, kissing me so hard that my head bent back.

With a move I could hardly process, he flicked open the clasp of my bra at my back. The black satin straps slid loose off my shoulders and I released my hands from where they clung to his biceps to shrug it free.

My legs came around his hips and his bigger hands were under me, cupping my bottom.

His lips moved against mine with the same request. "Tell me to leave."

Air crashed from my lips, fanning his mouth. I felt like I had sprinted a race. "No."

That single word spurred him to action. He was all movement again. Strength and power. His hands tore my panties off me, and I gasped, stunned and turned on and electrified.

He didn't stop kissing me. Never once. I didn't know kissing could be like this. Long, drugging, endless kisses that squeezed the coil in my belly tighter and tighter. I didn't want him to step back and put any space between our bodies. Even that brief separation would kill me. I was sure of it.

I heard the snap of his jeans and the sliding teeth of a zipper. There was a crinkle of a wrapper and it registered through the haze that he had a condom.

Oh, God. This was really happening. He'd given me plenty of opportunities to stop. To tell him to leave. This was my choice. I wanted this. I wanted him.

He pulled back and I whimpered at the loss of him, biting my lip as I watched him roll on the condom. Some of my excitement edged into anxiety as I stared at the size of him.

"Don't do that," he growled as his hands came back to my hips again and hauled me to the edge of the table in one sliding motion.

"Do what?" I gasped as he lightly bit down on my throat. I cried out, pleasure-pain shooting through me as he followed the nip with a stroke of his tongue.

"Think."

"I-I don't think you're going to fit."

"I'll fit," he assured, his hand diving between our bodies. His fingers glided against me, teasing me for a moment before easing one inside. I moaned. "See, Pearls. You're so wet for me."

I nodded drunkenly as he curled that finger up inside me, hitting some secret spot that sent me careening over the edge.

He made a sound of appreciation. "You're past ready."

I nodded again, insensible, aching, my body clenching in need.

And then he was there. Hard and big, pushing inside me. His hands held tight to my hips, anchoring me as he drove in to the hilt.

I whimpered, the sensation of his pulsing cock alien and

overwhelming. I wasn't a virgin, but he made me feel like one. All of this . . . him . . . felt so new.

His eyes blazed down at me. "God, you're tight."

"It's been a while," I gasped.

"I can tell."

I made an inarticulate sound in response to that as he moved again, stretching me. His shoulders and arms quivered and I could tell he was restraining himself from moving faster, but the slow friction of him sliding out and in again stoked the ache back to life.

"God," I moaned. "I can't take it."

His eyes sparked fire and he drove into me, sliding me back on the table. He changed his grip on me, fingers digging into the swells of my ass, locking me into position for the hammering of his body. "You can take it."

I nodded. Incoherent. Sensation rippled down my spine and twisted around to the pit of my stomach. I felt him deep. Deeper than I ever thought possible. I came in a flash, shuddering with a piercing cry. I'd never been loud and my face burned until the sensations started all over again as he continued to stroke inside me.

He laughed low and deep, the sound a purr that vibrated through me. "So you're a screamer," he breathed against my ear. "That's fucking hot. Keep screaming. Show me how much you love this."

I shook my head, for some reason defiant, even though I reveled in his body driving into mine. I didn't know why I fought it. He'd made me come twice tonight and now I was headed for a third orgasm. For a girl who never got off during a four-year relationship it was nothing short of a miracle.

Logan kept going, increasing his pace. He was far from done. My nails dug into his arms as he worked over me, the sound of our bodies smacking together filling the air. His biceps flexed and bulged under my fingers. Unbelievable as it seemed, the insistent friction of him moving inside me had me hurtling toward that crest again.

Unintelligible sounds choked from my lips again and he dropped his head into my neck, biting down on my earlobe.

He reached between our bodies and found my clit, rolling it once before pinching it firmly. That's all it took. I came apart in his arms, shuddering and gasping and moaning, my arms slipping around his shoulders and hanging on to him.

He followed fast, slamming into me with a ferocity that would have slid me right off the table if not for his grip on my ass.

His throat arched and I felt him jerk and pulse to a stop inside me. His body folded over me then, his firm chest sticky on mine. We were still joined. I held on to his shoulders, my heart pounding like an incessant drum in my ears.

My fingertips worked against his skin, fluttering slightly on the smooth surface, unsure where to go. What to do next. I'd never been here before. I'd only ever slept with someone I was in a relationship with. A fling was a new experience and I was lost on the protocol.

He lifted his head and looked down at me, his blue eyes deep and unreadable. He still didn't move his weight off me or slide out of my body. His deep voice rumbled up from his chest, vibrating against my bare breasts. "I knew it would be like this with you."

My pulse skittered at my neck and his eyes caught the flutter of movement. His fingers grazed my pulse point there like it was the most fascinating and tempting thing he had ever seen. As though I was.

It's as if he saw everything in me. Missed nothing. "Be like what?" I whispered.

A long beat followed before he replied, "Not enough."

My heart danced a little until I shoved it back down and forced my rioting emotions to behave. He almost made me feel relaxed and not completely awkward. "I bet that's what you tell every girl."

His expression turned grave. "I've never said anything I didn't mean to a girl. And I've never said that before."

Okay, now I was uncomfortable. I pushed at his shoulder with the heel of my palm. This wasn't the beginning of some grand romance. Relationships didn't start this way. I was looking for a forever kind of guy . . . eventually. And he wasn't that. "I need to clean up."

He lifted off me. I turned and snatched up my dress from the back of a nearby chair where it had landed.

Holding it against me as a makeshift shield, I hurried to the bathroom. Only once inside, I realized he had followed, his bigger body cramping the small space.

"What are you . . ." My voice faded as he reached inside the shower stall and turned on the water.

"You wanted to clean up."

I watched, gaping as he pulled off his shoes and then shrugged out of his jeans, revealing the lean lines and hardness of his body. There wasn't an inch of fat to him. He was corded and sinewy with muscle, skin smooth and golden except for the narrowing happy trail that led to that part of him I was already familiar with.

He tested the water, adjusted it with a nod, and then reached for me.

"What are—"

My voice died abruptly as he tugged my dress free and tossed it aside for the second time tonight.

He wrapped an arm around my waist and lifted me easily, depositing me in the shower. Warm water sluiced down me, plastering my hair to my face. Gasping, I quickly pushed the strands out of the way, slicking my hair back. He followed me inside, closing the door. The water hit him and he stretched his neck, angling his head to better wet his hair, turning the dark blond almost black.

His body crowded me in the small confines of the shower. Steam started to fill the air that wasn't infused by pounding water. I inched around him, moving in a small circle, staring up at him uncertainly.

He stared back down, watching me in that way that made me feel almost hunted.

"You never took a shower with a guy before?"

I shook my head. I was beginning to realize there was a lot that I'd missed out on with Harris.

His eyes narrowed, considering me. "Did you ever come before tonight?"

My throat constricted and I looked away. He grabbed my chin and brought my gaze back to him. "Don't be ashamed. Tell me the truth."

I shook my head and then added, "No."

"No what?" he pressed me, his expression fierce, his blue eyes like a storming sea.

"No. I've never . . . come before."

A slow, satisfied smile curled his lips and I wanted to smack him.

"Until tonight," he clarified. And the rest was there, unsaid but heard. *Until me*.

"Don't look so smug," I muttered, feeling as though I had just handed him the recipe to my undoing.

The water beat at my back and ran down my legs. Still watching me, he grabbed the bottle of body wash and poured some of the liquid soap into his hands.

I motioned tentatively to the shelf hanging off the showerhead. "I have a sponge—"

"I'll use my hands."

He set his soapy hands to my body, washing me and massaging me so thoroughly I couldn't stop from moaning. It was unbelievable. He started at my shoulders, then down my arms. He missed nothing, not even my fingers. He worked intently over every digit, my wrists, and then back up my arms to my shoulders again.

He stepped closer, his chest brushing the aching tips of my breasts as his hands worked their way down my back to massage the rounds of my ass. I arched my face up into the spray of water, mouth gasping wide with sharp whimpers.

Nothing had ever felt so good. It was like taking the best massage of my life and merging it with the hottest sex (which coincidentally had happened only ten minutes ago).

His foot nudged my feet apart and his fingers slipped down the cleft of my ass, skimming me until he found my entrance. He only teased there, soapy fingers softly circling my oversensitive button and giving it a roll.

"There it is," he murmured in satisfaction as a hiss escaped me.

Then his hands were gone from between my legs. I mewled in disappointment. He spun me around, lifting both my hands and flattening my palms to the tiled wall.

I heard the squirt of the bottle and knew he was getting more soap. I didn't look back, just stood there, quivering in anticipation, my hands on the wall. The tips of my breasts were cold against the tile but I didn't care.

His hands came around and cupped my breasts, warming them. His hands squeezed and fondled the soapy-slick flesh for several moments before palming his way down my stomach. One hand slipped between my thighs from behind while the other hand attacked from the front.

He eased one finger inside me the precise moment the other one found and played with my clit. I dropped my face to the wet shower wall, my cheek plastered to the wet tile as I convulsed. Moans rolled over my lips, endless and without break as I came in a flash.

His lips moved against my drenched hair as his finger stroked inside my convulsing channel, building the ache back to a simmer. "God, baby, you're so tight and swollen. Are you sore from that last fuck?"

I shouldn't love dirty talk like this, but my belly dipped and twisted at his words. He brought something out in me I didn't know existed. A darkness that needed to release itself into the world. If only for tonight. This felt like freedom.

I nodded with a hiss as he pushed his cock against my backside, sliding it against the cleft of my cheeks.

"I'll just have to get us off this way then." His erection ground against me while his finger pushed deeper.

My voice rose up, broken and ragged over the beat of the shower. "N-no. I want you again."

He paused for a moment. "You won't be able to walk tomorrow."

I spun around and the sight of his beautiful face, the stark lines and hollows sluiced with water, the dark glitter of his blues eyes brought that darkness in me swimming to the surface. "I don't want to walk tomorrow. I want you now."

To prove these words, I grasped hold of his cock and squeezed. He filled my hand, water-slick and hard as a rock.

I pumped my hand over him until he cursed and dropped his head into my neck, the hard bands of his arms gathering me up close. He groaned and thrust himself into my hand several times. I ran my thumb over the engorged tip of him, wondering what it would take for him to bury it inside me.

"Logan." He lifted his head to look at me and the battle was in evidence all over his face. "Make me come again. Please." I licked drops of water off my lips and went for the thing I knew would get to him. "Be the first guy to ever fuck me in the shower."

His eyes went black. I watched my words sink in and ripple across his features. He picked me up in one move, guiding my legs around his hips. He entered me in one thrust, impaling me to the shower wall.

I cried out, the pleasure white-hot and blinding, dancing the fine line of pain.

He groaned and held himself still for a moment, adjusting us both to the feel of him inside me. I was swollen, and if possible he felt bigger inside me than the last time.

"I can't . . . not move," he gasped into the wet snarl of my hair.

"Then move," I ordered, hands gliding down the slick surface of his back to seize his tight ass.

He unleashed himself. As though he had only been waiting my permission.

He wasn't easy on me. His hips moved, slamming into me like he was racing toward a destination neither of us had ever visited. A hard thing to believe with his level of experience, but the arms holding me up trembled around me like it was all new and overwhelming for him, too.

My thighs clenched around him as my orgasm came fast and hard. Loud cries exploded from my lips, only proving his earlier statement. I was a screamer.

His fingers dug into my hips and he drove into me several more times and then pulled out of me suddenly, reaching his own orgasm. It was this, the sight of him coming in the shower that obliterated the euphoria of my climax.

I just had unprotected sex.

Chapter 15

IDIDN'T EVEN KNOW myself anymore. I would have kicked any one of my friends' butts for doing what I just did. I'd even lectured Amber about safe sex when she started getting serious with her boyfriend, considering it my job as her older sister to do that.

And then I went and did this.

At least pregnancy wasn't a concern. I was on the pill and had been ever since I was seventeen. My mother hadn't asked if Harris and I were having sex. She would never have had so candid and uncomfortable a conversation as that with me.

She, however, had been that girl who got knocked up at twenty and then suffered the fallout—a broken heart and me—when the relationship didn't work out. I'm sure she had guessed that my relationship with Harris was escalating. Or she had assumed it would. Without any discussion, she took me to her gynecologist and got me on the pill. I'd been on it ever since. But just because I wouldn't get pregnant didn't mean there weren't other concerns.

Without a word, I quickly rinsed the soap off my body,

avoiding Logan's gaze. Not an easy thing to do in the cramped space of the shower. Especially with his beautiful body drawing my eyes.

"I'm clean," he announced as I shut off the water and reached for my thick, fluffy robe. I knew exactly what he meant. He wasn't talking about being shower-fresh. The words sent relief coursing through me, but I quickly shook it off. What did that even mean to him? I eyed him dubiously, suspecting our qualifications didn't match up. Was I just supposed to trust him?

Stepping out of the shower, I slipped inside my robe. It's like he could read the thoughts tracking through my mind.

"Georgia." At the firm sound of my name, I looked up as he stepped out onto the shower rug. Water sluiced down his hard body and my heart stirred at the sight. He really was beautiful. Right or not, I felt possessive of him, my mind struggling to disconnect from him after what we'd just shared.

"I got checked recently. At a clinic," he said. "I can show you my results."

I looked away for a moment before looking back at him. Those eyes of his compelled me, drew my gaze again and again.

He continued, "I've never done what we just did before, but—"

At my snort, he stopped and narrowed his gaze on me.

I yanked my belt tight around my waist with angry movements. I knew what he was. How dare he try to persuade me into thinking I was somehow an exception? And how stupid was I to want to believe him?

"You expect me to believe I'm the only girl you've ever been with without wearing a condom?"

"You think I'm lying to you. Is that where we are?" He planted his hands on his hips, indifferent to his nakedness. He stepped forward until only an inch separated us. His body heat radiated toward me . . . and something else. Something that was entirely him and his magnetism. His ability to reach me and touch me without touching.

I held my ground, refusing to back down like almost every other time with him. "You," he said. "Me bare-skinned inside you. That was the first time I've done that with any girl."

That declaration made my stomach dip with pleasure. I gulped at the intense way he looked at me. I wanted to believe that. It fit with what I knew of him. Logan was responsible. He'd been living as an adult for years now, taking care of himself, his father, Rachel.

I shook my head stubbornly. "It doesn't matter. I'm on the pill, but it still doesn't matter. It was reckless. We should have talked about it first."

He angled his head. "I seem to remember that you begged me for it."

I closed my eyes in a pained blink. Opening my eyes again, I nodded. "I'm not saying the fault is all yours. It's my fault, too. Maybe even more than yours. I did push you into it. You didn't want to—"

"Oh, I wanted to," he corrected, his eyes gleaming hotly.

I shook my head again, trying not to let him muddy my thinking. This had gone far enough. "Let's just agree we're both to blame then. Things got out of hand. We had . . . an itch. Scratched it, and now we're good." Done. Finished. I didn't say it, but he understood my meaning.

His jaw tensed. "So I was an itch? That's all?"

I threw up both hands. "C'mon, Logan. You have an itch every night of the week. This isn't anything more than that."

His eyes went cold. "That's right." He nodded. "I'm Reece's man-whore brother."

I flinched. "I didn't say that."

"Didn't you? Just so you know, I haven't been with a girl since I was checked over a month ago. I haven't even kissed a girl since you outside the kink club."

I blinked, stunned. He couldn't mean that.

He read my disbelief, and shook his head, clearly disgusted. He dragged a hand through his wet hair and muttered more to himself than me, "What am I even doing?"

A sharp pang hit me in the chest at the regret behind those words.

He leveled a dead-eyed stare on me. "Think what you want. You will anyway."

He marched out of the bathroom then. I followed, feeling queasy. I didn't want this to end like this.

I didn't want it to end . . .

I wanted to face-punch myself at my utter contrariness. I just needed to let this go. *Let him go.*

He stopped to hastily jerk on his clothes.

"Logan."

At the sound of his name, he looked back at me, waiting for me to say something. Anything. Words to fix this.

"Good-bye." It's all I could find to say. The only thing safe.

With a short, dry laugh, he said, "Right. Good-bye, Georgia."

He vanished down the steps. I listened to the thud of his

steps on the stairs and the door opening and shutting. Then there was nothing. Silence.

THE DAYS PASSED IN a monotonous blur sliced with regret whenever I thought about Logan and our night together—which pretty much happened with every other breath I took.

I jogged in the morning, hoping to make myself so tired I couldn't feel anything. I buried myself in Dr. Chase's research. Grabbed lunch with Emerson, where she grilled me about Logan and looked skeptical at my repeated assurances that it was just a onetime thing.

"So there's nothing going on between you two?" She twirled her straw in her soda.

I shook my head and stared out at the sun-splashed sidewalk in front of the café where we ate. "Nope . . . just a moment's weakness."

"Well, he is insanely hot. I can't blame you."

I turned my attention back on her. "It's not worth telling Pepper and Reece. It will make things awkward. You know that, right?"

She nodded. "Okay." Her blue eyes sharpened. "As long as it really was a onetime thing."

I stabbed a fry into ketchup. "Why do you sound so doubtful?"

"Uh, 'cause he's Logan Mulvaney. Girls line up for this guy. He's a kink club regular. You know that."

I nibbled on my fry. "Yeah." Except he hadn't been with a girl in more than a month. Well. Except for me.

I believed him. He'd been telling the truth. Just like I knew he got himself tested and was clean. I'd lived my entire life with a mother who taught me to be suspicious of men, to look hard at a person for the truth. To rarely trust. My father had made promises and broken every one of them. That made a person—my mother and me both—a bit of a cynic. I wasn't easy to dupe. And I knew Logan hadn't been lying. We'd already had sex at that point . . . multiple times. There was no reason for him to lie to me.

"Just watch out for yourself." Em twisted a short, spiky strand of her hair around her finger. "I saw what splitting up with Harris did to you. This guy . . . Logan could wreck you in a way Harris never could."

Her words rang with a truth I couldn't deny. I clung to them, letting them fortify me over the next week, memorizing Logan's work schedule and avoiding him to the best of my ability. I never came and went through Mulvaney's during peak hours so that I didn't have to come face-to-face with Logan.

Friday arrived and I knew from Pepper that Logan was graduating.

I told myself this should make me feel better. Less guilty for sleeping with him. At least he wasn't in high school anymore. Not that he had ever seemed like a guy in high school. In some ways, he felt more mature, more experienced than I was. He was real. He owned his emotions in a way that I didn't. I worked through the weekend, trying not to think about Logan graduating. Hard to do. According to his schedule, he wasn't working all weekend and I imagined him partying it up with teenagers who were out of high school and suddenly curfew-free.

I was grateful when Monday rolled around and I was able to resume working. Connor, Gillian, and I had a meeting on Tuesday with Dr. Chase, and I spent the rest of the week in the library. Dr. Chase revised our assignments and I actually had to spend Wednesday and Thursday working with sourpuss Gillian.

I was ready for some happy time that night, so when Pepper texted me and Emerson about a girls' night, I was in.

We went to see the new Bond movie. It was just like old times. The three of us laughing and talking over popcorn and getting shushed by people sitting near us. It was the kind of behavior my mother would frown at, but considering I'd been doing a lot of things lately Mom would frown at, this, comparatively, seemed like a small offense.

After the movie we grabbed a late dinner at Gino's, splitting an enormous Greek pizza that we devoured with utter abandon. We talked until the staff started cleaning up, signaling us that we needed to leave.

It was a good night. My best friends were happy. It was in their every move and gesture. In the way they smiled. And I knew why. They had found peace in their lives. In Reece and Shaw. Their futures were bright. It was hard not to let the envy creep in. I tried to remember if it had ever been like that for me with Harris. Maybe in the beginning, but we had been so young then. Just sixteen. The light that shined in Pepper's and Emerson's eyes . . . I doubt that light had ever been in my eyes.

I was glad we'd gone out and spent time together even if it meant I was returning to Mulvaney's after ten P.M. during peak hours *and* I happened to see Logan's Bronco in the parking lot, so I knew he was working. The risk had been worth it. And I couldn't hide forever. Not to mention it wasn't very adult of me.

So we'd had a fling. People do that. It happens. *But it never happens to you.* Squaring my shoulders, I stepped inside the noisy bar and sucked in a breath.

I was going to see him again. That was a given. He was Reece's brother. Determined to get over it, I pushed through the crowd lining up to place their orders at the counter. Still no glimpse of Logan, and there was an ache in my chest that felt a little like disappointment over that fact. I gave myself a swift mental kick, realizing that as much as I didn't want to see him . . . I did.

I made it into the kitchen. I was in the clear. Sighing, I rolled my shoulders, forcing myself to relax.

That's when I saw him.

He rounded the counter and stopped hard. A few feet separated us. He held a tub of clean glasses, and his biceps strained in a way that made me remember his strength . . . the ease in which he held me up in the shower. I was pretty average in size, no little thing like Emerson, but he had made me feel dainty.

"Hey," I blurted, my voice a little too high.

"Hey," he returned, his reply slower, his deep baritone sliding over me. Everything in me responded, my skin tingling and reacting with a sharp shiver.

"Congratulations. I heard you graduated."

He nodded. "Yeah."

I wet my lips, wanting to ask him more. Everything. I wanted to know everything about him and his plans for the summer and beyond. I gave myself a mental slap. *Get a grip, Georgia. This wasn't ending with happily ever after.*

"Did you do anything special?"

Why was I still talking?

He snorted, his sexy lips twisting into a self-effacing grin. "Yeah. Reece and Pepper took me to dinner and then I went home and peeled my old man off the floor where he had passed out."

He uttered it so matter-of-factly, his blue gaze flat. This was his life. He wasn't looking for pity. In fact, I knew he would hate that, but I still couldn't stop myself from reaching out and touching his arm.

His forearm contracted under my fingers. "Don't," he warned softly, glasses clinking as he adjusted his grip on the tub. "Don't touch me and expect me not to touch you."

I dropped my hand to my side, my heart beating wildly in my chest. Of course, those contrary feelings that always hit me around him resurfaced. *Run, stay, run, stay.*

It was so tempting to let him touch me. To lead him upstairs for another go-round, but that would just make things messier than they already were.

"I just thought we could be friends, Logan."

"Do you fuck your friends?"

I flinched.

"I didn't think so." He stepped around me, his eyes still that distant blue. "I have enough friends." The words stung, ringing in my ears. "With you, I want more. I want you under me. On top of me. In the shower again."

My mouth dried. Without another word, he walked away.

I looked up to find Cook watching me with an almost bored expression as he shook a fryer of pickles. Like he was accustomed to girl-boy drama unfolding in his kitchen.

I forced a wobbly smile as though nothing was wrong and turned to unlock my door. Once inside the loft, I kicked off my shoes and dropped facedown on the bed with a groan, thinking about Emerson's words. Logan could wreck me. She was right.

Only it might be too late.

Chapter 16

THE SOUNDS OF THE bar below greeted me like a rumbling growl when I opened my door to find Annie, dressed in a striped miniskirt and a tight tank top that glittered like the Vegas strip. I hadn't seen Logan since Thursday when we came face-to-face in the kitchen. I had vowed not to spend another Saturday night in, beating myself up and analyzing what we were or weren't a hundred different ways. Even if Annie was the only person available, I was going out.

She tossed her hair over her shoulders and stepped past me, marching up the stairs. At the top, she propped her hands on her hips and inspected the inside of the loft, examining my living quarters. "Well, isn't this convenient? If I don't hook up with anyone, I can just pass out up here." Her gaze slid to mine, assessing. "Unless you plan on hooking up tonight."

I lifted one shoulder like that was a very real possibility.

She laughed. "Little Georgia Peach. Who knew you had such a naughty side."

An image of Logan and me in the shower flashed through my mind, tormenting me. I did have a naughty side. Except I couldn't imagine myself being naughty with just any random guy. "You should come with me next weekend."

"What's next weekend?"

"Hello." She waggled her eyebrows. "What do I do once a month? Kink club, remember?"

"Oh, yeah." Actually I had forgotten about it, except in the context of Logan. That's where it had all began. Where I first kissed him. Would he be there? If Rachel went, he would be. That's why he went, after all. To look after Rachel. At least that's why he claimed to go. Maybe he'd hook up this time. There was no reason why he couldn't. Nothing stopping him.

"Half the members are gone for the summer, so this is going to be a signature event."

"What's that mean?"

"It will be an intimate gathering . . . it's at this phat house over on University Boulevard. I'm wearing a cocktail dress and these fuck-me heels I found on sale at Nordstrom." She motioned just below her hip. "Thigh highs. No underwear. I've had my eye on this guy for a while. He always pairs off with this one girl but she went home for the summer so I'm making my move."

"Sounds like it will be . . . a memorable night."

She nodded. "For sure. This house is supposed to have like twelve bedrooms. Plenty of space. It's not like I'm into ménage every single time. Usually that happens out of necessity."

But there would be plenty of space this time. Room for Logan to be alone with a willing partner. Or two. I know he claimed he hadn't kissed another girl since that night I kissed him on the porch, but I'm sure that was about to change. If it hadn't already. Jealousy sank its fangs into me as I envisioned him slipping inside one of those eight rooms with some girl.

"Let's go." Forcing a smile, I waved Annie out of the loft, closing the door behind us. We headed downstairs together, Annie clinging to the walls of the stairwell on either side of her so that she didn't fall in her lethally high-heeled ankle boots. "I'm sure you won't need to crash with me tonight. You're dressed to kill and you never have a problem getting a hookup," I dutifully reminded her.

She preened. "True, but pickings are slimmer in the summer months. I'm already ready for fall semester. I swear, next weekend is the only highlight of my summer so far. Hope it doesn't disappoint."

I was hardly listening to her anymore as we entered the bar and made our way through the crowd. This was Logan's stomping ground, and my every nerve was on high alert.

My eyes scanned the room, searching for anyone in a Mulvaney's staff T-shirt. On the lookout specifically for a shirt that was filled out nicely by a body so ripped that it made me dizzy.

It might have been days since I'd last seen Logan, but he invaded my dreams. I couldn't fall asleep without his image there, filling my head. Alone in the dark . . . thinking about him. It was a problem. It was like he flipped a switch inside me. My body ached for him, unwilling to go back to its dormant state. My hands tracked over the places he had touched and kissed and bit . . . caressing my breasts, skimming down my stomach and between my legs. It was embarrassing, this wanton creature I had become, touching myself like some kind of sex kitten who couldn't get enough.

My hands were a pale echo of Logan's touch, and it only made me hungrier for him.

When Annie texted me earlier in the day to see if I wanted to hang out at Mulvaney's with her, I'd agreed. Even if I didn't love the girl, she was single, and single girlfriends were few and far between. Suzanne was working a lot to save up money and make up for the time she was having to take off to house-sit for her parents' cruise, so she wasn't very available. Besides, I could just go upstairs to my room if Annie got to be too much.

We located a long stretch of table with two unoccupied chairs. A few people sat on the other end of it, drinking beer and playing dominoes.

"Want me to order us—"

She held up her hand. "Patience, grasshopper. Give it a few moments. Two girls alone in a bar . . . we won't be alone for long. And then we can drink for free."

Sure enough, within moments a couple guys ambled over carrying a pitcher of beer. They offered us some plastic cups and poured us drinks. Annie beamed at them and got her flirt on, beginning with the usual conversation.

Are you a student?

What's your major?

Oooh, you have a tattoo? Show me . . .

I was bored. Neither one of them could compete with the lingering effects of Logan's bright light. People eventually got up from the table, leaving room for the two guys to sit down beside us.

I forced the small talk, still scanning the bar. With every

minute that passed, I resigned myself to the fact that he wasn't working tonight.

"Are you looking for someone?" the guy in a knit cap beside me asked. His dark hair was long and peeked out of the sides. He was cute in a Hollister kind of way.

I shook my head. "No."

"Then I must be boring you."

I offered a wan smile. "Just tired. Had a long workweek."

That sent us into a conversation about what it was I was doing over the summer. I had to hand it to him. He was polite. He seemed interested as I described the goal of Dr. Chase's research.

My gaze still flickered around the room; I couldn't help myself. Now that I had a taste, I was maybe addicted to Logan Mulvaney. Fine. No maybes. But that didn't mean I wouldn't kick the habit. People overcame bigger obstacles every day. I would, too.

Of course, this conviction was blown out of the water when I suddenly spotted him across the room, standing near the bar. He didn't look like he was working. A posse of girls surrounded him. One kept her hand planted firmly on his chest as she talked, and the totally unacceptable urge to pull her off him by her hair seized me. *God*. I was such a cliché. I bit the edge of my tongue, disappointed in myself.

I wasn't the jealous type. I never had been. I hadn't even been jealous when Harris started studying long hours in the library with the girl he left me for, and I probably should have been. I guess I hadn't cared enough to be concerned, but I cared now and it sucked.

When her hand drifted down his stomach, pain sliced my chest. It only got worse as I watched her red fingernails stroke low, snatching hold of the hem of his shirt. He smiled. Like he used to smile at me, in the beginning when he was all teasing grins.

I wondered what she had said to make him smile. She tossed her long hair over a sleek, tanned shoulder, leaving no obstruction to the view of her ample cleavage.

Comparatively, I felt like a minister's wife in my pink wraparound blouse with a sash that tied smartly into a bow across my midriff.

I must have been glaring holes into Logan because suddenly he lifted his head and scanned the room, promptly finding me.

I tore my gaze and looked back at the guy beside me. Knowing Logan was watching, I tried to look really interested in what he was saying. I hated that Logan caught me gawking at him. Even though I was dying to know if he was still watching me, I refused to look in his direction again.

I was in the middle of asking Knit Cap Guy a question about winters in Maine where he grew up when a pair of long legs stopped beside my table. I looked up into Logan's impassive face.

"Hey, it's Little Mulvaney," Annie declared.

He flicked her a withering glance before looking back at me. "Can I see your ID, please?"

I shook my head and tucked a long strand of hair behind my ear, certain I had misheard. Of all the things I thought he might say, that was not what I expected. "Excuse me?"

"ID," he repeated.

Now I was royally pissed. He knew I was still twenty and he was asking for my driver's license? Jerk. I stabbed a finger where he had been standing moments ago with his little harem. "Don't you have something better to do?"

"C'mon, buddy," the guy beside me coaxed. He rested a hand on my shoulder as if offering his support. "Be cool."

Logan's eyes settled on that hand on my shoulder for a moment before sliding his blue eyes to Knit Cap Guy's face. "Stay out of this, and I'm not your buddy."

My would-be savior's smile faltered.

"You got to be kidding me, Mulvaney. Her best friend is together with your brother and you're carding her?" Annie's voice was loud enough to draw stares. "And she's living in the loft upstairs. That's just dick of you."

"Be quiet, Annie," I ordered without looking at her. I didn't look at anyone except Logan. Even as I dug around inside my handbag for my fake ID, I kept my glare trained firmly on him, positive that steam was escaping my ears. He glared right back at me, his jaw locked hard, arms crossed over his chest.

Finding the ID, I extended it to him with one angry flip of my wrist.

When he took it from me our fingers brushed and it was like a spark of heat flew up my arm from the touch. My body remembered him even though my mind was trying to forget. Even if my mind wanted to introduce him to my fist right now. I hated my body right then.

"Marianne Allison Kellog?" He read my cousin's name in a deadpan voice. I'd used her ID for the last two years without issue. We bore a resemblance.

"Who's she?" he asked.

"Me." I lifted an eyebrow in challenge.

Annie giggled. "That's right, Jack-off. She's Marianne."

He ignored Annie. "When's your birthday?"

My mind blanked. I hadn't been carded in a while, and even then no one had grilled me. "October eleven . . . no, seventeenth."

He grinned then. It was a nasty smile. Slow and satisfied. I felt it slither through me like a snake winding its way home. "Sorry, sweetheart. October seventh. I'll have to confiscate this, *Marianne*. And get rid of the beer."

I shot to my feet. "You . . ."

He clucked his tongue. "Careful or I'll have to escort you out. It's protocol for me to give anyone flashing a bogus ID the boot, but I'm feeling generous."

I quivered with indignation. "I live *here!*"

"Then maybe you need to go on home for the night."

I was so mad I saw red. How dare he interfere after I slept with him? Was this his MO? To punish the girls he slept with?

Without thinking, I reached for my half cup of beer and splashed it in his face.

You could have heard a pin drop. The bar went silent. The only sound was the rush of blood in my ears. Even Annie watched with her mouth gaping. The guy I had been talking to looked like he wanted to be anywhere else. He inched back in his chair as if he wanted to distance himself from the crazy beer-tossing girl.

Crap. What did I do?

A nerve ticked beside Logan's right eye and I knew he was

pissed. Even more pissed than when he first walked over here and demanded my ID. He was a bomb and I had just lit the fuse.

What was happening to me? I was normally a polite, drama-free girl. But there was nothing normal about this. About me and Logan. The air was charged, sparking with suppressed energy.

"It's time to go," Logan said, his voice lethally quiet.

"Hey . . ." Knit Cap Guy started to stand in one last effort at heroism on my behalf.

Logan swung his gaze to him. "Sit the fuck back down."

The guy sank down in his chair, avoiding my gaze. I rolled my eyes. Good to know he wasn't easily intimidated.

Taking my arm, Logan led me through the bar. Bodies parted liked the Red Sea. I could smell the beer on him and that only kept the moment I splashed beer over him on instant replay in my head.

As we entered the kitchen he grabbed a dishtowel off the counter and wiped it over his face and then tossed it down without a glance.

"Just what in the hell was that about?"

"You're not twenty-one."

"Oh, come off it! Like you give a . . . a . . . shit."

He *tsk*ed. "My, my, Pearls cursing? What would your mother say?"

"Fuck you!" This fell easily even as the thought flashed through me that my mother would be horrified. Being a lady was right up there with eating your vegetables in my house. It didn't matter how provoked you were. Staying composed under fire was a true testament to one's character.

He smiled, looking both dangerous and excited. "Oh, there she is. The real Georgia."

No. I wasn't this wild thing he made me out to be. He brought out this ugly in me. This beer-tossing, foul-mouthed, hot-for-his-body girl. I shook my head and bit my lip, bewildered. No. This wasn't me at all. It couldn't be.

I headed for my apartment door, tossing over my shoulder, "Why don't you head back to your little bar groupies?"

"Jealous?" His hand clamped on my arm, forcing me around.

"Ha. As if. I don't care who paws you, Logan. We're not even friends."

"No . . . we're more than friends. And you know that."

I swallowed against the lump in my throat. "No."

He took my face in both of his hands then, holding me still as his gaze scoured me like hot coals. "What are you so afraid of?"

You. Me. How I am with you . . . Us being something more, something real, and then facing the world . . . My mother, enduring her disappointment by becoming all her worst fears.

Releasing my face, he grabbed my hand and pulled me after him. At the door leading to the loft, I dug in my heels and stepped in front of him. "You don't get to come up." My chin lifted in a show of bravado. Courage that was hard to cling to when he looked so furious . . . with the front of his shirt wet with the beer I'd thrown at him.

"Key." The single word dropped like a stone between us. He nodded at my bag, that nerve still ticking near his eye.

I hesitated a moment before moving, my fingers fumbling

until I pulled my key out of my bag. He plucked it from my hand and unlocked my door.

I braced myself, determined not to move until he left. Me and him upstairs? Together as mad as we were? Alone? Yeah, not a good idea. I was so not on board with that.

Swinging the door open, I didn't stand a chance though. He ignored my sputtered protest and ushered us inside the stairwell.

He shut the door with a dull thud and we were engulfed in shadows. I moved up and turned on the third step, determined to go no farther. I would not let him bulldoze over me. This ended here.

I'd left a lamp on in the loft above and a dim gold light trickled down into the stairwell, gilding the lines and planes of his face. Standing one step above him, we were almost eye-level, and I seized the advantage, letting it embolden me. "You're not coming up here." My voice fell loudly, echoing in the tomblike space.

"Scared of what I'll do to you?"

My pulse jackknifed against my throat. His eyes glittered like an animal's in the shadows of the stairwell. The air was electric, like he would erupt any moment into fire and ash.

He was still pissed at me, but there was something else in the air, too. Something that brought to mind the hot press of his body pinning me to the bathroom door . . . ordering me not to move my hands from above my head.

"No one *does* anything to me," I countered.

He laughed almost cruelly. "Your whole life has been others *doing* things to you. Deciding how your life is going to be. Your parents. Your douche ex."

The accusation enraged me. I didn't want it to be true, but a piece of me buried deep acknowledged that he wasn't totally wrong.

He continued, "You're like that guitar of yours. Buried away from the world where no one can see or touch you."

"Shut up," I hissed.

"You're scared," he pressed. "From the moment you took me on you've been wondering what the hell you're doing getting tied up with a guy that doesn't fit into your vanilla life." He took another step, and damn it, he was taller than me again, encroaching like an invading tank. "But you want it. You want to be with the kind of guy who will retaliate when his girl has a tantrum and splashes a drink in his face."

His girl?

The words simultaneously thrilled and terrified me, sparking something deep and tugging at the part of me that I kept hidden. The Georgia buried deep. Just like my guitar. He was right. Panic blossomed in my chest with the realization. Everything he said was true. He saw me. I felt stripped bare. I couldn't hide anymore.

I swallowed. "I'm not your girl."

"That's where you're wrong. You are. You just haven't figured that out yet."

"Oh, so now *you're* deciding things for me," I charged, diving for the words almost desperately.

"No. I didn't decide it. You did. The moment you kissed me. I thought I would give you a little more time, some space to realize this, but I changed my mind."

I made a strangling sound. "Oh?"

"About ten minutes ago when I saw that asshat sitting next to you and looking at you like you were his next meal." He leaned in, forcing me to grab the stairwell wall and arch back from him. "I wanted to fuck him up and then throw you over my shoulder." One corner of his mouth lifted, but there was no humor in the play of his lips. "You've turned me into a caveman. I've never acted this way before." His eyes looked almost bleak right then. Like he didn't want to feel this way. I could relate. "You. Me. We're the real thing, Pearls." His eyes gleamed in the shadows of the stairwell, willing me to see that, too.

I just couldn't. The idea of us . . . it was too wrong . . . too crazy.

Shaking my head, I shoved at his chest. His hand locked around my wrist, fingers circling my bones completely, stopping me from pushing him away.

Feeling slightly panicked, I brought my other hand from behind me and shoved harder at him. The momentum sent me falling back on the stairs and he followed, coming over me, one hand circling around my back to soften my fall against the steps.

His knees settled on either side of my hips. I was enveloped in his hardness, in the beer-laced scent of him.

Suffocation by Logan Mulvaney wouldn't be a bad way to go. The giddy, absurd thought fed my panic and edged me into hysteria. I hit him in the chest with my free hand.

He removed his hand from my back to grab that, too. Now both my hands were trapped between us.

"Let me go," I growled, tugging on my hands. "Or I'll . . ." My voice faded as I glared up at his shadowy shape.

I didn't know what I'd do. I knew what I *wanted* to do and that scared the hell out of me. Every inch of me buzzed with an achy hunger. I actually hurt for him, but I couldn't surrender to this. Not again. Not after he just proclaimed me his girl. That would be like me agreeing with him.

He pushed his face close to mine, his voice fierce as he rasped, "You've slapped me. Thrown beer on me. I think I can take whatever you've got. Let's have it."

"Let go of me," I repeated, my mind working, not about to give up the battle. It suddenly felt life-or-death. We were not a thing. We couldn't be.

"All right." His hands loosened, but didn't release me entirely. His fingers glided from my wrists and up my arms, a feather-light, sensual stroke. He rounded my shoulders and skimmed down to my collarbone. With a flick of his fingers, he brushed back the hair from my shoulders, exposing my neck to his descending mouth, and I realized he had changed his approach. He was seducing me now. And this was so much worse. So much more threatening because I couldn't resist this Logan. The past had already taught me that.

Heart pounding, I grabbed a fistful of his short hair and yanked, pulling his head down hard with the motion, keeping that tempting mouth of his away from me.

A groan rumbled out from him, and before I knew it he had his fist in the back of my hair, too. He didn't hurt me. He simply held me prisoner, his unyielding fingers tangled in my hair, trapping me as much as I trapped him, our bodies twisted up in each other. And then I felt it, the hard ridge of him against the inside of my thigh. Need clenched ahold of me, throbbing between my legs.

Our breaths crashed hoarsely between us, and I knew what was coming next if I didn't get away. I released his hair and flipped over, ignoring his fingers still tangled in my hair. I'd leave hair behind to escape. As I scrambled up the steps, he let go of my hair, but then both his hands came down on my waist. He hauled me back with a growl.

I flipped over again, ready to hit him, but then his mouth was on mine and it was my turn to groan. He kissed me hard and I kissed him back just as savagely, my legs wrapping around him. The struggle of moments before became another struggle. A race toward getting each other off. We unleashed on each other. My teeth sank into his bottom lip. He made a snarling sound and I released his lip, licking it and sucking it inside my mouth until I felt him shudder against me.

The creak of the door only dimly registered. The flood of light against the backs of my eyelids only tapped at my awareness. I was so intent on the feast of Logan's lips.

It was the sound of my name that yanked me to harsh reality.

Gasping, Logan and I broke apart and I stared in horror at the trio standing framed in the doorway.

Chapter 17

L OGAN," PEPPER BREATHED HIS name like she had just caught him in the middle of a criminal act.

"Should have known." Annie crossed her arms over her chest.

"What. The fuck?" Reece choked, glaring at Logan like he was the one responsible for this scenario. Like I wasn't an equal participant. It made me think of Logan's accusation that people were always *doing things to me*. That I was just the recipient of others' actions. The notion didn't sit well with me.

"It's not what it looks like," I said, wondering what that even meant . . . and why I was trying to offer explanations.

Reece continued glaring at his brother with his hands curling and uncurling at his sides. "You couldn't have kept it in your pants just once? Huh, Logan?"

I flinched. Pepper put a hand on Reece's arm as though restraining him from saying more. I felt Logan stiffen beside me.

"I'm going upstairs," I declared, not about to endure an inquisition. I had to explain my choices to my mother. Not my friends. Standing, I looked at Pepper and Reece. "Was there something you wanted to see me about . . . ?"

"I just stopped in to check on the bar and heard there was . . . an altercation between you and Logan." Reece looked back at Logan, his gaze sharp with disapproval. "Now I understand the situation."

"I doubt you do," Logan shot back, his features set with annoyance.

"Oh, yeah. Then explain it to me, little brother. What am I missing here?" Reece waved a hand at us like the sight explained everything.

"It's not like you think," Logan returned.

I wished everyone would simply stop talking like this was something that even warranted a conversation. I was an adult. For that matter, so was Logan. What we did and didn't do together was no one's business.

Who are you kidding? You don't want people talking about it because Logan doesn't fit into your idea of who you are . . . or rather who you should be.

The cold hard truth was that I was embarrassed.

"Georgia isn't some fling. It's different with her."

At that declaration, my heart tightened in my chest with equal parts thrill and terror. Logan looked at me then, his gaze steady and deep.

Reece snorted and my gaze swung to him and Pepper, reading the doubt on their faces . . . the incredulity.

"Oh, please." Annie laughed. "Like we're supposed to believe you two are in love?"

"I don't care what *you* believe. Why are you even here?" Logan demanded.

She sniffed, but remained firmly in place.

"Georgia?" Pepper's soft voice drew my gaze. Her amber eyes searched my face, asking without words if he was telling the truth. Was there something between Logan and me? Something besides the physical display they had just interrupted? It was an uncomfortable moment and for some reason I was reminded of my mother as Pepper stared at me, her expression one of confusion because I had not lived up to her expectations of me. I shook my head. Pepper was not my mother.

I felt Logan's gaze and turned to face him. He stared at me, waiting, and I knew this was the moment. I either owned that I felt something deeper for him than mind-numbing attraction and saw it through or I shut this wild ride down now. Whatever I said would determine whether I would be his "girl" or not. The temptation to explore this thing between us was strong.

But fear was stronger.

I shook my head at him and almost immediately a shutter fell over his gaze, snuffing out the light that had been there. The light that had been there for me.

"No," I whispered. "This can't go anywhere between us, Logan. We're not right . . ."

Logan nodded once, turning to face his brother. He shrugged, looking so damnably unaffected that I wanted to cry. Which only made me a contrary idiot. Like always. "Guess I was wrong."

Something inside me crumpled as he stepped past me and left the four of us staring at one another in the stairwell. I wanted to be alone so badly right then to lick my wounds that I ached. But I wouldn't look exactly dignified running upstairs.

Annie whistled between her teeth. "I think you actually

just stomped all over his heart." She grunted in satisfaction. "Who knew he even had one?"

Pepper whirled on her, her hair whipping around her shoulders. "Shut. Up."

"Fine." With a shrug, Annie turned and left. "You guys are a buzzkill, anyway."

Pepper looked back at me, her expression uncertain, her deep amber eyes so damned pitying I wanted to scream. "Georgia . . . are you okay?"

I forced a smile that felt brittle as fractured glass. "Sure. That was a little awkward." I motioned to the stairs where we had been caught making out. "But I'm okay." I inhaled, filling my lungs.

Pepper bit her lips and looked between her boyfriend and me. "He looked kind of . . . crushed."

"Pepper," Reece cut in. "Leave it alone."

"He's not like you think," I blurted, glaring at Reece, my voice angrier than I intended.

Reece arched an eyebrow at me. "No? And what do I *think*?"

"He's not some irresponsible kid jumping from girl to girl. He's had the world on his shoulders forever and he's been handling it all on his own and he's just . . . lonely." And then it dawned on me.

Maybe that's what all the girls had been about for Logan. His way of searching for intimacy. Connection. Feeling something, filling in the void. "I think he's been lonely for a long time." And I'd just failed him. I hated myself a little right then . . . until I told myself that I wasn't the girl for him. He deserved someone who didn't have obligations holding her down. The expectations and pressure of her family strangling her. That was me.

The creases bracketing Reece's mouth tightened. "I know he's not irresponsible. He's had to carry more on his shoulders than he should have and I blame myself for a lot of that. I should have been there for him."

Pepper rubbed his arm, consoling him. "You were young . . ."

"So was Logan. Younger than me." Reece glanced at her before looking back at me and continuing. "As for Logan jumping from girl to girl . . ." His voice faded and he looked me up and down meaningfully, the implication clear. I was just one in a long line.

He did think his brother was a man-whore.

I shut my eyes in a tight blink and batted away the idea that I had somehow changed him. Even if he was looking for a relationship with me, he wasn't the kind of guy I could bring home to my parents. They would never accept him, and that wouldn't be fair to him.

Reece continued, "I don't know how far this thing between you two has gone."

My face burned and Reece's lips tightened, obviously inferring that it had gone far.

"Logan has never been into monogamy, Georgia." His voice gentled, his eyes full of concern. "I hate to see you get hurt."

"I've never seen him like he was just now over any other girl," Pepper interjected. "Maybe it's different this time—" She stopped when Reece sent her a look.

"You willing to bank on that?" He inclined his head to me,

still using that kind voice. "Georgia is our friend," he reminded her.

"And Logan is your brother," she returned.

"I'm going up to bed," I inserted, over and done listening to them talk about me like I wasn't even standing in front of them.

"Sure." Pepper nodded, moving to take a step upstairs. "Want some company for a little while?"

"No, I'm tired."

She continued to bob her head in that eager manner, watching me like I might fall and break a hip. She had been looking at me that way a lot. Ever since Harris dumped me. Things had finally been starting to get back to normal, with less pitying looks, and now this. She'd probably be watching me warily from the corner of her eye for another five months. Awesome.

"See you next weekend, right? At Emerson's gallery showing?"

"Oh, yeah." I'd almost forgotten Emerson had been offered an opportunity to show some of her pieces at a gallery in Boston.

"We can ride together if you want. Suzanne is coming, too. She actually got off work."

I nodded. "Great. I'll text you."

Once inside my loft, I stood alone and stared blindly into space. I quickly thought about my last glimpse of Logan's face before he walked away. So hard and impassive. As though he felt nothing when I rejected him in front of his brother and Pepper. I'd handled that badly, although I'm not sure, if it happened all over again, it could go down any differently. Some things just weren't meant to be.

THE WEEK PASSED IN numbing monotony. I walked around in a daze, functioning, but not really caring about my day-to-day tasks. It was reminiscent of when Harris dumped me. That same vague state of bewilderment. As though I'd just been punched in the gut and didn't quite know how or why that happened, only that it hurt like hell.

Where it differed was that this was worse than my breakup with Harris. I'd spent four years with Harris and just a few weeks fooling around with Logan, but this felt worse. My stomach was off like I'd eaten something bad.

I had successfully killed any chance of being with Logan again—even in a physical no-strings-attached kind of way. He had too much pride to come around me again. Not after I shut him down in front of Reece and Pepper. Which was what I had wanted. What I had set out to do. End it once and for all.

So why did my heart ache so damn much?

Saturday afternoon I was bingeing on popcorn and M&M's, zoning out as I watched a *Walking Dead* marathon. I'd deliberately avoided anything remotely romantic, flipping past *Bridget Jones's Diary* so fast I might have sprained my thumb. People running for their lives from flesh-hungry zombies fit the bill nicely.

I was in the same clothes I had worn to bed the night before, greasy ponytail and all. I may or may not have brushed my teeth yet.

When my phone buzzed beside me on the futon and I saw it was Mom, I suppressed a sigh and answered it. I'd dodged her call earlier this week and knew I couldn't do it again. Not without her sending out the National Guard.

"Hey, Mom. How are you?"

She dove straight from guilting me over not calling her back to pressuring me into coming home for a visit before fall semester began. She insisted there had to be time in my schedule for family. Even if just for a long weekend. And there was. I could leave on a Thursday and come home on Sunday. Except I didn't want to. Despite my current misery, I liked it here. I liked the cooler northeastern summers. I liked working for Dr. Chase. I liked my apartment above Mulvaney's with Cook slipping me fried pickles every time I passed.

But how could I explain that to Mom? I loved my family. Everything I did was to make Mom proud. To prove that my birth had not been a mistake.

I knew that was messed up. I should be confident enough in myself, but it was still an internal struggle, needing my mother to simply say she was glad I was born, that I was not a constant reminder of her lapse in judgment.

"Mom," I interrupted the latest news of my cousin Marianne's engagement to a plastic surgeon in Auburn. "Do you remember the little pool house we rented behind Mrs. Flanagan's house?"

"Why are you bringing that up?"

"I don't know. Because it's my earliest memory, I guess. I remember eating Popsicles on the edge of that pool with you." *You had seemed happy with me then. When it was just the two of us. I had seemed like enough for you.* These thoughts scudded across my mind, but I didn't dare say them. If I did, it would sound like I regretted what came after. My stepdad. Amber. Our very serious and respectable suburban existence.

"I try not to think of those days. Life was hard then. Being a single mom, trying to finish school and work. I don't think my life really began until I met your father." And by *father*, she meant my *stepfather*. Not my real dad who knocked her up and bailed on us.

It shouldn't have hurt to hear her say this, but it did. I was tempted to say: *but you had me*. Didn't that make it all worth it? Wasn't I enough, even then, to make you feel complete?

Except it would sound like I was bitter and resentful that she had married my stepfather. That she had Amber. And it wasn't that at all. I loved my stepfather and sister. My struggle was with Mom and this overwhelming compulsion I felt to be everything for her. To be the best so I could justify the mistake of my existence.

Mom dove back into the subject of Marianne's wedding and how I needed to be sure to reserve that entire week the following March because I, of course, would be one of the bridesmaids.

Mom circled back around to when I was coming home. She pressed me for a precise date. "I'd like you here before August third. That's when Harris is leaving. He and his family are going on a cruise."

A sour taste tickled the back of my throat. "Mom, what does Harris have to do with when I come home?"

"Georgia, I hear things are rocky between him and the other girl . . ."

"You mean the one he left me for? The one he cheated on me with?"

Mom ignored that and continued, "It's just like I told you. It would never last."

I sighed, rubbing the bridge of my nose. "Mom, I'm not getting back together with Harris. He left me for someone else, remember? I don't want to be with him anymore."

"We learn from our mistakes, Georgia, and we're stronger for it in the end. Better."

"Yes. I couldn't agree with you more. I've learned from mine."

"Oh, Harris was a mistake then? Four years of your life?"

"Yes . . . maybe. Look. He's part of my past, Mom. That's where I want to keep him."

"I don't know what's gotten into you, Georgie. First you wanted to stay up there for the summer, rejecting Mr. Berenger's kind offer to intern at the bank. Embarrassing me, I might add. Now you're not even interested in patching things up with Harris. I don't know who you are anymore."

The disappointment was there, ripe in her voice, and I felt suddenly suffocated. Like I couldn't breathe under the pressure of it. That I could break apart from it at any moment.

"Mom, I have to lead my own life and do what's right for me. Just because I don't make the choices you want doesn't mean my choices are wrong." *Did I honest to God just say that?*

"Georgia," Mom's voice sharpened with authority—it was her principal voice. "Let me remind you that these choices you make are at my expense. Your father and I are paying your way. You are not as free as you think you are. We had an understanding when we let you go so far from home—that you would be there with Harris had a lot to do with our agreeing for you to go to Dartford."

I sputtered and tried to remind her that he dumped me, but she barreled ahead.

"You were supposed to come home in the summers. And after graduation. You would get a sensible, useful degree and settle down here after graduation."

There was an edge of desperation to her voice as she flung out these reminders. Before I could stop myself I heard myself snap, "Deviating from your plan doesn't mean I'm like him, you know. It doesn't mean I'm less of a person. I'll still be your daughter. You can still love me."

Silence met my outburst and for a moment I wondered if we had been disconnected. I almost hoped we had. That she had not heard me bring up that most taboo of subjects—my father.

I tried to imagine her face. Was she sitting at the kitchen table or in her bedroom with shades of pastels all around her?

"Georgia," Mom began in carefully modulated tones and I released a breath, thinking this was it. We were finally going to have that talk—address the elephant in the room that happened to be my father and her need to create me in an image that was the antithesis of him.

"You will be here before August third. No ifs, ands, or buts about it. Do you understand?"

My fingers tightened around the phone until my knuckles ached. I was a fool to ever think we would have a conversation of substance. "Yes. I understand."

A few more empty words were exchanged and the call ended. A frustrated scream welled up from my lips. I tossed the phone down on the futon, watched as it bounced twice and then clattered to the floor. Like it was some living thing trying to get away from me.

She'd never understand. She didn't want to. I'd be what she

wanted or I could kiss good-bye her support. Financially. Emotionally. If I wanted her love and approval, I had to live the life of her choosing.

I pressed my knuckles to the backs of my suddenly aching eyes. I hated her right then . . . hated myself because I let her do this to me.

It was like Logan had said. I was buried away in my closet. Too afraid to let myself go. Well. Except for when I was with him. I'd embraced my wild nature then, shutting off the voice in my head that sounded a lot like Mom, warning me to be sensible, good, well-behaved, and dignified.

I hated that voice. I hated that me.

A sudden burn started in my gut. I scrambled for my phone. Hanging half my body off the futon, I snatched it from the floor and texted Annie. I hadn't forgotten what night it was or her offer.

My fingers flew over the keys, punching in just a few words, making certain the sensible Georgia that Mom insisted be home by August third was gone. At least for tonight anyway.

Me: Hey, A. Can I still come with you tonight???

Chapter 18

ANNIE HADN'T BEEN KIDDING. Pillared and eggshell white with a wide veranda that faced an infinite stretch of green lawn, the house was something out of *Better Homes and Gardens*. Jasmine crawled over the porch, and flowerpots brimming with colorful buds swayed in the evening breeze. It was elegance bordering on decadence. The kind of place I imagined Ina Garten hosting one of her cooking shows.

All the houses on the street sat on big lots, promising a semblance of privacy. Several cars were already parked in the large horseshoe drive. Annie parked on the street and we walked past the parked vehicles, our heels clicking in unison. I couldn't stop myself from scanning for Logan's Bronco. I didn't see it, but I also didn't know what Rachel drove.

At the front door, Annie pushed the bell, sliding me an approving glance. "You look hot."

"Thanks. So do you."

"Damn right. This is my night."

I smoothed a shaking hand down the skirt of my snug dress. After Annie told me what she would be wearing, I'd decided to dress up, too. As tempting as it had been to wear basic black, I had reached for the bright blue dress in the back of my closet. I'd bought it a year and a half ago to wear to a dinner that Harris insisted I attend with his parents. I probably weighed five pounds less then so it hugged me like a second skin now. Even if it wasn't so tight, it would be hard to fade into the background in the peacock blue.

I had vowed that the Georgia my mother had worked so hard to create . . . the only Georgia she would accept and tolerate . . . be nowhere in evidence tonight.

"Annnnnie, looking hot!" The guy who opened the door for us was familiar from the last kink club. His hair was shaved on one side and the other side of his scalp sported long, slicked-back hair. He wore glossy pink lip gloss a shade close to my own.

He pressed a quick kiss to each of our cheeks. "Well, bitches. What do you think?" He motioned widely to the foyer with beringed fingers.

"Beautiful," I murmured, looking up at the domed ceiling in awe.

"Yeah, I thought you were bullshitting about hosting this month in a twelve-bedroom mansion, but I stand corrected, Andy."

"I always deliver. No more orgies in a room the size of my closet." He linked his arms with ours and led us through the grand foyer, our heels clicking over the tiles.

I admired the expensive art hanging on the walls. Classical music piped in from hidden speakers somewhere. We passed a table holding a ginormous vase of fresh-cut flowers. "Andy, is this your place?" I asked.

He smiled elusively as we entered the living room. "It belongs to a friend. I have connections." He plucked up two wineglasses and thrust them at us.

I nodded my thanks and scanned the small crowd occupying the large space. No loud music or kegs of beers. No cheering as people made out on top of a pool table. It was dignified. A dozen people mingled throughout the room, drinking from wineglasses.

Annie spotted her guy almost immediately. She winked at me. "I'm going in."

Suddenly alone, I stood near the grand piano, fingers playing with the stem of my wineglass and trying not to feel uncomfortable. Tonight was about freedom. Doing what I wanted without fear of failing to meet the expectations that had been drilled into me since birth.

Even though it was summer, a fire crackled in the fireplace. I'm sure Andy thought it added to the ambience, and I had to admit it did cast enticing light and shadows throughout the room.

Within a few moments, Annie and her guy slipped upstairs, presumably heading to one of the many rooms available. And they weren't the only ones slipping away. A few minutes passed and Andy gave up on his hosting duties, exiting the room with another couple.

"Hello, I don't think we've met. I'm Lance." I turned to face the guy who stopped before me. A girl stood beside him. "This is my girlfriend, Opal."

We shook hands. "Hi, I'm Georgia."

They were an attractive couple. Maybe a few years older than me. Grad students probably.

"Are you new?" Opal asked. "We haven't seen you before."

"I've been once. Briefly."

"Ah." Lance nodded. "Decided to try it again then. Well, the summer meetings are the best. Less intimidating for a newcomer, right Opal?"

She nodded, her dark corkscrew curls bouncing around her shoulders. "Yes, far more intimate. It's more conducive to making an actual connection." I almost smiled. She made it sound like online dating. This was a bit of a stretch from that. "The rest of the time, it's just one giant meat market."

"It was a little overwhelming the last time," I agreed.

"Are you interested in going upstairs with us, Georgia?" Lance asked, his gaze cutting into mine directly. His hand lightly touched my arm. He was all politeness, but what he was asking was clear. Would I join them? *In a bedroom?!* Just the three of us.

I swallowed and stammered. "I-I appreciate the offer, but no, thank you."

Opal nodded. "Interested in something else, huh? Maybe we can help you find it."

I must have looked panicked at their invitation for her to take pity on me and make such an offer. I *was* looking for something else, I realized. Someone else. Someone else was the reason I had come here. I had been pretending otherwise.

I opened my mouth, but then closed it with a snap when Rachel and Logan walked in the room.

My gaze locked on him. He wasn't dressed up like everyone else. He was wearing jeans and a cotton T-shirt that looked soft and touch-worthy, falling flat against the cut of his pecs and abdomen. My palms tingled, ready to feel all the hard valleys and angles of his body.

"Ahh." Opal nodded, following my gaze. "You're here for Logan."

I shook my head in denial, even though I kept my gaze trained on Logan. I was locked on him like he was some kind of homing device.

Opal waved him over. "Logan!"

"Oh, no . . . Don't!" My face burned as his gaze lifted and found me. He took me in with a sweep of blistering blue, and I suddenly felt self-conscious standing there in my tight dress. Like a little girl playing dress-up.

He and Rachel strolled toward us. I risked a glance at Rachel, and her eyes flashed at me with some of the aversion that I recognized from our last conversation at the ballpark.

"Fancy seeing you here, Georgia," Rachel said, looking back and forth between Logan and me. Clearly, she was waiting to see his reaction. So was I.

I took a slow sip of my wine.

Lance and Opal looked from Logan to me and then to each other. The tension was palpable, thick and choking. Lance shifted on his feet.

Opal downed her glass of wine. "I'm going to get a refill."

Lance nodded eagerly and placed his hand at the small of her back. They walked away, leaving the three of us standing there. I struggled to hold Logan's gaze, waiting for him to say something.

Finally, he spoke: "What are you doing here?"

"Annie invited me."

"And this seemed like a good idea?" He motioned to the room.

I shrugged. "Why not? You're here." My gaze flicked to Rachel. "She's here. Why can't I be here?"

Rachel turned her gaze to Logan, looking very interested in his answer.

"You're not us," he replied flatly.

This answer seemed to satisfy her. She turned an almost smug smile on me. If he wanted to widen the gap even further between us and firmly stick me in a box outside of the one he occupied with Rachel, he had just succeeded. A bitter ache filled my chest. I guess I deserved that. I had rejected him in front of Pepper and Reece. I couldn't expect open arms from him tonight.

A muscle feathered along his jaw and he dug the blade deeper into my heart, saying, "This is my kind of place. Not yours. You've made it clear how different you and I are." He angled his head as if searching his memory. *"We're not right . . .* I think that's what you said." His gaze sharpened on me, his eyes glacier blue. "We can ask Reece if you don't remember."

I had said that. And now I was here at a kink club. Like that was *right*. What a hypocrite I was. That must be what he thought looking at me now. I couldn't muster the truth though. Especially with Rachel watching. I couldn't tell him I changed my mind. I couldn't just admit that I was here because of him. For him. That I couldn't leave him alone.

I tossed my head back and downed the rest of my wine, hating how my hand trembled. I wanted to apologize, but I couldn't bring myself to say anything.

I held up my empty glass. "I need a refill, too."

I turned my back on them and marched toward the bar, my spine ramrod-straight. A guy was there pouring wine. He grinned as I approached. "What can I get the pretty lady in blue? A refill? I can also make you a cocktail, if you'd like that."

I opened my mouth but I didn't have time to respond. Logan came up beside me. He plucked the glass from my fingers and set it down sharply. Seizing my hand, he turned and started walking me from the room, his footsteps biting hard into the floor.

His fingers laced with mine, and my breath hitched at his strong palm flush against my own. I could feel his pulse bleeding into me from this single contact.

My strides weren't as long as his—largely due to my too-tight dress—and I had to hurry to keep pace. A strong sense of déjà vu washed over me. It was like the last time he marched me out of a kink club. Except this time every nerve ending in my body sparked and hummed with the knowledge of him. His hands, his mouth, his body moving over mine. Against me. In me.

I knew what it was like between us. There was no wondering about it. There was only longing that curled in the pit of my belly. A yearning anticipation that went bone-deep and quickened my breathing.

We cleared the threshold and he pulled me down the wide hall with all the expensive-looking art. I tugged my hand free from his and stopped, rubbing it against my thigh.

Our gazes clashed.

"You're here because of me," he accused. "Just fucking

admit it. Go ahead. Reece and Pepper aren't here so there won't be any embarrassment."

That stung. Even if it was the truth. "There goes that arrogance again."

"Better that than delusional."

"What's that supposed to—"

"I don't know if you're lying to yourself or me, Georgia. You're not looking for some kink with a random guy here. The only reason you came back here is because you knew I might be here." He inhaled a deep breath, lifting his broad chest, adding, "Because you miss me as much as I miss you."

I floundered, unable to deny the truth of his words. But if I admitted that, I couldn't go back. I couldn't deny *us* anymore. "I meant what I said in my apartment. However badly it came out." We weren't *right*. This couldn't go anywhere between us.

"But you're here." He inched closer a step, his deep voice taunting. "Damn frustrating, isn't it?"

I inched back. "What?"

"Letting your head get in the way of what your heart wants . . . what your body needs."

My back hit the hall wall. He stopped, keeping a thin space between our bodies. His hand covered my heart then, his palm curving over my breast. I inhaled, my breast rising to fill his palm. I wasn't wearing a bra. The dress held me in so tightly I didn't need one, and my nipple beaded almost painfully hard, thrusting up into his palm.

My gaze searched his face, the deep-set eyes, the hard jaw, and beautiful mouth. He held my gaze, his expression almost challenging.

How could he see so much? It's like he understood me without me having to explain anything at all.

"You want me. You just have to stop living in your head so much. Listening to all the reasons why we can't be together." The hand that curved over my breast slid down my torso, molding itself to me, gliding over my rib cage, my hip.

"Easy for you to say. You don't live under any expectations. Any rules. You don't have—" I stopped abruptly, horror filling me at the insensitive words about to trip from my lips.

"A family?" he finished.

I shook my head, feverishly backpedaling. "No. You have a dad—"

"A drunk who doesn't even know when I move him from the living room to his bed after he passes out on the floor."

"Your brother—"

"Is my *brother*. Not my parent. And he has his own life. Pepper is his family now. But you're right. I don't live under anyone else's expectations. I follow my own rules."

And I envied him that freedom.

My breath caught as his hand slipped around to my bottom. He gave me a hard squeeze and then slipped down even farther, his fingers inching down my thigh to the hem of my dress.

His voice continued in a husky pitch, "You should try it."

"Try what?"

"Being an adult."

"I'm twenty years old," I shot back, an awful feeling trickling through me.

"That doesn't mean anything. It's just a number. Especially

if you're still acting like a scared little girl . . . too afraid to live the life she wants for fear of disappointing Mommy."

The languor that had been filling my body vanished. Fury blossomed inside my chest. Now I recognized that awful feeling . . . knew it for the fear it was. But he was right. That's what infuriated me the most. I grabbed his hand and halted it where it had started to slide up the hem of my dress.

"I'm a scared little girl?" I squeezed out from between him and the wall, thinking: *watch me.*

I started marching back down the hall toward the living room, following the sound of music and voices.

"Georgia, what are you doing?" The taunting quality had fled from his voice.

"Going to get my kink on with some random guy," I flung out.

"You know you're just proving my point." He was following. His voice sounded like it was right behind me, so I walked faster—as much as I could in the stupid dress. "You don't like hearing the truth, so you're throwing a tantrum."

"Then that ego of yours should feel great about being right."

"Damn it, Georgia." He grabbed my arm and swung me around. "You're out of your mind if you think I'm letting you go into that room to hook up with someone else."

"Maybe *you* need to stop treating me like a little girl." I cocked my head. "That's what you're doing. Bossing me around. Playing protector. I already have a mom and a dad."

"Oh, I'm perfectly aware that you have parents." One of his eyebrows winged high. "Even thousands of miles away they still manage to control you."

I hissed a stinging breath. "I'm not Rachel. You're not my protector. You don't have to follow me around to make sure I don't dive off the rails. I'm not going to swallow a bunch of pills."

It was a low blow. Hot color stained his cheeks, and I instantly regretted the words. I opened my mouth to say so, but his fingers flexed around my bare arm. "Oh, I know exactly who you are. No mistake there. I probably know you better than yourself."

He opened a nearby door and pulled me in after him. Shutting the door, he pressed me against it, his body aligning with mine, fitting against me so perfectly that the familiar ache was back, slamming into me full force. "I also know that all this fighting is just foreplay. This is what you really came here for."

His hips pushed into mine and I felt him there, his hardness nudging into where I most needed him. I shook my head even as a hot shot of joy raced up my spine. Why was I pretending? He was right. This was what I came here for.

I grabbed his face in both hands and kissed him hard, punishing him with my lips, hating and loving his taste all at once. I licked my way inside his mouth, swallowing his groan deep inside myself.

"That's it." He encouraged as I nipped at his bottom lip and sucked it deep before thrusting my tongue back inside his mouth.

One of my hands dropped from his face and worked its way down between us, sliding under his shirt. I scraped my nails over his taut stomach, the flesh smooth and tight over his ridged stomach. He quivered beneath my fingers, and I continued south, covering him with my palm, letting him know exactly what I wanted.

"Georgia," he choked as I stroked the hard shape of him, my excitement mounting as his erection grew against my fingers.

"Logan, I need you now."

His fingers reached for the hem of my dress, inching the tight fabric up my thighs. I wiggled, trying to help him. Cool air caressed the flesh he exposed. His fingers dragged a fiery path that made me squirm against the door and push into him. I broke our kiss and cried out when his hand slid around to cup my aching mound.

"What's this?" With his mouth at my ear, he released me to yank my dress up past my hips. With the fabric gathered at my hips, his big hands slid down my bare hips and circled around to my naked backside. "No panties?"

His voice sounded hoarse and I choked out a whimper as he kneaded my bare bottom.

"It wouldn't work with the dress . . ."

"You've been walking around without anything on under this little dress?" His eyes glittered at me in the dark room, the only light that from the outside perimeter lights that poured in through the French doors.

I nodded and then gasped as he brought one hand between us, unerringly finding and going right to that spot between my thighs that throbbed for him. His finger slid inside me, probing my aching wetness.

"I'd be pissed if I wasn't so turned on." He stroked that finger in and out of me as he rolled my clit slowly with his thumb, deepening the pressure until I was crying out and surging against his hand.

"That's it, naughty girl. This is why you came here," he spoke against my throat.

I nodded, beyond words.

He crooked his finger inside me, hitting my sweet spot that he always seemed to know where to find. I shuddered and came apart against him, my hands flying to his flexing shoulders.

I was still flying, ripples of sensations eddying through me when he pulled me away from the door. Dimly, I assessed our surroundings as I followed him across the room. It was a masculine room full of dark colors and rich wood furniture. He guided me to a large mahogany desk and bent me over it, shoving my dress up farther until it bunched high around my waist.

He smoothed both hands over my backside and everything inside me clenched and ached, desperate to be filled with him.

"Georgia," he breathed, kissing the small of my back and then lower, above each cheek. "You have the sweetest dimples here." He pressed a lingering kiss to each spot and all of me quivered. His mouth moved lower, kissing each cheek.

I propped my elbows on the desk and looked over my shoulder. His eyes, heavy-lidded and dark as smoke met mine over the rounded swell of my hip. He kissed me again, using his teeth this time to bite me, the barest nip followed by the stroke of his tongue.

"Oh," I sighed, instinctively parting my legs wider. He rubbed against me as I thrust back into his hard erection, his clothes a frustrating barrier. He pulled back slightly and I whimpered at the loss. Even when I heard his zipper and knew he was doing it just to free himself and give me what I needed, I didn't care. I was needy and achy and couldn't stand, even for that moment, to lose the pressure of him against the core of me.

I looked back over my shoulder at him again, feeling wanton and alive and totally unlike that girl I was desperately trying to leave behind for the night. "Logan."

He was reaching for his back pocket, but paused at the sight of me.

I locked my gaze on his face, my tongue darting out to wet my lips. "I want you inside me. Now."

He nodded once, his expression fierce, a savage light in his eyes as he pulled his wallet the rest of the way out—and I realized he was stopping for a condom. I hadn't even thought about it, which really should alarm me. I should be relieved that he was the responsible one and thought of it, but instead I heard myself saying, "No. I want you inside me. Like last time. I want to feel every inch of you moving in me."

"Georgia." His voice came out strangled. "You don't have to—"

I pushed my bottom back out toward him in invitation, in trust, rocking my hips. "I trust you, Logan." And I realized I did. There was nothing about this guy that wasn't as clear and honest as morning sunlight on my face. He was more than a gorgeous guy objectified by coeds. He wasn't just a jock or Reece Mulvaney's brother.

"We're safe," I assured him. He was clean. I was on the pill, and I wanted him in me so badly I shook like an addict craving her next fix.

He curved his body over mine with a groan, one hand tightening on my ass as he swept my hair aside with his other hand. His cock nudged at my opening and I parted my legs even wider, panting indelicately. His mouth dragged down the back of my neck producing a wake of delicious shivers.

"Logan," I begged. "Now!"

He gave me what I wanted. Finally. Surging inside me, filling me so completely that I screamed, dropping my head to the desk. I felt stretched, impaled, the sensation a searing burn, hitting that spot, going deep, right past it and pushing at every nerve.

He groaned my name and kept going, pumping his hips, our bodies coming together with loud smacks in the echoing silence. "God, Georgia. I think you're even tighter than last time."

I cried out, every slam of his cock inside me propelling me forward on the desk and wringing out a cry from my lips. It was fast and hard and wild in a way that totally undid me.

I clutched the opposite edge of the desk and shoved back into him, meeting his thrusts halfway, determined to reach that climax he was pushing me toward.

My cries got louder.

"That's it, baby," he urged. "Come for me."

I nodded and shook my head, frantic, wanting to get there, but also wanting to draw this out. Wanting the ache to keep building, the unbelievable friction of him to never stop.

"Georgia," he commanded. "I need you to come now. I'm almost . . . there . . ."

I whimpered, my inner muscles instinctively clenching tighter around him.

"Georgia," he said again.

The ragged sound of my name was followed then with a swift slap on my ass. I surged against him, my back making contact with his chest. It was all it took. I cried out and shuddered, splintering apart inside. My vision went fuzzy. The hard slide of him inside me coupled with that delicious sting made my mouth open on a silent scream.

I fell back down on the desk as he pumped one more time into me and then stilled. His hands clenched around my hips as he jerked a final time against me.

I gasped and shivered, never having felt this breathless even after racing sprints. It was truly the best sex of my life. Even better than the times before with him and somehow I knew that every time with him would be better.

I flattened my body against the smooth, cool surface, pressing my cheek against the wood and staring unseeingly at the wall.

"Georgia." He whispered my name, brushing sweaty tendrils of hair from my cheek. "Are you all right?" His voice sounded uncertain, almost afraid, and I loved him all the greater for it.

I loved him.

Crap.

I flipped over, disengaging our bodies, feeling shell-shocked, staring at him with eyes that felt wide and too dry. I couldn't even blink.

His expression grew alarmed. "What is it? Did I hurt you? God, I'm sorry, baby—"

"No." I swallowed. "You didn't hurt me." On the contrary.

He gave me what I came here for. And then some. He gave me perfection. I hadn't even known I was looking for it. For him. But he was my kind of perfect. It was everything he was and all he did.

I wasn't delusional enough to think anyone was actually perfect *perfect*. But he was *my* perfect. The thing I had been wanting . . . hoping that I might find someday . . .

It was Logan Mulvaney.

I wanted wild and reckless and unorthodox. Even if it came in a package that was slightly younger than me. And not Ivy League. A jock who was loyal to a fault and knew more about sacrifice and friendship and responsibility than the likes of Harris would ever know. Maybe more than I'd ever known, too.

All of this crossed my mind in a flash, and it must have crossed my face, too, to an extent. Something flickered in his eyes. Something tender and vulnerable in a way that I'd never seen in him.

"Georgia, I—"

Whatever he was about to say died abruptly when the door flung open. Voices flooded the room and echoed throughout the rest of the house.

I couldn't identify the source because Logan stepped in front of me, blocking me, which was a relief since my dress was still hiked up around my waist.

Sudden light blasted through the room as the overhead light flipped on. I struggled to push down my skirt, peeping out around Logan's body.

My stomach dropped to my feet. A half-dozen uniformed policemen swarmed into the study. Through the open door, I could see that there were more of them, too many to process, shouting and rushing down the hall into other parts of the house.

Chapter 19

L-LOGAN? WHAT'S GOING ON?" *Why were the cops here?* He looked over his shoulder at me. "Cover yourself."

Terse voices congested the air. From somewhere in the house a woman screamed. Static from a police radio scratched on the air.

"Hands in the air!" the officer closest to us boomed, his baton at the ready.

I shimmied my dress down my hips, my eyes going round in my face as the uniformed man got in Logan's face. "Stand aside with your hands in the air." I gulped. Clearly, he didn't approve of Logan hiding me from sight. Maybe he thought I had a weapon.

Logan's voice came out tight and angry as he lifted his hands but remained in front of me. "Not until she's fully dressed."

The police officer didn't appear to appreciate this. His hard eyes didn't show even a flicker of compassion. He grabbed Logan by the shoulder and tried to haul him away from me, but Logan dug in his heels, resisting. "I said stand aside—"

"I'm good," I blurted, tugging the last bit of my dress down and holding my hands up in the air. The last thing I wanted was Logan getting into trouble. Or worse—because apparently we were already in trouble. I didn't want him to get hurt.

I stepped around Logan and met the suspicious stare of the policeman as I held my hands above my head. "What's the problem? We haven't broken any laws, Officer."

Last time I checked, consensual sex wasn't against the law. My face burned facing the officers, knowing they knew what we had been doing. They were strangers to me and I shouldn't have cared, but they were authority figures and shame scalded the back of my throat.

"Sorry, but criminal trespass actually is a crime." Brackets of disapproval tightened around his mouth.

"Criminal trespass? But we're not trespassing. This house belongs to Andy . . . I think. It belongs to a friend of his." I paused beneath the weight of the man's frown. He reminded me of my high school gym coach. Mr. Kramer had been incapable of smiling, too.

I smiled in a placating manner. "I'm sure this is a misunderstanding. We didn't break into this house. Talk to Andy . . ."

"Your friend Andy, and the rest of you here, do not have the owner's permission to be in this house. A neighbor saw all the lights on and called it in. The residents are out of town right now. We have to bring you in."

Oh, God. Bitter realization washed over me. Andy had broken into this house. My gaze shot to Logan's face. Had we all unwittingly stumbled into his crime? Did Logan know?

As though he could read my thoughts, he shook his head at

me. "Georgia, I didn't know." He looked pissed enough for me to believe him.

My gaze moved to the desk. I just had sex on some stranger's desk. Suddenly everything that transpired between us felt cheapened. Logan knew exactly what I was thinking because his eyes grew flinty. "Georgia," he started to say. "Don't . . ."

"Spread your legs apart please. No, keep your hands in the air," the officer directed when my hands started to dip.

My face burned even hotter at the businesslike request. I obeyed, watching Logan from the corner of my eye. He followed suit, too. I didn't know what I expected—for him to resist in some hot-headed display of temper? The only outward sign of his anger was a nerve ticking near his eye. His feaures looked cast in stone.

The cop issuing orders jerked his head to another policeman who stepped forward to frisk us. He made short work of the task. His movements were brisk and impersonal.

I could hardly process it all. I was reeling from the fact that this was really happening.

I was being arrested. If my mother could only see—

I killed the thought, refusing to let it fully form. It was too much to bear contemplation.

"Hands behind your back."

We turned. My legs felt numb beneath me. Yeah. This was a real-life nightmare. I blinked. My eyes stung, and I couldn't stop the hot track of tears from falling down my cheeks.

Logan leaned close to whisper against my face. "It's going to be okay. It's just a misunderstanding. We'll get it cleared up."

I flinched as his mouth brushed my cheek, and he pulled back slightly, his eyes searching mine, inquiring.

I whimpered as the officer closed the hard steel around my wrists and flinched at their grinding *click*. With my hands cuffed behind my back, I felt like the prisoner I was. I had done this to myself. This was my punishment. This was what happened to good girls when they decided to step off the path. I played with fire and got burned. Mom had warned me. She had taught me to be better than this . . . but here I was, being led from a room. Handcuffed. The smell of sex still ripe on me. The censorious eyes of police all around me.

I tore my gaze from Logan as we were ushered out into the hall.

"Georgia, look at me," he commanded.

I shook my head and stared ahead. Other members of the kink club joined us in the hall. All of them were handcuffed like we were. I spotted Annie down at the end. Her shirt was inside out. She was shooting her mouth off to one of the police officers. Once they appeared satisfied that they had us all out in the hall, a female officer read us our rights.

I didn't think I could sink any lower in my misery, but as her voice rang loud and clear advising us of our rights, something inside me fissured. My tears dried and I felt numb. Dead to pain. It was like this thing broke inside me, taking with it my ability to even cry.

"All right. Let's go." The officer who handcuffed Logan and me guided us forward. Stepping out onto the porch, the number of police cars with their flashing lights against the dark night only hammered home the enormity of the situation. This was bad. I was being arrested. Me. The girl who had worried about my permanent record since kindergarten. This went far beyond the shame of after-school detention.

Drivers had parked alongside the road to observe what was happening. A few people even stood outside their cars, necks craning as they watched the group of us being led down the porch steps. Neighbors gawked from the yards on either side of us and across the street. Several even had their phones out snapping pictures. I fought to swallow past the lump in my throat. Didn't they have anything better to do than bask in the misery of others? I suddenly regretted every *Jerry Springer* episode I ever watched where I let another person's misery entertain me.

I was put into a police car with Rachel of all people. Logan went in another one with another guy, and I was actually relieved for that. I wanted to be alone with my shame. I wanted to nurse my regret, stir it into a bubbly stew inside me, and let it strengthen my resolve to get through this.

I just wanted to wake up tomorrow in my own bed and forget any of this ever happened.

And yet I wasn't alone. Rachel was with me.

"God." She eyed me with disgust. "You look scared shitless. You're not going to piss your panties, are you?"

I glared at her. Feeling mean and tired of her less-than-kind attitude toward me, I snapped, "I'm not wearing panties. Ask Logan."

Her eyes flared wide and then narrowed to slits. "Nice. I'm sure he appreciated the easy access."

I grunted, done with talking to the girl. "Look, I'm fine not talking to you."

"Just like you're fine jerking Logan around."

"What are you talking about?"

"You're the first girl he's ever given more than two damns about and you don't even give a shit."

"You don't know anything about me," I accused, rattling my cuffs behind me for emphasis. "I'm in handcuffs in the back of a police car because I came here to see him—"

She tossed her head back in laughter, her dark hair shaking all around her. "Oh, you're going to blame Logan for this?"

"No. I'm not saying that." I closed my eyes tightly in a pained blink. "It's not his fault. It's mine. I let myself get caught up in—" I stopped and swallowed. I wasn't about to confess to Logan's obviously jealous best friend that I was in love with him. "I came here tonight for him." No matter how much I kidded myself, it was for Logan. "And now here I am. If this isn't proof that I need to let whatever this is just die between us then I don't know what is."

"I agree." She nodded, dropping her head against the backseat. "That sounds like a fanfuckingtastic idea. I can't imagine a better graduation gift. You're no good for him."

"And I suppose you're what he deserves?"

"Oh, I know he's too good for me. But you? You're too much of a coward to even own up to how you feel about him. I can resign myself to not having him as long as he's not with you."

Her words pelted me like jagged rock, but in her face I saw that she was as much of a coward as I was. She was in love with her best friend and she had never dared to confess that to him either. I could have pointed that fact out to her, but I decided to spare her. Logan didn't love her. Not in the way she wanted him to. Nothing would change that so why remind her?

Instead, I let her continue to vent her spleen on me. "He's about to leave for college and he'll meet girls who don't look down their noses at him. And someday when he's playing in the majors and you're living your little boring suburban existence, you can tell all your little country club friends that once upon a time you banged Logan Mulvaney."

I wanted to argue. Wanted to open my mouth and explain that I didn't look down my nose at him . . . that I knew he was good. He was honest and real, but he lived his life outside the box and I had to stay inside mine.

Swallowing past the words, I inhaled, the odor of days-old sweat filling my nostrils. Another smell tickled my nose. The faint, coppery edge of blood. I scooted forward on the seat, hating for any part of me to touch anything in the back of the police car.

Turning, I dropped my forehead against the cool glass of the window. I stared into the night as we pulled out of the driveway past the gawking onlookers. Glancing down, I noticed my too-tight dress has ridden up indecently high on my thighs, but there was nothing I could do about it, and this just made me feel more helpless than ever. I flexed my fingers behind me where my hands were trapped.

I should have gone home this summer like always.

Right here at this moment, on the way to jail, why I stayed seemed kind of minor and petty. To avoid Mom talking about Harris? To pretend I was something I wasn't and do wild things like go to a kink club and have no-strings sex? Clearly, I'd failed on the whole no-strings sex. I'd gotten myself trapped and tangled in those strings . . . tangled up in Logan Mulvaney. I'd

taken what should have been fun and casual and made it serious. I wasn't made for casual.

Rachel sighed and I glanced at her. "I was imagining handcuffs tonight, but nothing like this," she muttered.

I looked back out the window again, a sob trapped in my
chest that refused to rise and spill. I kept it locked up in there—
with the rest of me.

"YOU'RE FREE TO GO."

I looked up from where I sat on cold concrete in the holding
cell. It was me with all the other girls from last night—in addition to one very inebriated self-proclaimed prostitute named
Darcy who wanted to know where I bought my dress.

"Not you." The female officer waved at Darcy when she
popped up from the bench and wobbled on her dangerously
high high-heels. "Everyone else."

Darcy plopped back down with a curse, stretching out her
long legs. Her knees looked like someone had taken a cheese
grater to them and I shuddered to think how they got that way.

"Hey, Blondie," she called to me and made a pretend phone
out of her fingers. "Call me. We'll hang."

I winced and waved good-bye.

Facing the guard at the door, I asked, "So all of us can
leave?" I glanced at Annie, thinking it a coincidence that we
were all being released at the same time. "All of our friends are
here to pick us up then?"

It had taken a couple hours to process us. The indignity of
having our mug shots and fingerprints taken would stay with

me for a long time. After that we had been allowed our phone calls. Annie called her roommate. I don't know who Rachel called. I called Emerson. I knew she would come running and had no issue bringing bail money. Emerson hadn't asked any questions. Not what I did to get landed in jail. Nothing. She simply said she was on her way and hung up the phone.

I knew if I called Pepper she would have come, too, but I wasn't ready to face her and Reece and explain that I had been arrested with Logan at a kink club. That on top of everything just made me feel slightly ill.

They'd hear about it soon enough, I'm sure. That secret was too big to keep from them, but I was hoping to get out of this dress first. Maybe take a shower and grab a few hours of rest. The peaceful oblivion of sleep sounded like a luxury above and beyond a trip to Paris right now.

The officer shrugged. "I don't know. You're free to go though. The charges are dropped."

"Dropped?" I echoed, stopping in my tracks.

"Thank God," Annie erupted, lurching forward.

"How?" I asked, skepticism leaking out in my voice.

"Who cares?" Annie hissed, closing a hand around my arm. "Let's get out of here."

The officer answered me though. "Turns out one of your friends confessed that he broke into the house and didn't tell any of you. We're letting all of you go and holding him."

Him. Andy, of course. I knew without having to be told. I guess I should be grateful he did the right thing and admitted that we were all innocent.

"See!" Annie exclaimed, eyes flashing. "We should sue."

The officer's lips thinned and she looked tempted to slide the cell door shut on us again.

"Annie," I tugged on her arm. "Let's go."

By the time we were all discharged with our few belongings returned to us, predawn light was creeping in through the blinds of the police precinct. I didn't see Logan or any of the other guys from last night around and I figured they had already been released. Or maybe we were being released first and they were now getting discharged.

When we stepped out into the lobby, Emerson was there waiting for me.

And so was Pepper.

I groaned internally. Reece and Shaw stood behind them. Mortification washed over me. This was the scene I had wanted to avoid.

"Georgia, are you all right?" Emerson and Pepper stopped before me, looking me up and down. Here, in the fluorescent light of the police station, my dress looked even more shocking. I'm sure I looked like a train wreck . . . hair a mess, makeup smeared.

"I'm fine. It was a mix-up. The party . . ." I didn't feel like admitting at the moment that I had gone back to the kink club. I was satisfied to just call it a party. "Well, the guy throwing it broke into the house . . ."

"Yeah. It's all over campus." Emerson nodded, her eyes wide.

My stomach twisted sickly. "It is?"

"Yeah, on the news, too," Pepper added, looking grim.

"Oh, God. On the news? W-why?" I shook my head, wondering why something like this was so noteworthy.

"Really, Georgia?" Emerson looked at me as if it should be evident. "A sex club broke into the Dartford dean of students' house. You think that wouldn't get out? Just tell me. Was Chippy the Squirrel there?"

Emerson's attempt at humor fell flat.

Acid surged up my throat. Clearly, there was no keeping the kink club a secret. "The dean of students?"

If Andy was in front of me right now I would seriously throat-punch the guy.

"Georgia, are you all right? What were you doing there?" Pepper's brow knitted with worry. "This is so not like you."

That's right. Stepping outside the box wasn't like me. I looked from her to Reece. They made no mention of Logan, and I could only guess they didn't know he was involved yet.

Her gaze flicked back to my dress before returning to my face. "And you missed Emerson's show. At the gallery in Boston, remember?"

I closed my eyes with a groan. I had totally forgotten. On top of getting arrested, I sucked as a friend. Another consequence for living life outside my box. "I forgot. Em, I'm so sorry."

She shook her head. "Forget about it. It's okay."

Rachel chose that moment to join us.

Craptastic. Things kept getting better.

Reece looked at her, then me. His nostrils flared and he swung his stare around the room, clearly searching for his brother. "Where is he?"

I shook my head miserably.

Rachel laughed. "Guess you weren't his one call."

"Logan was there, too?" Pepper asked.

Annoyance started to prick at my nerves. "Look, I appreciate y'all coming here, but I only called Em." I so did not feel like a group interrogation this morning.

Pepper looked crushed, so I amended my tone, wondering why I was tiptoeing so much around them. They weren't my parents. And I'm the one who spent the night in jail with a prostitute who wanted wardrobe advice for a crime I didn't commit. "It was a mix-up. They let us go. They're not pressing charges."

This didn't alter their expressions. Emerson and Shaw looked at me like I was some kind of curious creature that might perform tricks for them. Pepper just looked worried, as though I might spew pea soup next. Reece looked tense and unhappy, ready to rip into his brother at the first opportunity. Which was right about now.

Logan and the other guys emerged through the doors. His gaze took in the group of us at once. He hesitated before shaking his head slightly and walking over to us, resignation clear on his face.

He looked slightly rumpled, exactly like he had slept on a bench in a police holding cell. His gaze fixed on me. "You okay?" he asked, his voice low, intimate, even though everyone was watching, listening.

I nodded, an inexplicable lump rising to my throat.

He glanced next at Rachel. She shrugged with a wry grin. "Sure. What's a night in the slammer? Our new friend Darcy gave me her pimp's number in case I ever need a job."

Logan rolled his eyes at her joke.

"What the fuck, Logan? I'm pretty sure getting arrested could cost you your scholarship."

Logan settled cool blue eyes on his brother. "Yeah, if I was actually charged with anything. It was a misunderstanding."

"A misunderstanding that landed you and Georgia in jail."

"Me, too," Rachel piped in with an overly bright smile. "Not that anyone cares."

Reece turned his blistering gaze on Rachel. "Considering you were the one to get him involved in that club in the first place, no, I don't really give a rat's ass."

"Back off," Logan growled.

Rachel shrugged. "It's all right. He's not wrong. Of course he shouldn't care about me. I'll go wait for my ride outside."

I watched Rachel go, for some reason wanting to call her back. I felt bad for her.

"Reece." Pepper touched his arm.

Reece looked down at her and then back at Logan. Remorse clouded his face, which he quickly chased off in favor of looking obstinate again. "When are you going to start making smart choices, man? I get that you and Rachel have been friends a long time, but you can't let her drag you down anymore."

"You don't get it. Rachel is family. When you left me with Dad, I didn't have anyone. She was there. She understood."

Reece nodded at me. "And what about Georgia? You gonna ruin her life right along with yours?"

I jerked at the reference to me. "Don't drag me into your family drama," I whispered, the quiet of my voice capturing my churning anger. I had my own shit to deal with.

"Reece," Pepper snapped, looking at me with apology in her eyes.

"I don't stick my nose in your personal life," Logan reminded him, facing off with Reece. "I never have. I'm almost nineteen. A little late to be playing the father role now."

Both brothers looked ready to take a swing at each other. Right there in the middle of the police station. Not the best move.

I squeezed between the two of them, so pissed. "No one can ruin my life." *I can do that all by myself.* "And your brother isn't ruining his. Shit happens. This was just one of those things."

I looked at Logan then. His broad chest lifted with breaths. He stared down at me, his gaze unreadable, but I felt like he was waiting for me to say something. *Do* something.

I moistened my lips and repeated myself, my voice small and only for his ears. "This was just one of those things," I repeated, shaking my head, silently beseeching him to understand.

Comprehension crossed his face, and then his eyes iced over.

I meant more than getting tossed in jail. I meant us. We were just one of those things. Something that happened without logic. Or planning. Like a meteor hitting the earth, leaving its impact forever deep, a scar on the ground that would never heal.

"So *we're* just one of those things," he clarified, not bothering to keep his voice at a whisper. He laughed then. A short bark of laughter that held no humor. I cringed and shot a quick glance around to our friends. They looked as uncomfortable as

I felt. "You're right, Georgia," he announced. "That's all we are. The *shit* that happens."

I flinched. Hearing him confirm my words hurt more than I could have imagined. I tried to speak but it felt like I was choking on rocks. My hands opened and closed at my sides, dying to reach out and touch him.

"We can never be anything else." He nodded once, his jaw rock solid. "Not until you figure out your shit and grow up."

His words rippled through me and settled like a writhing serpent in my belly. *I* needed to grow up? Shock and indignation spiked through me. And fear. Fear that he was right. Fear that he was more of an adult here, owning his feelings, and I was the little girl still afraid of making a misstep, disappointing my parents when they weren't even here to witness my actions.

"And I can't sit around waiting for that to happen anymore." He angled his head, resignation hard in his eyes. "Goodbye, Georgia." His gaze flicked to his brother, his voice flat. "Can I get a lift?"

Reece nodded, his eyebrows drawn tightly over his eyes in concern as he looked between Logan and me. Without another glance at me, Logan walked out of the precinct, taking my heart with him.

"Georgia . . ." Pepper squeezed my hand, her heart in her eyes. Shaking her head sadly, she released my hand and followed Reece and Logan out.

Turning, I faced Emerson with a smile that felt as brittle as glass. The ache in my chest went so deep I had to fight wrapping my arms around my middle to keep myself from splintering apart. I just had to get out of this place. I just needed to shut myself in my apartment before I crumbled. "So. Can I get a ride?"

She nodded, her vivid blue eyes wide and absorbing on my face. "Sure."

I walked out of the precinct, commanding my legs to move, to hold it together, to follow Em and Shaw to their car.

Chapter 20

I SHOWERED WHEN I got back to the loft, functioning like a robot, not thinking, not allowing myself to feel. When I approached anything that resembled emotion, the pain was too raw, too deep. I stuffed it far down inside me, right alongside the image of Logan walking away from me.

I ate a slice of cold, leftover pizza, which settled like cardboard in my stomach, and then collapsed into bed, sleeping twelve hours straight. When I woke, it was dark and I fumbled for my phone to see what time it was: 8:19 P.M. stared back at me. So did nine missed calls and countless text messages.

Pepper. Emerson. Suzanne. Mom. My sister even. No Logan, though, and pain that shouldn't be there sliced my chest.

I started scrolling through the texts. One from Em caught my attention because it was all in caps. GO CHECK YOUR FB PAGE!!

My heart slid into a faster rhythm as I jumped over to Facebook on my phone. I didn't regularly visit my page. Given that I wasn't very active, I didn't get a lot of interaction there.

As soon as my wall popped up a strangled sound ripped from my throat. There I was in my blue dress, handcuffed beside Logan and being led from the dean of students' house. There were multiple pictures for all the world to see. Well, all my world, anyway. All my followers.

Friends, fellow students I slightly knew but whose friend requests I had obligatorily accepted, were LOLing and OMGing all over my wall. I was getting dancing and laughing emoticons and things like:

WTG!
High-five!
You dirty girl!
Didn't know you had it in you!
Crazy biatch, why didn't you invite me to the party?
I know who I want to party with!
Who's the hottie with you???

As fast as I could I deleted all the posts and then I sat there in the dark, heart hammering so hard I thought I might pass out.

What were the odds that any family member saw it?

I wasn't an asthmatic, but right then I thought I needed an inhaler.

With a trembling hand, I lifted my phone back up and stared at my missed calls. Four from my mother. One from my sister. Their voicemails were there, beckoning.

Why, oh, why had I taken a nap? If I had been awake I could have deleted the posts as soon as they appeared and no one

would have likely seen them. At least no one in Muskogee, Alabama.

You still don't know anyone from home saw them.

Mom called me a lot. She liked to keep tabs on me. And
today was a Sunday. She always called on a Sunday. Even multiple times.

My thumb hovered over my phone, inching closer to the
play feature of my voicemail.

Suddenly a sharp rap on the door had me squeaking and
my phone flying. I jumped to my feet and turned for the bedside lamp, stubbing my toe.

"Motherfucker!" I grabbed my toe, feeling my shattered
nail against my palm. At that moment I didn't feel the slightest
bit guilty for the profanity. My throbbing toe . . . and the last
twenty-fours warranted it.

Tears spilled from my eyes that were only partly due to
pain.

Another knock sounded.

"Coming!" I flipped on the lamp and limped to the door,
blinking back my tears and swiping at my cheeks.

Expecting to see Emerson or Pepper or Suzanne there and
totally ready for someone to talk me off the ledge, I pulled the
door open.

The impeccably coiffed woman staring back at me pushed
me off that ledge.

"Georgia. Good of you to answer the door. I don't imagine
'motherfucker' was the greeting you intended for me."

"You heard that?" I said numbly.

"I think the entire bar heard that." The way her lips curled around the word *bar* told me exactly what she thought of me living above one.

I dragged a ragged breath into my lungs. "Hello, Mother."

IT TOOK LESS THAN an hour to pack up my things. Mom insisted we could pay someone to pack the rest and ship it back home. As far as she was concerned, she wanted to get me out of this cesspit—her words—and back home where I belonged. Permanently.

I didn't argue. She hardly looked at me as she moved about the loft, grabbing my things and stuffing them into my luggage. Her inability to meet my gaze conveyed just how disappointed in me she was. I didn't need to ask why she was here. Whether or not she'd seen the photos on my wall. She had.

My heart felt like a twisting mass in my chest. I wasn't going to get through to her in her present mood. My best hope was to go home and visit for a few days until she cooled down.

She zipped my suitcase with flourish. "There. Let's go. We don't want to miss our plane."

I nodded.

"You have your ID and phone?"

It was the same question she had asked me every time I left for the airport. Ever since I took my first trip. I nodded again. "Yes, ma'am."

Mom walked downstairs ahead of me. I paused on the threshold and looked around the loft, telling myself it wasn't the final time I would be seeing it. I liked living here. My own space. And I had so many memories of Logan wrapped up in the place. With an inhale, I closed the door and locked up after me.

MUSKOGEE WAS THE KIND of place that changed very little over time. A relatively affluent community half an hour outside of Auburn, the male population lived for football and good barbecue. The women lived for church and gossip. Teenage girls in Muskogee lived for cotillion. As I was reminded as I stood in my sister's bedroom.

I peered into Amber's closet, admiring the white gown that hung from her door, and tried to look genuinely interested.

I had dragged myself from my bedroom, where I'd been hiding the last two days, to see it. She had been bugging me to check out her gown ever since I arrived—indifferent to the circumstances of my return or Mom's black mood.

Mom had yet to talk to me since we got back. A fact that told me how truly angry with me she was. I'd texted my friends and called Dr. Chase, explaining that I went home for a short visit. No one pressed me as to when I would return, which was a good thing, since it wasn't a subject I had addressed with my parents yet.

"Do you love it?"

I stroked the silk flounces. "It's beautiful."

"Here." She pulled a heavy scrapbook off her desk. Together, we sat on the bed and flipped through the pages that captured every moment leading up to and through the night of her cotillion.

"Did you have a good time?" I asked, pausing at a picture of her with Mom before the fireplace. Mom looked happy. Proud. It made me think of my own cotillion.

I'd attended with Harris as my escort. It had been the highlight of high school for me. Shopping for the perfect dress with Mom. My photograph in the newspaper alongside all the other debutantes. Waltzing in Harris's arms at a fancy hotel ballroom.

I remember thinking that night was so magical. But now it seemed a dim memory. That girl someone from a very long time ago. The pride in my mother's eyes a faint recollection.

I glanced at my sister. She was blond like me, but with my stepfather's green eyes. I had been her—without the fear of rejection. My real father's legacy was always there. Still to this day. Like a snake ready to strike and release its venom.

I glanced around her room. The pink canopied bed. High school pennants on the wall. Pictures of her friends and boyfriend all over her mirror and in frames on her dresser. My world had been like this. It should feel more familiar. This should feel like home.

Instead, I felt like a visitor. I always assumed I would return to this place someday, but now the urge was gone. I wanted to go back to Dartford. To my friends. To my life there.

"I saw the guy on Facebook," Amber's voice interrupted my thoughts.

"What?" I looked at her.

"The guy walking beside you. When you were handcuffed in the blue dress."

"Logan?" I frowned at her.

"Is that his name?" She returned her attention to her scrapbook, flipping the page. "He was smoking hot. Is he your new boyfriend?"

I studied her bent head before replying. "No."

It felt weird talking about him here with Amber. He was part of another world. A different world.

And so are you. *Now.* I had another life. One I liked.

"Well, that's good. Mom has been on the phone with Harris's mom a lot lately."

I tensed beside her. She kept talking as she flipped through her scrapbook, looking at photos she had doubtlessly looked at a hundred times. Amber in front of a limo with her boyfriend and another couple. Amber grinning as a corsage was slipped on her wrist.

I wondered if she ever got tired of looking at these photos.

Suddenly, I was glad that I had dated Harris. If for no other reason than that I followed him to Dartford and expanded my horizons and found friends like Pepper and Emerson and Suzanne.

And Logan.

"It's just a matter of time," she was saying.

"What is?"

"You and Harris. That's what Mom thinks."

I shook my head. "No. Not happening."

She looked up. "Good."

"Good?"

"Yeah." She closed her book with a snap. "I always thought he was a prick. Walking around Muskogee with a huge ego because his dad is the mayor. I mean Muskogee is this big." She pinched her fingers together in the air. "It's not like he's the president's son or something."

I smiled. "No. He's not."

When I saw that guy in the photo with you . . . I confess I was hoping you had moved on. Especially with someone as yummy as that."

My mouth sagged. Maybe my little sister wasn't such a Mary Sue after all.

A gentle knock sounded at the door. Mom pushed the door open. "Hey, girls."

She might have been addressing us both, but her gaze was fixed on me. Mom crossed her arms and cleared her throat in that way she did when she was settling in for a long talk.

Amber rose and set her book back down on her desk, not missing the cue. She grabbed her keys and phone. "I'm going over to Jeremy's."

"Back for dinner," Mom said.

We didn't say anything for several minutes. Sitting on the bed, I listened to my sister back out of the driveway until her Prius faded from hearing.

It was a little bit after noon. Mom was off for the majority of the summer, but Dad was working. I did wonder why she didn't wait for him to get home before having this talk. He might be my stepfather, but they had always handled the big conversations together. It gave me hope. Maybe this wouldn't be so bad since he wasn't present.

"Georgia." Mom pulled out Amber's desk chair and sank down onto it. "I've taken these two days to cool down . . . I admit this latest debacle of yours greatly upset me. Me and your father." She crossed her legs. "But you know I don't believe in making decisions in the heat of anger."

I nodded, relaxing. I liked where this was headed. She had cooled off. There was no real harm, after all. No charges had been pressed. It was just a misunderstanding. As for the fact that I had been at a "sex club," maybe she could just pretend she never knew that. You know, like how she knew I was having sex and took me to the doctor to get me on the pill but a conversation about sex never actually took place.

"You're going to withdraw from Dartford and move home."

We stared at each other, her words sinking in. Home. *Home.* The word reverberated through me. I tossed it around and turned it over, tasting it in my head.

I glanced around us. According to her this was home. Only it didn't feel like home to me anymore.

When I found my voice, it came out a hoarse scratch. "What?"

She uncrossed her legs and closed both hands primly around her knees. "It's too late to apply to Auburn, so you can attend community college in the fall or intern at the bank. That might be great experience for the future. In the spring you can transfer into Auburn and finish your degree while living here."

Pain slicked through my chest at her words. "You'd do this to me?"

"Oh, don't look so stricken. I'm looking out for you. I always have. You've had this . . . side to you, Georgia." She shook her head. "It's always worried me." She meant my father. I had his blood running through my veins.

Helplessness raged inside me. What had I ever done to concern her? Enjoy music? Play the guitar? *Almost* get into trouble with the law one time in twenty years?

"So you're just going to plan my life out for me?" My heart galloped eighty miles an hour in my chest.

She cocked her head. "You don't seem very capable of doing that yourself these days, Georgia."

I opened my mouth to tell her that this was my life. That she couldn't dictate my future, but then she added in succinct tones, "Let me be clear: This is not a suggestion, Georgia. You're done at Dartford. We are no longer paying your way unless you do this. Your tuition. Your living expenses. It's all gone. Oh, and your car isn't in your name. That's gone, too. Insurance. Everything. If you go your own way, you're paying your own way."

I sat there, the air sucked out of me, stunned.

Mom *tsk*ed. "Don't look so miserable. This is for the best. There was a time when you cared about what I thought. You wanted to please me and listened to me."

I nodded. I still did, but pleasing her was harder. Impossible maybe. Nothing I ever did seemed to be enough. And she didn't really mean listen . . . she meant obey.

She continued, "You'll see, Georgia. Harris will be home in two years, and he's already expressed to his mother that he can still see the two of you settling down someday. Isn't that great? You'll be here waiting for him after he graduates from Dartford."

I stared at my mother in disbelief. This was who she thought I was. A girl who would live at home, waiting for Harris to take her back on his terms when he was ready?

Mom thought that was good enough for me. That I couldn't possibly want more? Or deserve more?

She rose from the chair. Lifting it, she slid it back beneath Amber's desk. "I'll let you think it over. I know you'll come around."

Because she had just taken away my freedom. And what freedom was that really, anyway, if it could be seized with a snap of her fingers? I never really had it to begin with, I realized. I was at the mercy of her whims.

The enormity of returning to Dartford and supporting myself—covering tuition, room, and board all on my own—overwhelmed me. Oh, and without a car or insurance. If I left here, I'd be on my own. An orphan, essentially.

"I'll think it over," I agreed, my lips hugging the words numbly.

"Of course, you will." Patting my shoulder, she turned and walked from the room.

As soon as she left, I fell back on the bed, every part of me suddenly as heavy as lead.

Chapter 21

THE DAY AFTER MY conversation with Mom she left the application forms on my bed for Muskogee Community College. It was her not-so-subtle way of moving things along.

A week passed before I forced myself to start filling out the paperwork. Something withered and died in me with every swipe and scratch of my pen across the paper. Still, I couldn't bring myself to sign my signature on the last page. Instead, I shoved the application forms in a drawer in my room.

But out of sight wasn't out of my mind. I couldn't forget they were there. Nor would Mom let me. She reminded me every day that there was a July twentieth deadline.

"Maybe you don't want to finish college," she suggested over breakfast one morning.

I looked up from my cereal, watching her warily, wondering if this was some new tactic, because surely she wanted me to finish college. She was an educator for God's sake. A principal.

Mom shrugged. "You can live here and work at the bank. Of course, I'd like you to complete your degree. I tell all my students that, but college isn't for everyone. Even I know that." She lifted the coffeepot to refill her mug. "And how important will it be for you to have a degree once you marry Harris anyway? I'm sure you'll stay home after the wedding. Start a family."

Oh. My. God. I looked down at my bowl and spooned another mouthful of Cheerios into my mouth so I didn't have to tell her just what I thought about that idea. When had my life turned into this world of suck?

I HELD BACK MY tears through the phone call with Pepper. I didn't need her to know how upset I truly was. I tried to sound practical.

"I can't afford tuition, Pepper . . . and all my other expenses on top of that."

"You can live at Mulvaney's. You don't have to pay rent, and we can float your utilities for a while. You use so little anyway and it's all rolled into the business."

"I appreciate that." And it really was generous, but that still left tuition and all my other expenses. I could get a job, but that still left tuition and books. It was a lot to wrap my head around. Mom knew that. She expected me to fall in line. I rubbed the center of my forehead where it was beginning to ache. I'd taken a run after breakfast but the endorphins had done little to alleviate the pressure building up in my skull.

"Look. I'm not saying I'm *not* coming back. I just need time to figure out a plan . . . how I can make it work without my parents supporting me. I might not be coming back until the spring."

"Georgia, you know if you drop out it will be harder to get back into Dartford. Have you called Dr. Chase?"

"Yes. I explained I had a family emergency and wouldn't be back for the summer. He was very understanding."

"Maybe he can help you, if you explain . . ."

"We'll see," I say, the ache in my head unbearable now. I rubbed harder, beating the heel of my palm to my head a few times as if that might kill the pain. "I have to go. It's dinnertime."

Pepper paused and I realized how lame that came out. I sounded fourteen having to hang up the phone because I was wanted at the dinner table. Not that it was even the truth. I already ate an hour ago.

"Georgia, what are you doing?" Her voice was almost a whisper here, but no less demanding.

"I'll be fine, Pepper. It's not the end of the world if I have to move back home." It only felt like it was.

She sighed. "What about Logan?"

Everything inside me seized tight at her question. "What about him?"

"You and Logan—"

"You heard Logan. He's not sitting around waiting for me."

"Yeah, I heard Logan."

Embarrassment sizzled through me. "Well, then you know."

"I know you're both totally into each other, and you're going to blow it if you don't come back here."

I already blew it. I pressed a hand over my chest, directly over my constricting heart. Great. Now my chest hurt, too.

"It was a fling, Pepper. What else can it be?" Bile surged in the back of my throat at the lie. It was so much more than that but what else could I say? I couldn't tell her that I loved him. She would only protest harder for me to come back. She might even tell Logan.

"Look, I know Reece and I came down on you two like a pair of disapproving parents. Sorry about that. We were kind of assholes. But I've been thinking . . . why can't you and Logan be together? He's going to school forty minutes from here. He's a good guy and I've never seen him act this way over any other girl. I've never seen *you* act this way over any guy. If you come back here you could both—"

"It was just sex, Pepper."

My blunt words fell on the air, the lie tearing something open inside me. The line crackled in sudden silence. My head felt like exploding. Tears streamed silently down my face.

Then she laughed.

"What's so funny?" I snapped on a wet, tear-soaked breath.

"Yeah. Well. Once upon a time I was hooking up with Reece just for foreplay lessons so I could land another guy."

"Yeah, I kind of remember that." I might have been involved in some of that scheme, crazy as it sounded now.

"I know all about deluding myself. And I almost lost him because I was too stubborn and too afraid to admit what was between us."

I filled my lungs with air. Yeah. I was afraid. I could admit that. I'd felt out of control since the first moment things heated up between Logan and me. But I was more afraid to embrace it all. To turn my back on the life I was supposed to lead, the one that had been planned for me since birth—or since my real father walked out and abandoned me and Mom.

Even if I wanted to embrace a relationship with Logan, it

couldn't happen anymore anyway. I was here. He was halfway across the country. If I went to him, I was turning my back on my family permanently. On the me I was supposed to be.

"Logan and I aren't you and Reece."

"You sure about that? You might be more like us than you think. How does it feel? Knowing you might stay forever in Muskogee while he goes off to college? The next time you see him down the road a few years, maybe at my wedding . . . if your mother lets you attend, that is."

Her words hit their mark with all the accuracy of a well-aimed arrow. I flinched.

"Of course, he'll probably be seeing someone by then," she added. "He'll have a date with him. Probably a girlfriend."

"Stop. Stop it."

"It hurts, right?"

I nodded, pressing my fingers to my mouth, holding the tears inside.

"Well, it wouldn't hurt if there wasn't something there. If you didn't love him."

I nodded, but didn't let a sound escape. I didn't dare. Not for her to hear.

"Georgia," she pleaded softly. "I almost lost Reece . . . and myself. Don't let that happen to you. Your home is here. Come back. It will all work out if you just come home. I'll help you figure it out. We all will. That's what friends do."

I inhaled, closing my eyes tightly. "I have to go."

Her answering sigh rippled through me. "Good-bye, Georgia."

I hung up the phone and clutched it in my hand for a few moments before flipping to my photos. There was a group shot in there at Mulvaney's taken a few months ago. Pepper, Reece, Emerson, Shaw, Suzanne. Even Annie was in there, tagging along with the group—whether we wanted her or not. I laughed, the watery sound filling the silence of my room.

And Logan. He was there, too. Coincidentally, he was next to me, his strong arm draped over my shoulders for the picture. My chest clenched. Not coincidental. I knew that now. There had been something even then, drawing us together before either one of us realized it. Or at least before I did.

I zoomed in on his face and let the ache in my chest intensify as I studied his strong features. The deeply set eyes and the square jaw. The golden-brown shadow of a beard growing in. The brilliant blue of his eyes seemed to stare directly into my heart.

I curled into a tight ball as dusk slid into night, tapping the screen of my phone every minute or so, stopping Logan's face from going dark.

I don't know how long I did this. Half an hour? An hour? Staring at his face, sodden in my longing and misery, a breath shuddered past my lips. I flipped to my contacts, to Logan's name, and started texting before I lost my courage. I started several messages, deleting them all before settling on one.

Me: I'm sorry

At the very least he was due an apology. I went back to the photo of us, not expecting an immediate reply. Not after our last exchange at the police precinct when I had let us both down. When his message popped up, my heart tripped a little, feeling

suddenly connected to him through this tenuous thread of dia-
logue. Even if he was halfway across the country.

> **Logan:** What for?
>
> **Me:** Everything

I wish I could take back the words I had said. I wish I had
been more honest with him . . . with myself. I'd still be stuck
in Muskogee, but there wouldn't be the foul taste in my mouth
whenever I thought of my last sight of him.

> **Logan:** Where r u?
>
> **Me:** Still at home. Alabama.

I'm sure he'd been apprised of my change in location by
Pepper and Reece. For a moment, it appeared he was typing,
and then nothing. I was reminded of his resolve that night in
the police precinct. He was finished waiting on me. Inhaling a
watery breath, I typed again.

> **Me:** I wish I could do things over . . .

He didn't reply. I stared at the screen for a few moments,
resigning myself to the fact that he wouldn't. Those words were
enough. As much as I could offer. I wouldn't tell him that I loved
him. That wouldn't be fair. Not with me stuck here and him there.
He had moved on, and I was taking his advice and growing up.

The most adult thing I could do was let him go.

Chapter 22

"GEORGIA! CAN YOU COME down here?"

I left my room and descended the stairs, assuming Mom wanted help with dinner.

When I stepped in the living room I noticed my sister's face first. Jeremy was with her. They'd been watching a movie, but the big screen was frozen on pause. Pity gleamed in her green eyes, which I didn't quite understand until my gaze shifted and collided with Harris.

For a moment, it felt like déjà vu with Harris standing in my living room, Mom beaming beside him, Dad sitting on the couch with an absent expression on his face as he read the latest Clive Cussler novel.

I opened my mouth, but words wouldn't come. They were there, trapped in my head but couldn't get past my lips. *What are you doing here? Go away. Go away. Go away.*

"Hi, Georgia." He stepped forward and touched my elbow as he leaned in to kiss my cheek. My skin shivered. "Good to see you. You look great."

I didn't look great. I hadn't washed my hair in two days and

I had pulled it tight in a slick ponytail to try to hide the fact. As for the rest of me. I wore yoga pants and a Dartford T-shirt. Yes, the former me was making a silent protest.

"Isn't it nice Harris decided to drop by? He's home for a visit." Mom stared at me with wide, almost pleading eyes, willing me to say something nice.

"Hello."

There. That was civil.

Awkward silence filled the air. Mom jerked her head toward Harris, looking at me meaningfully, trying to convey only God knew what she wanted me to do.

Suddenly she clapped her hands together. "Well, it's almost dinnertime and we haven't made any plans yet."

Um. Liar much? Any fool could smell the roast that was cooking in the oven.

"Oh." Harris glanced between me and my mother, reading her unsubtle maneuvering. "Maybe we could all go grab something to eat?"

Mom waved a hand. "Oh, no! I'm not dressed to go out." And I was? "You two kids should go to dinner."

I glared at her. Was she really doing this? It wasn't going to work. The ploy might have worked in *The Parent Trap*, but forcing me alone with Harris wasn't going to get us back together.

Maybe I needed to let him know that. No matter what our mothers plotted, I wasn't interested in reconciling. For all I knew, neither was he and he was only here because his mom had pressured him. I knew something about pressuring mothers, after all.

Harris lifted an eyebrow and grinned suggestively—a grin

that used to make my heart melt but did nothing for me anymore. "How about it, Georgia?"

I held silent for a long moment, considering him, and then, "Sure. Give me a minute to change."

IT TOOK THE WALK to Harris's car to confirm that our mothers had arranged the night's impromptu dinner date.

"I have a reservation at Guido's Kitchen." It was the only establishment in Muskogee that could be considered fine dining.

I nodded, pissed, even though I had surmised as much. "So when did you get in?"

"Yesterday," he replied, backing out of my driveway. "And it took five minutes for my mom to inform me that I had to take you out tonight."

"Nice."

"I kind of knew it was coming though. She's been on my case ever since we broke up."

"Same here with my mom."

"Mom never liked Tiffany."

I didn't really care to talk about the girl who had briefly replaced me. I supposed I should be curious. Weren't ex-girlfriends always curious about their replacements?

Shaking my head, I looked out the window at the passing lights of the Muskogee's main street, aptly named Main Street. It was a short ride to the restaurant. It wasn't very crowded. We probably didn't even need a reservation. They seated us near the large brick-oven fireplace that they cooked their pizzas in and the heavenly aroma of rosemary and olive oil and bread washed over me.

Harris didn't even open the menu. When the waiter brought our water he ordered his usual, chicken picatta, and my usual, baked ziti. It was my old life again. Harris in the driver's seat. Ordering for me. Shit, how did this happen? I hate this life.

"Wait," I said, stopping the waiter and quickly glancing over the menu. "I'll have the small Hawaiian pizza."

Nodding, the waiter took our menus and left.

"Pineapple on your pizza?" He wrinkled his nose. "Since when?"

"I do a lot of things now I didn't use to do."

He stared hard at me for a long moment. "Yeah. So I've heard."

Ah. Facebook. Suddenly, I was thankful for my life being plastered all over social media. I was glad he knew that I was different now and not the girl he broke up with all those months ago. I smiled thinly and took a sip of my water.

"So let's talk." He flattened his hands on top of the table like he was about to discuss some important business negotiation.

I shrugged. "Let's."

He frowned. "You sound bitter, Georgia."

"Oh, why would you think that? I'm on a date with you against my will. My mother is doing everything in her power to keep me here instead of going back to Dartford."

"Maybe it's for the best. Those friends of yours . . . I never liked them."

I laughed harshly. "Pepper and Em? Oh, they're bad influences, are they?"

"Yeah." He looked me up and down, and then leaned across the table to hiss, "You went to a sex party."

I laughed even harder, indifferent to the stares swinging our way from other tables.

"Who would have ever thunk it, right?" I took a savoring sip of water. "Boring Georgia getting kinky. An old dog can learn new tricks."

That succeeded in pissing him off. His face flushed. He always got splotchy when he got mad. But behind his anger there was something else in his eyes. A light of interest as he looked me over. Like the things I might have learned without him intrigued him. Pig. Suddenly I had no appetite.

When he reached for my hand across the table, I tried to slide it away, but he tightened his grip and squeezed my fingers. "I missed you."

"Did you?" I angled my head, the end of my ponytail sliding over my shoulder.

"Did you miss me?" he asked, sticking out his bottom lip. I knew he thought he looked adorable when he did that because he had told me so.

I studied him, thinking, trying to feel inside whether even a small part of me had missed him. That first month after the breakup I had been crushed. Hurt. Angry. But had I really missed him?

The last couple years of our relationship had felt like a lot of work. It had been a long time since I'd felt relaxed and enjoyed myself around him.

Kind of like how I felt here with Mom. Tense and unhappy. I didn't enjoy myself. I never felt relaxed or at ease in my skin. I felt like an imposter, trying to be someone else—the person who made them happy and not me.

I only felt like myself at Dartford. After Harris and I broke up, I'd finally uncovered myself. And then I met Logan.

I thought about the way he made me feel . . . the things we did and shared. Being with him . . . it felt like freedom. I never knew it could be like that with a guy.

I remembered how easy it was to be with him—when I wasn't pushing him away.

I met Harris's gaze. "No."

"Huh." The sound escaped more like a grunt than a word, and his expression revealed every bit of his disgust with me for confessing that bit of truth to him.

"Look, Harris, I know our mothers have this grand plan for us. But I'm not going to marry you. I'm going back to Dartford."

It was his turn to laugh harshly. "Really? Without Mommy and Daddy supporting you?" He snorted his skepticism.

"Yeah. I like it there. No"—I stopped to correct myself and shook my head—"I love it there. I love my friends. I love . . ."

Logan. I love Logan.

Something ugly flickered in his eyes as he stared at me. "You're kidding me, right?" He stared at me for a long moment. "There's someone else. Was it that guy you were arrested with? The one with you in the pictures?" So he had seen the photos. He inhaled. "I forgive you, Georgia. Whatever you did, we weren't together then. I can forgive you."

I laughed lightly then. "You're really incredible."

He grinned, mistakenly complimented. "I know. I can be generous and admit that we both made mistakes."

"No, Harris, I don't want to get back together with you. Even if there wasn't someone else . . . but yeah. There is."

His nostrils flared. "You little . . ." He stopped himself short, showing some restraint. He glanced around to make sure no one was watching us. "We're going to finish this dinner, Georgia, and then I'm going to take you home and give you some time to reconsider."

I stood. "We don't really need to finish this dinner."

He looked up at me, his mouth gaping like a fish. "We ordered already—"

"You can eat. I'm going home. I'll get my sister to come and get me." I dropped my napkin on the table then and marched across the restaurant. In the lobby, I stopped and pulled my phone out. I'd had it on vibrate, but I immediately saw there were several texts from Amber and even a missed call. Hoping everything was all right, I clicked on the voicemail first. Her breathless voice filled my ear.

"Georgia! Georgia! Oh. My. God. I can't believe—"

"Georgia."

The deep voice hit me like a punch to my solar plexus. Breathing was impossible. I lowered the phone from my ear, my heart a painful thump in my chest. I turned, forgetting about my sister.

"Logan?" He looked amazing. A little rough. Like he hadn't shaved in days. His clothes were wrinkled against his tense body. But that only made him more beautiful. More dangerous looking. "What are you doing here?"

"Did you mean what you said? In your text?" he demanded.

I moistened my lips and took a step toward him, trying to remember what I had texted, but I couldn't think beyond the sight of him.

"You said you wish you could do things over," he supplied, the blue of his eyes washing over me.

I nodded, remembering.

He continued, his voice deep and raw and hitting me in places that I never knew a voice could touch. "Because I don't want to do anything over. Every minute . . . I'd do every fucking minute of it again even if that's all I could have. But I gotta know. Is it? Do you want more?" He lifted a hand, motioning vaguely to where I stood. "Or are you staying here?"

"I don't want to stay here," I said in a rush.

"Good. Because I drove all this way hoping to hear you say that."

The air released from me in a *whoosh*. Home. Dartford. Him. Yes. YES. Tears welled up in my eyes.

"Is everything all right, miss?" The hostess, an older lady, looked Logan over in his faded jeans and T-shirt disapprovingly.

And I didn't care. I nodded dumbly, happiness rolling through me.

Logan watched me closely, his blue gaze intense, peeling away my layers.

"Everything is . . . great."

Logan closed the distance between us then. He seized me by the face, his touch all at once gentle and rough. His need was palpable. I knew it, recognized it, because it was the same for me.

His hands cupped my cheeks. His fingers splayed wide, each finger a burning imprint. "People wait their whole lives for this. Sometimes half their lives pass before they find it. Sometimes they never do. They settle for something else. Or nothing at all. But we found each other now, Georgia. Do you know how lucky that makes us?"

My chest tightened, emotion clogging my throat, but reality was there, biting at the edges of this beautiful moment, threatening to burst the bubble with the question of how I could make this all work. Love wasn't going to feed and clothe me and get me through school. "I know, but . . . my parents—"

"What do *you* want, Georgia?"

He was the first person to ask me that. To care what I wanted. My mother never once asked me what I wanted. She never asked what was important to me.

"I came here for you, Georgia, but if you really want to stay here . . ." He released a deep breath and dropped his hands from my face. "I'll go."

A sob burst from my lips. "No. I want you! I want to be with you." I reached for him, grabbing hold of his head and tugging his face down to mine. "Don't you dare stop fighting for me now. For us."

I couldn't let him go. I chose him. The rest I would figure out.

He kissed me, swallowing the sound of my sob. His hands flattened against my back and hauled me against him.

The hostess sputtered from where she stood a few feet away, but we ignored her.

"I won't," he muttered between hot, fevered kisses. "Never."

"You little whore."

I tore my mouth from Logan with a gasp to see Harris standing just beyond us with hands balled at his sides. "I came here tonight willing to give you a second chance and you're ready to spread your legs for this loser who got you arrested." Logan's arm tensed under my fingers.

"Harris, enough!" Words burned on my tongue. I wanted to hurl insults at him—and not even for calling me a whore. I wanted to hurt him for calling Logan a loser.

"No, this was good," Harris continued. "I needed to see this. Like I would even want to put my dick where this punk has been."

Logan slipped from my grasp before I could even snatch hold of his arm again. He was across the lobby in quick strides and struck Harris in the nose.

Harris flew back into the hostess stand. He shook his head as though to clear it and then charged Logan, wrapping his arms around him and tackling him to the floor.

They went down with a crash on the floor, limbs flailing, fists connecting. The terrible sound of bone on bone filled the air. The hostess screamed.

I danced around them, trying to look for a way to separate the two of them, but they were a tangle. Logan landed more hits, but Harris wouldn't give up. Somehow they managed to get on their feet again. Locked together, they rammed into a wall, rattling pictures depicting the Tuscan countryside. The hostess danced around them, screaming for them to stop.

I grabbed Harris's shoulder. "Harris, stop it!"

He twisted halfway and gave me a push that sent me

careening into the wall. I slipped down to the ground, a frame falling with me, shattering glass everywhere.

Logan shouted my name and rushed to my side, both hands gently closing on my arms as he lifted me to my feet.

"Georgia! Are you all right?"

"I'm fine." My voice trembled past my lips, a warble on the air. My hands shook.

Logan frowned, his forehead knitting with concern. He didn't see the sucker punch coming, but I screamed as Harris's fist connected with his cheek.

Logan slammed into the wall and I forgot all about my fall and shaking limbs. I attacked, jumping on Harris like a monkey. I clawed his face, leaving bloody scratches. I didn't stop there, raining my fists on any part of him I could reach. Face, shoulders, chest.

I was still cursing him when Logan peeled me off. Gasping, I looked around. The lobby was suddenly full. Waitstaff, gawking restaurant goers. And two uniformed Muskogee police officers, their steel-eyed gazes fixed on me.

Chapter 23

ARRESTED FOR THE SECOND time in less than two weeks. That had to be some kind of record. Of course, I wasn't alone in that ignominious distinction. Logan was with me. We sat side by side, hands handcuffed behind us on a bench inside the county sheriff's office, and shared a smile. He shook his head at me and leaned in to press a kiss on my lips, forgetting about his bottom busted lip. He hissed.

"Oh, baby." I pressed a tiny butterfly kiss to his mouth.

He chuckled against my mouth. "Remind me to bring you to my next bar brawl, tiger."

Harris made a sound of disgust and leaned back on his bench across from us, beating his head on the brick wall. He was handcuffed, too, but they made a point to put distance between us. I didn't care if he was watching though. I didn't care that I was arrested. I was happy.

Deputy Milo Henderson was my second cousin. He'd grown up with my mother, and besides seeing him around town all my life, I saw him every Easter at Aunt Charlene's. He pushed through the swinging doors and I breathed a sigh of relief, ready to explain everything that had happened. And then my mother and father followed, entering the room behind him. *Of course he had called them.*

Logan must have heard my swift intake of breath. "Georgia?"

I sent him a reassuring glance and rose to my feet. "Mom—"

"Georgia!" She pushed past Milo. After sweeping me with her stare, presumably to assure herself that I was all right, she flicked her gaze back and forth between Logan and Harris. Her lip curled as she assessed Logan. He was sporting an angry split lip with one black eye. He'd never looked hotter. Or more dangerous.

My father turned to Milo, motioning to me. "Are the handcuffs necessary?

Milo stepped forward, uncuffing me first, then Logan, then turning to Harris. "I just got off the phone with the manager. I convinced him not to press charges against any of them."

Harris stood, flexing his shoulders and angrily brushing his hands down his starched button-down. "Don't come crawling back to me, Georgia. We're through."

"Harris, don't be hasty." Mom made a move toward him. "This was just a misunderstanding. I'm sure tomorrow you'll feel—"

"Sweetheart." Dad reached out and placed a hand on Mom's shoulder. She swung a bewildered glance at him. "Enough," he said, his voice firm even though his look was gentle.

Mom stared at Dad, her mouth working for speech. I could have hugged my father right then, so grateful that he had decided to shake off his usual apathy.

Harris brushed past Mom and walked out of the station without another word.

Mom stared after him for a moment, as though he were her last great hope for me. Turning, she found us all staring at her. She fixed a plastic-looking smile to her lips and patted her cousin's arm. "Well. Thank you so much, Milo. We really appreciate it. I promise you won't be seeing Georgia in here ever again. We'll have a stern talk to her as soon as we get home. We'll get her straightened out and on the right path again, I promise." Mom laughed awkwardly. "You would have thought we'd have had this trouble with her in high school, not now."

I bristled and rubbed me newly freed wrists, hating that she was talking about me like I was a delinquent fifteen-year-old.

She faced me again, sent Logan a dismissive look, and then, taking my elbow, tugged me forward. "Let's get you home, Georgia."

I dug in my heels. "Mom, this is Logan."

Her eyes narrowed on me, refusing to glance his way and acknowledge him. She was never this rude, which only told me she didn't think he was deserving of good manners. "I know who he is. He showed up at the house and spoke with your sister. She lied and told me he was a friend of Jeremy's. I'll be taking that up with her later."

So that explained all the texts and calls from my sister. She had told Logan where to find me.

"Now let's go home, Georgia." Her clasp tightened on me, growing more determined.

I pulled my arm free and moved to Logan's side. "I'm not going home with you, Mom."

Her panicked gaze flitted from me to Logan. "W-what?"

"I'm going back to Dartford. I'm going to finish my degree there, and when it's done I'm going to look for a job that best suits me . . . which I doubt will be in Muskogee." I looked up at Logan and wrapped my arm around his waist. He in turn wrapped his arm around me. "And I'm going to be with my boyfriend."

Logan stared down at me with such pride in his eyes. The pride I had always been looking for from my mother but never found. It was there, given so freely in his gaze.

"Georgia." Mom had moved closer to whisper her words, clearly embarrassed that others were listening. "What are you doing?"

"I'm choosing my fate. I can't live for you. I can't live fighting every day to prove to you that I'm not my father."

It was like I struck her. The blood left her face. Her chest lifted on a ragged breath. "You do this on your own."

I nodded, smiling slightly. "I'm okay with that."

She stared at me like I was a stranger in front of her. And I guess I was. I was new to myself, too. It was going to take her a while to learn to accept this Georgia, but she would. Eventually. I believed that. At the core of it all, she loved me. And yet, I wasn't going to fall apart if she didn't accept me. Because this new me was strong enough to be who I wanted to be regardless of what she did or didn't do.

I faced Logan. "Let's go. We have a long drive."

Logan nodded, his hand sliding down to mine. Our fingers laced together, palms flushed. Together, we walked out of the station.

WE MADE IT THREE hundred miles before stopping at a hotel for the night. Once in the room, we made it three seconds before getting naked. He was inside me in less time than that. We made love, fierce and tender. Tears leaked from the corners of my eyes as I came apart in his arms, his mouth fused with mine.

"Hey, why are you crying?"

"Because I've never felt this free . . . and this happy. Or scared. I love you, Logan."

He smoothed the tangle of hair back from my face and tucked me against him. "I love you, Pearls. I've never loved another girl before . . ." He sucked in a hoarse breath. "There's only a handful of people in my life I can even claim to love at all. It is a little scary. You chose yourself—me—over your family today. I promise you won't regret it."

"I know I won't." Even without Logan, it had to happen. I would have gone back to Dartford. He just helped me reach the decision that much sooner.

"Hey," I said suddenly. "You know this is the first time we've had sex in an actual bed? We're getting boring."

His chest rumbled with laughter against me. "I've been arrested twice in the last month. I'm okay with boring for a little while. Something tells me with you it won't last."

I pouted at him and he kissed me again, drawing my bottom lip into his mouth. My fingers ran down his chest, over his quivering stomach and even lower. He was already hard. I lifted wide eyes to him. "Again?"

"Every night you've been gone I've thought of you. Of being with you again . . . inside you. I missed you."

Smiling mischievously, I glanced around the hotel room. "This *is* kind of a nice room." I smoothed my hand over the crisp sheets. "A nice bed."

"Good." He kissed me long and slow and deep. "Because I got us a late checkout."

Epilogue

One year later . . .

Logan pressed a kiss on my neck as he came up behind me in front of the bathroom mirror as I was applying mascara. He was naked and wet from the shower. His hand drifted to my belted robe, nudging his erection against my backside.

"Hey." I *tsk*ed, covering his hand with my own and stopping him from completely disrobing me right there. "None of that right now. We're going to be late. I should have started getting ready sooner but someone emailed me this awesome new chapter . . ."

His gaze locked on mine through the mirror. "Did you like it?"

"*Like* is an understatement. I loved it. When do I get the next chapter?"

He grinned. "Oh, I don't know." He gripped my hips, better positioning himself against me. "Maybe you can bribe me for more—"

"You already make me barter for chapters," I reminded,

motioning vaguely in the direction of the living room, where my guitar sat near the futon. It no longer hid in my closet. It was a well-loved and well-played instrument. At Christmas, Logan had surprised me with guitar lessons. In addition to everything else on my plate, I now took lessons once a week. We teased that we had a bartering system going, but Logan liked to hear me play and I liked to read his stories. Win-win.

"I had something else in mind this time . . ."

I groaned, nerves sparking, everything in me responding to him. "Logan, we're already not going to be on time."

"Half an hour. Max," he coaxed.

"It's Pepper and Reece's engagement party," I reminded him as he brushed back the hair from my neck and nibbled along my throat, sending a delicious shiver through me.

"They won't notice if we're a little late."

Turning, I gave in and kissed him. We'd been like this ever since he moved into the apartment above Mulvaney's with me for the summer. Insatiable. There was something to be said for waking up together every day. Sleeping together every night. There was forever in his eyes, and it never got old.

As soon as I returned to Dartford last summer, I went to Dr. Chase and explained how I was suddenly without finances. He helped push my paperwork through the campus's financial aid department. I'd missed all the deadlines for aid, but his influence went a long way, and I was able to continue my courses and pay for my textbooks in the fall.

Reece and Pepper let me remain in the loft, so that saved me from paying for the dorm. They refused any efforts I made to pay them. Dr. Chase hired me as his assistant throughout the year. I was learning a lot, making great connections, and earning some money. Enough to eat at least and cover the essentials. And there was Logan.

During the year, he lived in the dorm, which was covered by his scholarship, but spent weekends and a couple nights a week with me—when he didn't have baseball practice or a game. Occasionally, he still worked at Mulvaney's, catching a shift here and there. Over the holidays I worked downstairs, too, helping Cook in the kitchen.

I didn't have money for pedicures anymore or extravagant shopping trips, but what I had was enough. It was more than enough. I was happy. I had Logan and my friends and a future I was excited about.

Mom and I had talked a few times. We were getting there. She was still struggling with the choices I was making, but she had stopped trying to bully me into her way of thinking. Mostly because it wasn't going to change anything, and she knew that now. It wasn't going to change me. She had agreed to let me keep my car and even covered the insurance. I'm pretty certain my father had a hand in this—he'd mailed me a check at Christmastime, which went a long way to cover my bills. I wasn't too proud to accept the help.

On our last call, she had mentioned coming to see me. I told her that would be nice. I looked forward to her getting to know Logan. She had started to ask questions about him. His baseball career interested her. Knowing Mom, she was readjusting her fantasy for me, envisioning me being married to a Major League baseball player.

"Thirty minutes," Logan repeated, his blue eyes beyond

inviting as he unknotted my belt and slid the robe off my shoulders. The terry cloth pooled at my feet.

I shook my head and used my sternest voice on him. "Logan, this isn't happening."

He stopped and sighed. "All right." Bending down, he picked up my robe and handed it to me.

I plucked it from his hands and tossed it across the bathroom. "Thirty minutes isn't going to cut it."

He laughed, wrapping his arms around my waist and lifting me off my feet, bringing our naked bodies flush with each other. He walked me out of the bathroom, my toes not so much as grazing the floor. I didn't need to see to know he was carrying me toward our bed.

"So . . . forty-five minutes?" Grinning, he came down over me on the bed, his arms bracketed on either side of my head.

I cupped the side of his face, reveling in the love for me shining in his eyes. Reveling in touching him, having him, loving him. A pang punched me in the chest. Love was this. Exhilarating and lifesaving. I could never give it up and never place a time limit on it.

I kissed him, whispering against his lips, "We have all the time in the world."

IT WAS MORE LIKE an hour later when we left the apartment and another thirty minutes before we walked into Reece and Pepper's house. Happy shouts greeted us. We hugged the bride-and-groom-to-be and endured the friendly jibes for being late. Em eyed my still-damp hair with a knowing smirk. I blinked innocently.

Pepper and Emerson cornered me in the kitchen as I was getting a drink.

"Um. Did you miss the start time on the invitation?" Em teased, munching on a chip.

"Sorry," I said unapologetically, searching for Logan and finding him standing across the living room with his brother and Shaw. My chest fluttered at the sight of him.

Pepper grinned. "There's something about being in love. It suddenly makes you chronically late."

Em sighed and stared at her boyfriend. "Tell me about it. I don't think I've been on time to anything since that man walked into my life. Suddenly other things seem vastly more important than showing up on time." From the glazed look in her eyes, I had a good idea of what she was talking about.

"It's a small price to pay." Pepper nodded in agreement. "But I don't plan to be late to my wedding."

"Yeah. We'll make sure of that." Emerson held up her hand. "Bridesmaids' oath."

"Thanks, guys. I promise to do the same for you when it's your turn."

Our turn. *My* turn.

I didn't expect it to happen anytime soon for me—not until Logan and I both finished school—but the idea of it felt natural. So right. We already spoke in terms of forever when we were together, and nothing about it felt forced or uncomfortable. We just knew. This was *it*. I'd found with Logan what my best friends had found.

As if sensing my stare—or maybe even my thoughts—Logan's eyes found mine. He smiled a slow, devastating grin and mouthed the words across the distance: *I love you.*

Acknowledgments

I cannot adequately express how much I've loved writing *The Ivy Chronicles*. Yes. Me, the writer = total loss for words. I can only say thank you for reading *Foreplay, Tease,* and *Wild*. I'm going to miss Pepper, Emerson, and Georgia maybe more than any characters I've written to date. And who could forget their guys: Reece, Shaw, and Logan? These girls felt like my girlfriends and the guys my buds. I hope you felt the same way, too.

Believe it or not, when I sat down to plot Georgia's book, I never planned on Logan being her romantic "match." With so many readers clamoring for more of Logan, I was toying with the idea of giving him his own novella. I could imagine the perfect girl for him, too. Someone his complete opposite. Someone conservative, bound by the influence of her parents and afraid of letting go. Then it dawned on me that Georgia was *that* girl. She had been staring me in the face all along. The moment I realized that, the pages of *Wild* just flew. I can't imagine a better way to wrap up the series than with these two finding their happily ever after together.

The Ivy Chronicles couldn't have happened without the support of my agent, Maura Kye-Casella, and editor, May Chen.

You both always trust in me and embrace my ideas. From the very beginning, y'all were fully on board and as excited as I was—which only added to my joy in the writing process. Thank you! Pamela Spengler-Jaffe, Caroline Perny, Molly Birckhead, Jessie Edwards, Chelsey Emmelhainz, and the entire Harper team, how lucky am I to have you all? You work so hard and I appreciate all your efforts.

I can't write proper acknowledgments without a shout-out to my family and friends. To my husband, children, parents, and in-laws, I couldn't ask for more love and encouragement. Jared, I know you love these books best, and I love you all the more for that . . . especially for being the kind of husband who reads his wife's books . . . even if that means ignoring her on vacation until he finishes the last forty pages of one. I'm lucky to have you. To my cop-cousin, Ben, thanks for answering all my questions.

Here's the scary part. Where I list all my friends who've been crazy supportive with me as I wrote *The Ivy Chronicles* and pray that I don't forget anyone. Sarah MacLean (thanks for always asking the hard questions that get me to the end), Jennifer Armentrout (your input is invaluable), Jay Crownover (thanks for being the one to insist "holy hot teenage boy" toe the dom-line!), and Lindsay Marsh (what would I do without your keen eyes?). Massive thanks and hugs to the rest of my crew: Tera Lynn Childs, Shana Galen, Mary Lindsey, Carrie Ryan, Rachel Vincent, Sarah J. Maas, Tessa Bailey, and Lisa Desrochers. To my bookseller friends at Katy Budget Books and especially bookseller extraordinaire, Crystal Perkins! You guys humble me with all you do for my books. I also want to give a special thanks to super fan Susan for giving me words from her own life to inject into Georgia's story!

And you. My dear reader. Thank you for taking this journey with me and I hope you'll follow me through my future endeavors (aka more books!).

Happy reading,
Sophie

About the Author

Sophie Jordan is the internationally and *New York Times* best-selling author of the Firelight series and Avon romances. When she's not writing, she spends her time overloading on caffeine (lattes preferred), talking plotlines with anyone who will listen (including her kids), and cramming her DVR with true-crime and reality TV shows.

GET BETWEEN THE COVERS
WITH NEW BOOKS FROM YOUR
FAVORITE NEW ADULT AUTHORS

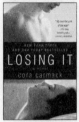

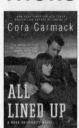

**Available in
eBook**

**Available in
eBook**

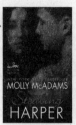

**Available in
eBook**

**Available in
Paperback
and eBook**

**Available in
Paperback
and eBook**

**Available in
Paperback
and eBook**

**Available in
Paperback
and eBook**

**Available in
eBook**

**Available in
Paperback
and eBook**

**Available in
Paperback
and eBook**

**Available in
eBook**

**Available in
eBook**

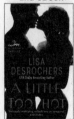

**Available in
eBook**